A collection of novellas inspired by
Shakespearen romantic comedies

Much Ado about
ROMANCE

Susan Page Davis
Shannon Sue Dunlap
Linda Fulkerson

Scrivenings
PRESS
Quench your thirst for story.
www.ScriveningsPress.com

Inspired by The Tempest
by William Shakespeare

The Tempest
IN THE BAY

a novella by
Susan Page Davis

ONE

Barney Scott entered the café and looked around. There she was. He glanced down at his jeans and frayed shirt cuffs. Probably should have put on something a little more presentable. He gulped and started toward the woman, feeling underdressed and outclassed.

Natalie Wrenn looked every bit the sophisticated publisher that she was. When she requested a meeting with Barney, he'd been shocked, even more so when she agreed to drive way up here, more than a hundred miles north of the city, just to talk about his brother. Paul's books were valuable to Wrenn Publishing, but still ...

Barney had only met her once before, at a New Year's party his brother and sister-in-law had thrown twelve years ago, but he should have remembered how classy she was when he agreed to meet her for coffee. Too late to change now.

"Ms. Wrenn."

She didn't stand, but she smiled and extended her hand.

"Mr. Scott. Thank you so much for agreeing to meet with me."

"Not sure what I can do." He shook her hand briefly, noting

3

her perfect manicure, and dropped into the chair opposite her at the glass-topped, wrought iron table.

She already had a cup of brew in front of her, half full.

"Guess I should have put in my order." He glanced toward the counter.

"What would you like?" She put up a hand and fluttered her slender fingers.

Barney had never known a server to come to the table to take the order in this place, but sure enough, here came the cute waitress with her hair in braids. Penny, that was it. Her folks owned the café.

"What can I get you, ma'am?" she almost gushed. Her nametag was pinned to the front of faded overalls. She shot Barney a sidelong glance and nodded.

"Whatever Mr. Scott would like this morning," Ms. Wrenn said.

"Oh, uh, black coffee, Penny. Thanks."

"Coming right up."

Natalie gave him a smile that was only a little stiff. "Do you come here often, Mr. Scott?"

"Some. It's Barney."

She nodded. "Barney."

"You wanted to talk about Paul? Because, like I said on the phone, he won't come back."

"Why are you so certain?"

Barney shrugged. "I've been out there a few times. He doesn't want to leave the island."

She frowned. "I don't mind if he wants to continue living in isolation, provided he'll send me a manuscript now and then. It's been what—ten years?"

He was certain she knew exactly how long it had been.

Penny placed a mug in front of him. "Can I top off your mocha, ma'am?" Penny held up a bronze and black coffeepot and arched her eyebrows at Ms. Wrenn.

Mocha. That was the sweet smell.

"Yes, thank you." Ms. Wrenn slid her cup a few inches toward Penny. When it was full and Penny had retreated, she looked over at Barney and pulled out that smile again. "He is still writing, isn't he? I can't imagine Paul sitting anywhere this long and not writing."

"Maybe. He doesn't discuss it with me." Barney recalled his last attempt to talk to Paul about his living situation. It was one thing for his brother to be a hermit, but it wasn't fair to Paul's daughter. Violet deserved to know what the rest of the world was like—but no way was Barney going to bring up that sore point with Natalie Wrenn.

"What *does* he discuss with you?" she asked.

"Not much." Barney took a sip of his coffee. "I think he's just enjoying nature."

"He's all alone out there?"

"No, his daughter's with him."

Ms. Wrenn's forehead wrinkled. "I seem to remember him bringing her to the office once or twice. She was quite small. How old is she now?"

"Must be twenty?" Barney wasn't really sure. Violet had seemed all grown up last time he'd laid eyes on her, but he hadn't calculated it out.

"And is she content to live out there offshore?"

"She must be. She's still there, so far as I know."

She took another sip from her mug and set it down. "Mr. Scott, when Paul moved to the island, I assumed he would keep on working and sending me his manuscripts. That hasn't happened. To be frank, I *need* his work. He was our top-selling author. But that's not the only reason I'd like to reconnect with him. We were friends, or I thought we were." She looked away.

Her cheeks flushed a little. It made her look prettier, but it surprised Barney. Was she interested in Paul romantically? He cleared his throat.

"Paul and Violet moved to the island after his wife died."

"Yes, I know."

"I figured he just needed time and space. But he really loves it there. Last time I visited, he didn't say one word about coming back."

"And you don't know if he's still writing?"

Barney pressed his lips together. He'd seen stacks of paper on Paul's desk and piles in a bookshelf nearby. He'd assumed they were new books. But if Paul didn't want this woman—his old publisher—to know, then why should Barney tell her? Maybe Paul was submitting his work to a different publishing house, although he hadn't heard of any new releases.

"Have you talked to him since your last visit to the island?" she asked.

"Talked to him? No. You gotta understand. They don't have phone service out there. They only have lights because they've got a generator."

"Sounds primitive."

"Maybe a little, but it's a big generator. They have heat and a stove and washing machine, all that stuff. But no phone or Internet."

"Hmm."

"So, no, I haven't talked to him. I did get a note in the mail a while back. I made him promise with me to touch base at least a couple of times a year, so I'd know he and Violet are okay."

"How long ago was this last note?"

Barney shrugged. "Four months? In May, I think."

She sat in silence for a bit, and Barney finished his coffee.

"Well, if there's nothing else, ma'am?"

She pulled in a breath. "Oh. I was thinking ... could someone do a wellness check, maybe?"

"Well, there's Darrell. He goes out there once a month in his boat, to take them supplies. He carries any mail they have and brings outgoing back to shore for them."

"So, Paul does receive mail."

"Yes, ma'am. If there was something marked 'urgent,' Darrell would probably make a special trip."

She nodded slowly. "They don't even go ashore to shop?"

"I don't think so. Not much, anyway."

"Hmm. This Darrell. How would one contact him?"

"I'm not sure. He lives in Pinecone Harbor, the closest shore community."

"Do you know his last name?"

"Uh ... Clipton, maybe? Or Clifton." Barney pushed back his chair.

"May I contact you again, Mr. Scott?"

"Sure. You've got my number. But I don't really see how I could help you."

Two

Violet Scott picked up the shopping list. It always ran two or three pages on the narrow list pad.

"Darrell's coming today," she said.

Her father looked up from the book he was reading while slowly eating his breakfast. "Let me know if you need my help."

"I probably will. You asked for a bundle of shingles, remember? For the porch roof."

"Oh, yeah." He sighed and shoved his chair back.

"Anything else that should go on the list?"

"Nothing comes to mind."

Violet understood that all right. It was impossible to know what you'd wish you had a month from now. By the time Darrell arrived with their next delivery, probably half the things on the list would no longer be needed.

Of course, they always tried to keep their stockpile of food topped off, and Violet kept a list of staples to check every month, but they tended to order the same items over and over.

"Batteries," her dad said.

"Right." She always had to order different sizes of batteries, and gas for the generator.

As for foodstuffs, she wished she knew what was on the shelves at the store. Probably a lot of delicious things she never thought about. Once in a great while, she'd remember something they ate when she was a kid and hanker for it. Sometimes Darrell could get it for her, and sometimes not. When he'd brought her jellybeans, she'd wondered how she'd ever liked them. They were too sickishly sweet.

"Turn on your walkie."

"Hmm? Oh, right."

Violet grabbed the new list for Darrell and her own walkie-talkie.

"'Bye, Dad." She hustled out the door and down the path toward the dock.

Their house wasn't visible from a distance but was effectively hidden by healthy evergreen woods on the side facing the mainland. Her path wound through the trees. A few hardwoods on the in-island side were leafed out, providing contrasting shades of green to the pines, fir, and spruce.

She heard Darrell's motorboat before she could see it. Emerging from the woods, she ran along the trail that skirted rock outcroppings and blueberry bushes.

The dock was situated on the windward side of the island, only visible from boats that came close. By the time she reached it, Darrell had cut the engine and drifted up against the pilings. He secured the cabin cruiser and turned to wave at her as she walked out the wooden pier.

"Hey, Darrell."

"Morning, Vi." He stooped to heft the first carton of groceries onto the dock. "Best bring your wagon."

"Right." She retraced her steps to the little shelter on shore. They parked the wagon there under a low roof, so it wouldn't fill up with rain and pine needles between uses. It was a small utility trailer, really, but with a bar handle on the front, so she could pull it like a child's wagon. It rumbled on the boards as she trundled it over the dock.

When she got back, three cartons, a cooler, and a big bundle of asphalt shingles lay on the decking.

"Oh, good, you got the roofing stuff."

"Tar and nails right here." Darrell set a smaller box out of the boat. "Your dad gonna come get that?" He eyed her testily, as though fearing she'd ask him to lug it up to the house for her.

"Yeah." She pulled out her walkie-talkie and wiggled it in his direction and then pushed the call button. For a second, she was afraid her father wouldn't answer, but then his voice came loud and clear.

"Hold your horses. I'm comin'."

"Roger that." She slipped the walkie into her pocket and smiled at Darrell.

He'd set four large plastic gas cans up where she could get them.

"Is this it?" she asked.

"Ayuh."

She pulled out the new list. "This is for next time. What do we owe you?"

He reached into his pocket for a batch of receipts and gave her the total. Violet took out the checkbook. Her dad had put her name on the account with his as soon as she turned eighteen —one of their last trips ashore. More than two years ago now. She blinked away the memories and signed her name.

As she tore off the check and passed it to Darrell, her father came strolling along the path. She and Darrell stood in silence until he reached the shore end of the dock.

"Mr. Scott," Darrell called.

Her dad nodded. "Everything good this month?"

"Yes, sir. Oh, I almost forgot."

Violet smiled at her dad as he walked out to join her on the far end of the dock. Darrell opened a small locker near the helm and took out a plastic shopping bag.

"Here's your mail."

"Can't forget that." Violet gave him a big smile and reached for it. Would this be a good month, when they received a personal note or two? Or would it be another disappointment, when all they got was junk mail?

Her dad never seemed to care much, but a quick peek into the bag told her at least two white envelopes were in there with "Paul Scott" heading the address, and one of those was handwritten. Her Uncle Barney, maybe? She wasn't sure, but there seemed to be several other small envelopes too. A large manila envelope and a couple of catalogs or magazines made the bag heavy.

She handed the bag to her dad. "Here. I've paid Darrell for the order, but I haven't given him his pay yet." She quickly wrote out the check for the amount they paid Darrell every time he made the island run. When she handed it over, he ducked his head and tucked the check securely away with the one she'd written for the supplies.

"Thanks, Darrell," she said.

"Anytime."

She smiled. Darrell's runs were definitely not "anytime."

Watching him push off and start the outboard, she waved again. When she turned, her dad was already hefting the cooler into the wagon.

"Looks like we'll need two trips."

"I can take those up—"

He waved a hand to silence her. "The gas and the shingles won't all go in one. You bring the wagon, and I'll carry a couple of these jugs. Leave the rest, and I'll come back for 'em with the wagon."

She was somewhat surprised. He usually left the ferrying of their supplies to her, even if it took her two or three trips with the wagon. The shingles, she decided. He figured she wasn't strong enough to heft them onto the cart.

"You could have waited for me to bring up the first load," she said.

Her father shrugged. "Didn't know how much there'd be."

He eyed the full wagon dubiously. "You sure he got everything? This doesn't seem like enough for a month."

"It's everything we had on the list."

"Okay." He bent and grasped the handles of two jugs and plodded down the dock. Violet followed him, tugging the laden wagon behind her.

Half an hour later, all their supplies were put away, with the shingles and other roofing supplies on the porch.

"Guess I'd better get on the roof this afternoon," her father said.

Violet sighed. It was necessary, but she didn't like the idea of him working up there. What if he fell? How could she get help in a hurry?

She couldn't. That was the worst thing about living on this beautiful island. That and the loneliness.

"It's not urgent, is it?" she asked.

"Need to get it done before the next storm."

She stared at him in dismay. "That's right, we're heading into hurricane season. But I haven't heard anything on the radio about storms." The battery-powered weather radio was one of their few links to the mainland.

"Good thing," he said. "If a big wind tore off more shingles where the porch hits the main roof, it'd be leaking here in the kitchen."

She looked up at the ceiling over the front door. "We don't want that. I'll help you."

"I don't want you up there."

"But—"

"I'll be fine."

She opened her mouth and closed it. Her dad didn't need to hear a string of what-ifs.

"Okay. Just be careful."

THREE

B arney got out of his ten-year-old pickup at the marina. He was a little early this morning, but he wanted to get to work on Leo Sutton's trawler. The faster they got it fixed, the sooner Leo could get back to fishing, and he had a family to feed.

His cell phone rang as he stepped away from the truck. He frowned. Fool things. Sure, they were a convenience, but they were also a nuisance. Maybe his brother had the right idea—go where there weren't any phones. But then he wouldn't have any boats to repair either.

He swiped the screen and put the phone to his ear. "Yeah?"

"Barney Scott?" said a woman's voice.

"Ayuh, that's me."

"Natalie Wrenn here."

Of course. Barney grimaced. He didn't say anything, but she hurried on.

"I wondered if we could get together again."

"What, you didn't get enough of the highway last time?"

"As a matter of fact, Mr. Scott—Barney—I've just pulled into the parking lot at the café where we met two weeks ago."

Barney blinked. "That so?"

"Yes, and I'd like to talk to you again if you're free."

"Free? I work, Ms. Wrenn. I'm just about to start my day. My very busy day."

"I see. Well, my son is with me, and we have something we'd like to discuss with you. An opportunity."

Barney hesitated. Smelled fishy to him. "What kind of opportunity, ma'am?"

"Perhaps we could come to your workplace and discuss it with you. Just a few minutes of your time. The Spruce Point Marina, isn't it?"

Clenching his teeth, Barney hesitated. He didn't like people digging into his life and finding out things about him without asking him directly. Computers! They were worse than phones.

"Let me square it with my boss, and I'll come there." He begrudged her the time, but he didn't want her traipsing into the marina and invading his private life, especially not in front of his boss. And she'd brought her kid along. He shook his head. Women.

The marina's owner drove in as he disconnected, and Barney sauntered over to meet him as he emerged from his truck.

"You're early," Ollie said.

Barney shrugged. "I was gonna be. Listen, something came up, and I need to go tend to it. I might be an hour."

"Awright. I'll see you whenever."

Sometimes, Barney wished Ollie wasn't so agreeable.

He climbed back into his pickup and drove the mile and a half to the café. There was her fancy car, all right, parked right in front of the door. He edged around it and walked inside.

She waved those fluttery fingers. A young man sat across the table from her. Barney gave a curt nod and strode to the counter.

"Coffee, Penny. And I'll pay for it now." He shoved a dollar bill across the counter. "That do it?"

"For you, it sure does."

Barney wasn't sure he liked that. What did she mean, "for you"? He glanced up at the menu over her head, something he hadn't done in a long time. What? Five bucks for a fancy coffee drink? He scanned the board quickly but didn't find a mention of plain old coffee. Was she giving him special treatment? He liked Penny, but still.

He reached into his pocket and pulled out two quarters, the sum of his extra cash, since tomorrow was payday. "That's for you."

"Well, thank you." Penny set a mug before him with a cheerful grin.

Barney picked up his coffee and carried it to the table. The way the chairs were arranged, he had to sit at one side, between Natalie and her son. He didn't like the hemmed-in feeling.

"Ms. Wrenn."

"Barney, thank you so much for coming. This is my son, Kevin."

The young man looked a bit like Natalie. Dark hair and brown eyes, a neat appearance, but not city-dressed the way his mother was. Kevin wore Dockers and a long-sleeved, button-up shirt with a muted green-and-black check. Barney's own blue work shirt and jeans probably looked rustic to them.

"Nice to meet you, Mr. Scott," Kevin said.

"What's this about?" Barney focused on the woman, since she seemed, as always, to be the one in charge.

"Kevin and I have a plan, and we hoped you'd execute it with us."

Barney frowned. He knew what she meant, in general, but he wasn't used to people who talked about executing plans. When Ollie gave him a boat to work on, there was no talk of execution. Just patch, paint, caulk, fix. Words like that, small and plain.

"What sort of plan?"

Ms. Wrenn raised her chin. "I'd like to visit your brother."

Barney picked up his mug, more to delay answering than anything else. He took a sip. The liquid was still very hot, and he set it down again.

"You mean ..." He focused on her eyes, brown like pecans. "... on the island?"

She smiled, which made her look a whole lot younger. "Exactly. We have a boat. Are you game?"

He glanced at her son and pulled in a deep breath. In the parking lot, he hadn't seen any boat trailers carrying a boat big enough for a cruise of several hours across the bay. If any had sat out there in the lot, he'd have noticed.

"What kind of boat?"

Before Ms. Wrenn could speak, Kevin said, "It's a forty-foot yacht. Mom and I go sailing on it a few times every summer, but not so much since my dad died."

Forty feet. Yacht. Sailing. Barney took a gulp from his mug and instantly regretted it. He sucked in cool air until his mouth didn't feel quite so scalded.

"It's got a 50-horse motor," Kevin said, "but we like to sail whenever we can."

"That so?"

Kevin rattled off more stats on the engine, and Barney nodded, thinking. The boy—who looked to be between twenty and twenty-five—knew his stuff and had apparently been sailing all his life. Barney hadn't supposed a book publisher made enough to buy a boat like that. But then, who knew what salaries were like in New York? He sure didn't. And Kevin's now-deceased father may have been a multimillionaire, for all he knew.

"How long would it take to get to the island?" Ms. Wrenn asked, leaning toward him.

"Well, if you left from here, it'd be half a day, I suppose. If you launched from Pinecone Harbor, Maine, it would only be about an hour."

She nodded soberly. "We'd have a crew, although Kevin and I can handle the *Prospero* when we need to."

Kevin eyed him keenly. "I suppose you're handy on deck yourself, Mr. Scott."

"It's Barney. I'd like to think so."

Kevin nodded, grinning.

"We'll have a crew of three, nevertheless," his mother said. "I don't want to have to worry about the boat. I want to concentrate on Paul and convincing him to give me whatever he's written in the last ten years."

Barney shook his head. "I'm not sure he's written anything, ma'am."

"Well, no one else has published anything by Paul Scott in all this time, and I can't imagine him sitting on his thumbs for ten years and not writing. Once an author, always an author."

Gingerly, Barney sipped his coffee. The liquid was cooler now, but he wished he hadn't been in such a hurry before.

"Has Paul got room to accommodate us on the island, or will we need to make it a day trip?" she asked.

"Well, the house is pretty small. I stayed there once, and Violet gave me her room and slept on the couch."

"We can all sleep on the boat if we need to," Kevin said quickly. "But, Mom, if we leave from here early in the day, surely we'll be back ashore before nightfall."

Her brow puckered. "We could moor up there, I suppose, if we had to."

"Have you written to Paul?" Barney asked.

"Yes, but he didn't respond."

He wasn't surprised. Barely two weeks had passed since his first meeting with Ms. Wrenn. Paul generally sent mail out once a month, and he liked to take his time and think things over before acting. Sometimes he decided not to act at all. If she'd been pestering him over the years, he was probably ignoring her letters.

He drained his mug and set it down. "Well, as I said before, ma'am, I don't think I can help you. Good luck."

"Oh, wait. Of course you can. We want you to go with us."

"Why?"

"Because if you're along, Paul will at least be open to talking. Won't he? I mean, you are on good terms, aren't you?"

Barney hesitated. He'd suggested more than once that Paul should move back to the mainland, for Violet's sake if not his own. In fact, he'd considered offering Violet the chance to come and stay with him and go to college onshore. But he hadn't voiced that idea to his brother or his niece yet. He should do it soon. Violet was beyond the age when most young people entered college. Maybe if he took the Wrenns up on this offer, he could sway Paul on that, even if he didn't want to publish any more books.

"I'll consider it," he said.

Kevin Wrenn smiled. "We'll bring the boat to your marina later today. We can leave on the morning tide."

FOUR

The porch roof was watertight now, and the house was snug. The Scotts had a good supply of firewood inside and in the woodshed off the kitchen. Their food stash would last them the rest of the month and more. They always kept at least a three-month supply of non-perishables, more in winter.

"Dad?"

"Hmm?" Paul took a slug of coffee but didn't look up from the newspaper he'd been reading at the breakfast table.

"What about that letter from Wrenn Publishing?" Violet asked. "Are you going to answer it?"

He sighed, folded the outdated newspaper in half, and laid it on the table beside his plate. "Can't send an answer till Darrell comes again."

That was true, but still ...

"Didn't she say she'd like to visit?"

The sound her father made was almost a snarl.

"Have you even decided what to say to Ms. Wrenn?"

"Not really." He wouldn't meet her gaze but glanced toward the newspaper.

"You can't just ignore her," Violet said.

"Don't know why not. I don't have what she's looking for."

"You've written at least a dozen books since we moved out here."

He shook his head. "They're not what she wants."

Violet considered that for a moment. "The ones you've let me read are really good."

"Thank you. But they're not the kind of books I used to write."

She hadn't been allowed to read her dad's books when she was a child, and when they'd moved to the island, none of the old editions had come with them. She wasn't sure why.

"How were they different?" she asked.

His mouth tightened. He picked up his mug, and she thought he wasn't going to answer, but after he took a swallow, he said, "I used to write thrillers. I didn't realize how reading those might affect people. Lots of violence. And they got pretty steamy."

Violet nodded slowly. That meant they contained sexual content. She was mildly surprised, but not shocked.

"They didn't mention God," he added. "In the first fifty books I wrote, none of the characters believed in God, or if they did, they were disdained by the main characters."

Now, that was surprising. Violet was ten when her mom died. Eleven when they moved to the island. She vaguely remembered her father smoking, but he'd never done that here. Never ordered cigarettes. She recalled him saying what her mother called "bad words." "Paul, don't say that in front of the child." Yes, she could hear her mom's troubled voice as she said that.

Mostly, her memories of Mom were happy. Sweet. Loving. Mom had been upset if her husband said or did anything she felt was inappropriate. And she'd taken Violet to Sunday school and church every week. Dad never went with them. And yet, after she died, he'd taken his daughter every week.

Violet hadn't ever connected the move to the change in her father. He was a different man now. Before, he was brash and a little arrogant. He went off frequently on speaking engagements and book signings. People clamored for his autograph. He liked to be the center of attention. He'd drunk alcohol moderately, and he sometimes got loud when he did that, and a little overbearing.

Now, he avoided people in the extreme. She'd asked him if they were ever moving back to the mainland, and he'd given her vague answers. Was he afraid to meet people now? Afraid he'd go back to his old way of life?

She'd asked him once why he hadn't brought any of his published books along, but he didn't give a direct answer. Was it because of their objectionable content? And what about all those awards he'd won? The walls in his den had been plastered with plaques ten years ago, and shelves were jammed with medals and trophies. If she'd had prizes like those, she wouldn't have left them behind.

Reaching for his empty plate, she said, "Dad, what happened to all the stuff in our old house? We didn't bring much when we came here."

"I sold it or put it in storage."

Ah, so some things were in storage. She'd been packed off for two weeks to her grandmother's house, and when she came home, the house was all but empty. That was when Dad told her they were moving.

The adjustment was hard for Violet. Less than a year earlier, she'd lost her mom. Now she was losing her home, her school, and her friends. Her loved ones. Uncle Barney had sent word six years later that Grandma had died. Violet would always regret not having a chance to say goodbye to her, but it would do no good to bring up the subject with her father. He got Barney's message the day after the funeral service. They'd stayed on the island.

She put his dishes in the sink and turned to study his profile. He'd gone back to the newspaper.

"Dad." She waited until he looked her way. "Why not let Ms. Wrenn read one of your new books?"

He grunted.

"I'm serious," she said.

"It's not the same. Once you're a thriller writer, you're branded. You have to keep up with the action, the suspense, the violence. She wouldn't like my new books."

"Maybe she would. They have good stuff in them." She thought hard, pulling up things she'd read in some of the many writers' craft books he had in the island house. She'd gone through them all and even written a few stories herself. Not good enough for publication, probably, but she'd tried to learn and implement what the experts said. "They have great character development, and they're suspenseful too. Maybe not as violent or as ... spicy ... as your old books, but they're terrific."

"Publishers don't want you to change. They want you to produce the same type of thing over and over and over. Because that's what your readers have been trained to want, and they crave more of it. If you put out a totally different kind of book, they won't buy it."

She thought about that. "Well, if Ms. Wrenn didn't like it, maybe another publisher would. There must be other houses that print the kind of books you're writing now."

"Maybe."

She frowned. What could be so interesting in the old newspaper Darrell had brought them last week?

"I know. You could use a pen name."

"I don't think so."

"Why not?" The idea excited her, but apparently, it didn't have the same effect on her dad.

He didn't answer. Did he not want to give up the fame attached to his real name? But he'd already walked away from it, hadn't he?

As she washed the dishes, she sent up a silent prayer. *Lord, show me what to do—if I should do anything.*

There was a lot she was missing out there. Her father had home-schooled her since she was eleven. He insisted she had as good an education as any high school could give her. But what about college? Sure, Dad could teach her about writing, but what if God had another career for her out there? If they'd stayed ashore, would she be preparing for medical school now? Running a small farm? Acting on Broadway? Fixing computers? There was so much she'd like to explore.

Should she leave the island, even if Dad wouldn't go? The idea scared her a little, but it set her pulse tripping.

BLACK CLOUDS ROILED OVERHEAD. The *Prospero* plunged down between huge swells. Natalie clung to the rail, the wind tearing at her hair and clothes, staring at the unforgiving sky.

Kevin staggered across the deck and grasped the rail beside her. "I thought we'd be there by now."

"It's getting dark early," his mother said.

"That's because of the storm. We should have taken heed this morning and not set out."

Natalie closed her eyes for a moment. Kevin had heard Asa Landry's warning that the approaching storm could arrive sooner than forecasted. Meteorology was not an exact science, he'd said. Kevin was apprehensive when his mother ignored his advice. She always thought she was smarter than the people she paid.

Asa, the fifty-year-old leader of their hired crew, lurched across the deck toward them holding two lifejackets.

"Put these on," he yelled.

Ordinarily, Kevin didn't like to wear them. They hindered his free movement about the boat. But this was a time when safety was more important than agility, even he recognized that. He looked toward the stern. Barney Scott and the other two crewmen were wearing their safety gear.

As he took the lifejacket and strapped it on, another huge wave rolled beneath them, lifting the *Prospero* higher than he would have thought possible. In the twilight, he could see the low, dark island only half a mile away. With luck and finesse, they'd be able to make land. Otherwise, they might drift in this nightmare the entire night.

He quickly snapped the buckles in place, grateful Asa was helping his mother with hers.

"All set?" he asked as Asa stepped back.

His mother nodded.

A strong gust tore at her, making strands of her hair snap horizontally beside her face. The wind yanked down the hood of Kevin's rain jacket.

"You should go below," he shouted.

Yes, she should take cover. Natalie longed for a quiet, warm, safe room. But she didn't want to go below and leave Kevin and the others out here at the storm's mercy. If something drastic happened, she didn't want to be cowering clueless in the cabin.

Their hired crewmen had long since secured everything not nailed down. Barney, who knew these waters better than any of the others, had sat at the radio, trying to communicate with authorities on shore.

They'd left the marina around ten that morning, certain they could run ahead of the storm. Well, they had for a couple of hours. The wind had picked up, and Natalie had thought that was good. It would push them along faster to their destination. Then sheets started tearing free, and the *Prospero* rolled unpredictably, with waves surging over the gunwales. They took down all sail and put the engine to use, but navigating in this—doing anything in this—was arduous.

Natalie clenched her teeth and clung to the rail as the yacht rose on a huge swell. They hung for a moment at the crest and then plummeted down. She let out a yelp she hadn't intended. Kevin grabbed her arm.

"Mom, go below!" He held her bicep firmly.

"Aren't we nearly there?"

"We should be, if we can hold our bearing, but this is wild. Please. I'll feel easier if you take cover."

Might as well do it. She wasn't doing any good up here, just worrying him and keeping him from accomplishing anything constructive. The deck was still on a treacherous slant, but she let go of the rail and pivoted toward the companionway with Kevin still holding her arm just above the elbow. Best get below before the next big one.

When she was halfway there, the deck heaved violently, throwing them off their feet. Kevin lost his grip on her arm, and freezing water washed over her, pushing her, pulling her, carrying her where she didn't want to go. She slammed against something solid and gasped for breath.

More water. She clamped her mouth shut and groped for anything to hang on to—anything that wouldn't move.

At last the swell ebbed away, leaving the deck soaked and dotted with seaweed and foam.

The men were shouting. Half dazed and coughing, she pushed up off the drenched boards and looked around her. Barney and two of the crewmen were clustered at the aft rail, shouting and pointing.

She sat up, still muddled. What—

"Is that him?" Barney yelled.

Her heart squeezed. Where was Kevin?

FIVE

Violet's father opened the front door, and a frigid blast of air tore into the room. He grimaced and stared out at the storm. Violet leaned to the side and looked past him. Rain poured down on the roof, and the wind buffeted the little house. The evergreens swayed, and a pine on the edge of the woods snapped off and plunged to the ground. The Gulf of Maine was letting loose her fury.

"Dad!" Violet's cry reached him over the howling and thrumming.

He leaned against the door, shoved it closed, and slid the deadbolt.

"Come have some cocoa," Violet said.

Cocoa was her go-to when they needed soothing or comforting. They'd secured everything they could that morning, and she'd helped her dad manhandle the storm shutters over all the windows. They couldn't afford any broken panes out here, where it would take weeks to get replacements.

"Is it already made?" he asked.

She turned to the stove, where the teakettle steamed. Quickly, she poured hot water into the two mugs she'd loaded with chocolate mix.

"Okay." He plodded to the kitchen table and sat down, his face somber.

Violet let out her pent-up breath. He would let her pamper him for an hour, and maybe the storm would pass.

"Think it will blow out to sea?" She plunked a steaming mug in front of him.

"Hard to say. But it will pass."

She sat down opposite him with a cup of her own.

"Dad, if something really bad happened, how long would it be before we could get help?"

He hated it when she brought up questions about the weakness of their position on the island. He picked up his mug, blew across the surface, and took an experimental sip. "Remember when you broke your leg?"

Did she ever! Violet cringed, just thinking about the pain. Her dad had made splints from sticks, carried her to their fifteen-foot aluminum motorboat, and taken her to shore.

"I had you to shore in less than an hour, and an ambulance came to the dock," her father said.

She nodded. "But what if ..."

"What?"

"If we were both hurt? Or if something happened to the boat? This storm could be really bad. The boat ..." She'd heard radio reports and read about them in old newspapers—how hurricanes had driven boats ashore or driven them out to sea.

"I took the boat out of the water yesterday," he said.

They had a little boathouse near the shore but well above the high tide line. The boat stayed in there during the winter.

"Okay." Violet didn't ask the next question—what if they weren't physically able to get the boat into the water? She could envision the boat smashed under the rubble of the boathouse, or even worse, the two of them crushed when a tree smashed onto their house.

"Don't fret so. God knows our needs."

That much was true, but sometimes God allowed painful

things to happen to His people. Look at Mom. She didn't deserve to die in a snowmobile accident. Violet's parents had been out having fun, and it ended in tragedy. If Dad thought he could escape the dangers of modern technology by retreating out here, he was delusional. Accidents could happen out here in the flick of an eye.

"I'll write something to Wrenn Publishing."

She wanted to say, "Promise?" but that might annoy him. He'd said he would. She forced a smile. "I'm sure Ms. Wrenn will appreciate hearing from you, even if it's to deny her request."

Her father tipped up his mug and took a sip.

KEVIN FLOUNDERED for the rail and caught it with one hand. He clung to it as the deck dropped from beneath his feet. Sucking in a breath, he squeezed his hand around the rail. The deck was nearly vertical. Before he could take another breath, the boat rose again.

At the worst moment, he hung, almost vertical, and then the deck fell back the other way.

His mother! He wanted to look around to make sure she was all right. Kevin turned his head and gasped at the wrong moment. A wave smacked him in the face. He lost his grip and plunged over the side.

"Mom!"

He hit the surface with a crash, as though it were solid, and immersed in the turbulent sea.

The lifejacket kept him from going too far under, but even so, when his head emerged from the water, he spluttered and coughed. The yacht was several yards away. Before he could cry out, yet another wave submerged him for a few seconds.

He came up disoriented, unable to see the boat or to hear anything but the howling wind above a ringing in his ears. He paddled frantically, turning around. A wave lifted him, and he scanned his surroundings, blinking and gasping.

There were the boat's lights! How could it already be so far away?

Six

Natalie staggered to her knees and clutched the handle on a sail locker. Asa reeled across the deck toward her and clamped his hands on the rail as the boat rode down the back side of the wave.

"Come on," he screamed. "We've got to get you below!"

"Kevin—"

"I know. We don't want to be looking for you too."

His words made sense. She reached toward the big man, and he wrapped his arm firmly around her.

"Now!"

As they plodded toward the hatch, she registered vaguely that the two sailors, Willy and Jake, were fastening lines about their waists.

Asa nearly threw her into the cabin. She stumbled and caught herself against the edge of the berth.

"Stay in here!" He wrestled the door shut, and the noise decreased by about half. The wind and the creaking of the vessel were still louder than ordinary, and the deck heaved beneath her feet.

Natalie rolled onto the berth, thankful for the side rail. She huddled, wrapped in a blanket. One second, she was smashed up against the bulkhead. The next, she was clinging to the grab bar, holding with all her might so she wouldn't be flung to the deck.

She didn't know how long she stayed there alone. In her mind, the worst scenarios played out. The storm would end, and she would go on deck to find she was the only person left on board. Or worse, they'd have found Kevin and hoisted him aboard, only to learn he was dead.

At last the hatch flew open. Asa stood clinging to the woodwork and squinting, with water streaming off his raingear.

"What is it?" Natalie managed to pull herself up and sit with her feet dangling over the side of the berth. "Have you found him?"

"No. We tried to put about, but it's all we can do to stay afloat, let alone steer this thing. I'm afraid we've lost him, Ms. Wrenn."

"No!" Her heart raced, and her chest squeezed. The fear was far worse now than at any time since the storm began. Was she to be alone for the rest of her life? "No." She tried to stand, but the *Prospero* lurched, hurling her back onto the berth.

"Stay here," Asa yelled. "We'll circle back if we can. If not, we'll get the Coast Guard out to search for him."

Natalie cowered on her narrow bed. She wanted to join the men on deck, but what could she do out there? She'd only be giving them one more person to worry about. She found herself whispering a broken prayer.

"Not Kevin, God. Please, not Kevin."

Amazing. She'd never put much stock in religion. She sat still for a moment, but she didn't feel anything other than the painful heaviness inside her.

Kevin could not be gone.

NATALIE'S WATCH told her only twenty minutes had passed since Asa's visit to her cabin, but it seemed like a lifetime. A knock came on her cabin door, loud and insistent.

"Come in!"

Barney Scott entered. He seemed better able to keep his footing than the others, and he made his way toward her with a rolling gait that accommodated the boat's movement. Water dripped from his orange life vest.

"Have you found him?"

"No," he said. "I'm sorry. We're close to land now, but they're having trouble steering."

"What? How—"

The throbbing of the engine stopped, and although the wind still whistled and howled about the vessel, the cabin seemed quiet.

"The rudder's damaged," Barney said. "They've cut the engine. We're getting close to shore, and they can't seem to pull away. The surf is too powerful, and the wind—"

"Are we going to wreck?" she screamed.

"I don't know."

"Where are we?"

"I'm pretty sure it's Paul's island, but I've never approached from this side before. We're not near his landing, and it's pretty rocky. Asa said if we didn't kill the engine, it would be worse."

"So, we just drift in?"

Barney sighed. "On a normal day, yes. But this gale won't let us glide in peacefully."

She looked up at the low ceiling. Above her, she could hear footsteps, thumps, and the everlasting wind.

"Can we veer off and go farther out?"

"They're trying, but ..." He shook his head. "Even if we could go around, we'd pile up on the mainland shore within half an hour."

"It's that bad?"

"Bad enough so Asa and the others have tied safety ropes to themselves, so they won't be washed overboard."

Like Kevin. She tried to swallow, but her throat was like sandpaper. "I felt the boat swing around. I thought we were going back to look for him."

"We tried. What you felt was likely resistance from the waves. It's no good, Ms. Wrenn."

"I'm coming on deck." Natalie swung her legs over the side of the berth.

"That's the worst thing you could do. Stay here and brace yourself. Put any extra pillows and quilts around you." Barney plodded to her and pulled the thin, narrow mattress off the top bunk. "Put this over you."

The *Prospero* lurched, and she clutched the edge of the berth. When she opened her eyes again, Barney was gone.

The yacht slammed against something with a crash, and she was flung against the bulkhead, banging her temple. The boat rocked, and she rose cautiously on her elbows. Overhead, the men shouted. The wind still howled, and a glugging, pouring sound reached her. Were they still floating? The rocking was punctuated by creaks and groans.

With horror, she stared at a gush of water seeping in under the hatch door.

Natalie leaped from the berth onto the inclined deck. No way was she staying below if the *Prospero* was going to sink. An image of the receipt with the exorbitant amount she'd paid for the yacht flitted through her mind.

That didn't matter now. What mattered was surviving. She patted her pocket. Phone still there, but it would probably do her no good. By some miracle, her designer purse still hung from its hook on the back of the hatch panel. She grabbed it and threw the door open.

The yacht shifted, rolling almost to its side, and she staggered toward the steps. Could she make it up the ladder? The stairs were nearly on the wall now, and she lurched along with one foot on the bulkhead. She grasped the railing and hung on as more water poured down, sloshing over her leather shoes and soaking her pants.

~

PAUL ENTERED the house and stripped off his raincoat. He shook it outside then shut the door and hung the coat on a peg.

"Everything all right?" Violet asked.

"Basically, yeah."

"What about the leak in the woodshed roof?"

"I'll get up there as soon as things dry out. I think I have enough stuff left over from the porch roof."

Violet nodded, satisfied. "Supper's almost ready."

"Well, it's still raining steady, but the wind's let up some. I think the worst of it is past us." Paul sank into a chair and toed his boots off.

"So, Dad ..."

"Hmm?"

"I was thinking maybe we could get a dog or something."

Paul straightened and stared at Violet's back. "Whatever for? We don't need a watchdog out here."

"For company."

"Ah." He'd known she was lonely from the day they moved out here, but she'd seemed to adjust and get used to the life—enjoy it, even. Now and then she'd ask him if they were ever going back, but he never took it seriously.

"We'd have to buy food for it all the time," he said.

Violet kept working at the stove and didn't respond.

He sighed. One more thing to worry about, if they had a pet. But he couldn't ask her to stay here all her life with no one to talk to but him. Maybe he should think about letting her go ashore and look for work. But she'd have to find someplace to live, and how could he be sure she could find a trustworthy landlord? He'd sold the old house. Maybe he should have kept it and rented it out.

Sometime soon, they'd have to have a serious talk about the future. He could see that. Actually, he was a bit surprised she hadn't pushed him about it earlier. She'd wanted to go to school, he knew it.

Paul got up and walked to the doorway. He leaned on the jamb and gazed across the room at his desk and the shelves beyond. He had twelve good, solid books and several partials. But would anyone buy them? Would people actually pay for the kind of prose he was writing now?

"It's ready, Dad," she called.

He turned back to the kitchen. Yes, he had some sober thinking to do.

SEVEN

N atalie clung to Asa's hand as he pulled her from the tilted deck onto a large rock.

"All right, Ms. Wrenn?"

"Yes." She drew in a shaky breath and looked around. The sky was still black, and mist sifted down, soaking her clothes. The bay still undulated, and large swells crashed against the shore, throwing spray up yards above her head. The *Prospero* lay atilt, shuddering with every wave that hit the stern. At least the bow had found a resting place on the shore without being smashed to bits.

Asa turned off his flashlight. No lights welcomed them, just the dark water and sky, with the darker shoreline sandwiched between.

"Jake and Willy are trying to get a fire started, but there's not much dry stuff to work with," Asa said.

Natalie tried to read his expression, but there wasn't enough light. All she could see was his large bulk, black against the background of swirling charcoal water.

"We have to have a fire. That's got to be our priority."

"Yes, ma'am. Are you cold?"

"Not for me, Asa. For Kevin!"

He drew in a slow breath and looked out toward the relentless sea. "Yes, ma'am. Come on."

They climbed over a few rocks to the pebble shore. It was no easy task, but Asa turned on his light and managed to take her above the surf. No sandy beach here, but at least the waves weren't sloshing over her feet every few seconds.

Barney Scott and the two crewmen who answered to Asa were muttering and casting about. As they approached, Barney met them on the damp pebbles.

"Ms. Wrenn, are you okay?"

"Yes, Barney. Under the circumstances, I think you should call me Natalie. No sign of my son?"

"No, ma'am," Barney said.

A brief beam of light showed behind him.

"The men have flashlights?" she asked.

"Only one, ma'am. Willy's using his phone, but he doesn't want to run down the battery, since we have no way to recharge it."

She huffed out a breath. "We have flashlights on the *Prospero*. Flares, too. And we can charge batteries when the engine's running." She rounded on Asa. "Is my yacht going to sink?"

"No, ma'am. We've tied it off with a couple of stout lines. There's damage to the keel, and the rudder's smashed."

"Smashed? So we can't steer it."

"That's right. There's a small hole in the hull that has to be fixed before we can go anywhere. I think the boys and I can hoist the bow high enough so's water can't get in, but it's tricky."

"Tricky how?"

"Well, as you saw, there's some water in the hold already, and it'll be hard to raise it high enough to work on without it getting slammed around by waves and damaged worse than it is."

"But—"

"I know, ma'am." Asa placed a huge paw on her shoulder. "If it's humanly possible, we'll save the *Prospero*."

She nodded. "Thank you. But my main concern at the

moment is Kevin. We have to build fires quickly, so he can see them if ... if ..."

"Yes, ma'am." Asa lumbered away toward the crewmen.

"I'm so sorry," Barney said. "We'll do whatever we can, but until morning ..."

"That's a long time from now," Natalie choked out.

"Yes, ma'am."

Full darkness had scarcely fallen when they'd hit the rocks. How long before dawn? Six hours in these northern latitudes? Eight? More?

Flames flickered, and Barney reached for her hand. "Looks like they've got a fire started. Come on, you need to warm up a little."

Her lips were shivering, and goosebumps rose on her arms. She let Barney lead her to where the men were working, putting sticks on the blaze. Making sure she stood on the landward side of the fire so she wouldn't block the view of it from the sea, she held out her hands. The warmth felt good.

Asa said, "Mr. Scott, can you keep that going, and the boys and me will see what we can do with the boat?"

"Yeah, sure," Barney said. "If you can get into the cabins, maybe you can find a coat for Ms. Wrenn."

"We'll try. But first, we need to keep it from ..." Asa glanced at Natalie and let it trail off.

"Is there anything dry on board we can burn?" Natalie asked, looking doubtfully at the pile of wet sticks the men had assembled.

"Well, I suppose we could unload those crates in the hold and burn them."

"Do it." Natalie had packed a couple of wooden crates with wine and treats for Paul and his daughter. Not bribes exactly, but she'd thought it wouldn't hurt to remind them of what they were missing out here in this godforsaken place.

"Can we use the dinghy?" she asked.

"Yes, we'll use it to bring supplies ashore, ma'am, after we've done what we can to keep water out of the vessel."

"Not that," she almost screamed. "For Kevin! We have to look for him. He'll drown if we don't find him."

"Natalie." Barney touched her arm. "It's been more than half an hour since … Nearly an hour. This water's too cold. If Kevin's still in it, we won't find him tonight."

Her stomach clenched, and she wanted to slap Barney Scott. He was saying Kevin was likely dead. But he couldn't be! Not her boy.

"We have to try." It came out as little more than a whisper, but he heard her.

"We'll build the fire larger, for a beacon. If Asa can find the flares, we'll set one off. Maybe the Coast Guard can come. But for you, I think we need to find my brother's house right away."

She stared at him blankly, her teeth chattering. "Paul's house?"

"Yes. This island isn't that big. Right now it's dark, and we're disoriented. But we should be able to locate the house. You can rest there. And we'll be out here at dawn with boats and binoculars and—and anything else we can come up with to try to find him."

She grabbed his wrist. "The radio." Asa and the other two men had already moved away, scrambling over the rocks toward the yacht. "Asa—"

"He tried to send out a mayday before we hit," Barney said. "We don't know if anyone heard it or not. After we struck, he tried again, but the radio was dead."

"But that's impossible. It's up top. That's not where the collision occurred."

"We don't know if the radio itself is disabled, or if something was disconnected, or what," Barney said. "When it's daylight, they'll figure it out. But for now, as you said, we need to build up this fire, and then I think we need to find Paul's house."

She stared at him. Sparks reflected in his eyes, but the flames were falling lower. They had to replenish the fuel supply. "But ..." She couldn't think of anything else they could do immediately to help Kevin, so she turned toward the scrubby trees and pulled out her cell phone.

After a few minutes, using her phone's light, she found a stick on the ground. She picked it up and carried it back to the fire. Barney was bringing more wood.

"We'll build this up and go find the house," he said.

"No. I'm not leaving here." Natalie tossed her stick onto the fire and faced him. "If Kevin comes ashore, it will be near here. I don't want to be half a mile away in the woods when he needs me."

"But Paul can help us. He may even be able—"

"No! I'm not leaving this spot."

Barney sighed.

A streak of red shot through the night. Asa had found the flares and set one off from the tilted deck of the *Prospero*.

"There," Barney said. "Chances are good someone will see that."

Natalie had her doubts. Who would be looking out over the bay in this storm? Everyone ashore would be huddled in their homes, waiting for it to pass.

"Can you keep the fire going?" Barney asked. "I need to find my brother's house. It can't be far."

She looked doubtfully at the small pile of damp wood. "I'll try."

He nodded. "The flare's our best bet. Asa will probably send up another after a bit."

Kevin will see it. He has to!

"Sure you won't come with me?" Barney asked.

"I'm sure."

He was gone, lurching along the shore by the light from his phone.

∾

"Hey!"

The shout came from the dark shore behind Natalie, and she swung toward it. The glow of a flashlight waved farther down the verge of the sea.

"Natalie," Barney called. He'd only been gone twenty minutes or so.

"Hello," came another man's voice.

She took two steps toward the sound. "Paul? Is that you, Paul?"

Natalie stared toward the men who had hailed her. Could Barney have found Paul that quickly? Natalie hesitated, not wanting to get too far from the fire. She'd fed it sporadically after finding she could break off low branches from the nearby pines. But they burned quickly, so she had to ration them.

"Natalie," Barney called, and he approached with two others, making their way slowly over the rocks with the aid of flashlights.

"Paul Scott?" She peered into the darkness.

"Yes, it's me, Natalie. We met Barney on the trail, and he told me you wrecked here in your boat."

A young woman stepped out from behind him, squinting toward the dark shape of the *Prospero*. "That's quite a boat."

"This is my daughter, Violet," Paul said. "You remember her, don't you, Natalie?"

"Yes, I met you a couple of times when you were eight or ten years old." Natalie wished she could see Violet more clearly. She recalled her as a bouncy little girl.

"Hi." Violet shook her hand, and the whole situation seemed dreamlike.

"My son—" Natalie's voice caught.

"Kevin Wrenn was washed overboard," Barney quickly told his brother. "We tried to go about to look for him, but the wind and the waves pushed us ashore. There's some damage to the yacht."

"I see."

Barney laid a hand on Paul's shoulder. "I thought maybe you could take Ms. Wrenn to the house. She needs dry clothes."

"No! I want to stay here for Kevin."

The dinghy pulled up, and Asa leaped out and waded ashore. "Mr. Scott?"

"Yes?" Barney and Paul said at the same time.

"It's my brother," Barney said. "He saw the flare from his house. This is his daughter, who lives out here with him."

The other two crewmen were ashore now, and Barney introduced Asa, Jake, and Willy, to his brother and niece.

After more discussion, Natalie saw she was outnumbered. None of them thought Kevin would suddenly appear on the boulder-strewn shore. And if his body washed up, heaven forbid, none of them wanted her on the scene.

"Come to the house, Natalie," Paul said gently. "You need to rest. And in the morning, we'll talk."

She opened her mouth, but she couldn't form a reply.

"You're shivering. Come, let me and Violet give you some hot tea and dry clothes."

"You can sleep in my bed tonight," Violet said. "We have a cot in the storeroom, and I'll stay there. Come with us, please, Ms. Wrenn."

Natalie looked helplessly at the others. "But the men ..."

"We'll stay here," Asa said. "Me and Jake and Willy. We've got the yacht secured, and we've got a tarp we can put up. We'll keep the bonfire going for Kevin, no fear." As he spoke, Willy brought an armful of wooden slats from the dinghy and tossed them onto the fire.

"Well ..." Natalie looked anxiously at Paul.

"You come too, Barney," Paul said. "We have a lot of catching up to do. I'm sure these men are competent to see to the boat."

"Yes, sir, we are," Asa said.

"There, you see?" Paul took Natalie by the hand. "I should have brought our boat, but I didn't."

"You'd never have made it safely to shore in this, sir," Asa shouted over a new blast of wind.

Paul reached toward Natalie. "Come this way. The path smooths out in a little bit, and it's not hard getting to the house from here, really. Ten minutes and we'll be there."

EIGHT

Paul was carrying an armload of typewritten manuscripts toward the stairs when Violet tiptoed down toward him the next morning.

"What are you doing, Dad?"

"Putting these out of sight."

Violet's eyes flitted to the empty shelves near his desk. "You don't want Natalie to see them?"

"That's right. And if she asks you about my work, keep quiet, okay? Let me be the one to decide how much she knows."

Violet frowned. "Sure, if that's what you want. Let me help you."

"You can't go in my room. Barney's still asleep in there."

"I'll carry them up to your door, and you can take them from me and put them where you want them."

Paul glanced toward the shelves. "Okay, but don't mix them up. I had everything in a certain order."

Five minutes later, they were down to the last stack. Paul looked at it and then looked again. "Wait. How many did you take in your last trip?"

"Just two, like you said."

He frowned. "There should be two left, but there's only one."

"Are you sure?"

"Yes, I'm sure." He picked up the last manuscript, which was held together with rubber bands.

"Maybe we miscounted. Take that one, and double check."

Paul picked up the typewritten pages and followed her back to the door of his room. He set it down on the dresser, beside the other ten, two per stack, and went through the stacks, one by one.

"Everything there?" Violet whispered, peering at him from the doorway with anxious eyes.

"No." He tiptoed out and stood with her on the landing. "The one that was on top of *Angry Falcons* is missing."

"What's the title?"

"*Androscoggin Journey.*" Paul pulled in a breath. "You know what this means?"

"No, what?"

"Someone took it."

"Oh, come on, Dad. They were all right there in the living room, and I slept in the box room, next to Natalie last night. I didn't sleep very well, either, on that camp cot. Surely I'd have heard her if she got up and came down here and took a manuscript."

He looked at her and then back at the empty shelves, unsure of what to say. He'd slept on the couch himself. Could Natalie have sneaked in and grabbed a manuscript without him noticing?

"Okay, but there's definitely one missing."

Violet shrugged. "What's the big deal, Dad? Ask her when she gets up. Now, what should I make for breakfast? Should we take some to the crew?"

"Uh, no. Barney said they had enough supplies to fend for themselves this morning." Paul shook his head. It wasn't that simple, but Violet didn't understand how important this was to him. Because he'd never talked to her in detail about his work.

Maybe he should have.

"Well, we could send them some sandwiches later and see

how they're doing," his daughter said. "I think we still have eggs. How about pancakes this morning? Everybody loves pancakes."

"Do they?" He gave a little shrug. Ultra-thin Natalie might not like to eat carbs in the morning.

"Okay," Violet said. "I'll fry up some bacon too, and I'll make coffee. Anything else?"

Paul strove to banish thoughts of the manuscript from his mind. "We got any fresh fruit? I seem to remember Natalie loathes fat."

Her lips puckered. "The fruit Darrell brought is pretty much gone. I think there are a few tangelos and, of course, apples, but the bananas are gone. But we have lots of canned fruit."

She hurried off toward the kitchen, and Paul spirited a couple of file folders off his desk, to the cabinet next to the window. He tried to remember last night, after he'd left Barney in his room. He'd settled down on the couch with a pillow and a blanket. Sort of. He'd lain awake for a long time and then tossed and turned until daylight.

But he hadn't heard anyone stealthily sneaking into his office area. If Barney had risen in the night, he'd have known. His brother was like a moose calf blundering around, especially in unfamiliar spaces. But maybe not Natalie. Maybe he'd drowsed and missed a foray in the wee hours. And he had gotten up once and visited the bathroom. How long was he in there? Not very long, he was sure.

When Paul eased the bedroom door open once again, a snort came from the bed. Barney, it seemed, was still out cold. He tiptoed in and started to move the manuscripts off the dresser. Was he being paranoid? On the off chance Natalie hadn't discovered them, he wanted them out of sight. And if Barney saw them sitting on the dresser, he might spill the beans.

Paul tiptoed to the closet and carefully turned the knob. The door creaked a little as he swung it open, and Barney gave a little moan and rolled over.

After shoving his shoes aside, Paul stacked the reams of

paper, carrying them two by two from the dresser top. There wasn't much closet space, but he stacked them in three piles—four books in two, and three in the last pile. He sighed. It would take him a while to sort them out after this batch of company was gone.

Immediately he felt guilty. Natalie's son was missing, likely dead. Sure, she'd brought up the subject of contracting a new book last night, but today, Kevin's tragedy would have set in. She'd be filled with grief and not be able to think about business.

On the other hand, if she hadn't spirited away the missing manuscript, who had?

He shut the closet door and walked stealthily across the room. Barney was stirring again as he went out.

He turned in the hallway and came face to face with Natalie.

"Oh, hi," he said. "Sleep all right?"

She hesitated. "The bed was fine. Is there any news?"

"Nothing yet."

She closed her eyes. Would she collapse?

"Come on, Natalie. Come eat something. Violet's probably got the coffee ready, at least."

"I'm not sure I can eat." She opened her eyes, and she was talking. That was a good sign.

"Right this way." He guided her down the stairs. Passing through the living room, where he had his desk beneath one window, he was glad he'd put the manuscripts away in time.

Violet gave their guest a strained smile as they entered the kitchen. "Good morning, Ms. Wrenn."

"Hello, dear." Natalie sank wearily into one of the chairs.

Usually, Paul and Violet were the only two at the table. They had an extra chair, in case Darrell helped carry a load to the house and stayed for coffee, or in case Barney made one of his rare visits. Paul pulled it over, so Violet could join them if she wished.

"The boat radio is probably the best communication?" Natalie fixed Paul with an almost accusing gaze.

"Probably. We don't have a two-way here, other than little walkie-talkies so Violet and I can communicate here on the island. We have the weather radio for forecasts. But it's not like we can transmit from here."

"How can you—" Natalie waved a hand as though realizing it would do no good to lecture him now. "If Asa got the boat's radio working, he'd have sent one of the men to get me."

"Maybe," Paul said. "If they heard anything about your son, I'm sure he would."

"I need to know if they got hold of the Coast Guard."

Paul sighed. More than once, he'd vacillated over whether or not to install more reliable island-to-shore communication. "Reception was spotty last night. I'm surprised we even heard the weather reports. And I only saw the flare because we'd left the curtains open." With no one else on the island, he seldom saw a reason to shut them.

"What's the word?" Barney spoke from the doorway, and they both turned toward him.

"Nothing yet," Paul said.

"Morning, Uncle Barney!" Violet gave him a huge grin. "Coffee's ready."

"Fantastic. Make mine a double."

She laughed and opened a cupboard for mugs.

When she brought three full mugs to the table a moment later, she had sobered, no doubt feeling her laugh was inappropriate in light of Natalie's situation.

"Can we go to the *Prospero* and check with Asa?" Natalie asked. She gave Violet a distracted nod and moved one of the mugs closer to her.

Barney got up and went to the refrigerator. "Got milk?" he asked Violet with a sly grin.

"I'm afraid it's condensed all the way."

Barney found the can and took it to the table, where he poured a generous dollop into his mug. He held up the can and arched his eyebrows at Natalie and Paul.

"No, thank you," Natalie said, and Paul waved him away.

"I can go down there after we eat," Paul said.

"Or I can go," Barney offered as he resumed his seat. "You two probably need to talk business."

Paul frowned at him. Trust his younger brother to put his foot in it. "I'm sure Natalie is more concerned about Kevin than she is about my work."

"Actually, it might be a distraction, if there's nothing else I can do."

Natalie held Paul's gaze with a challenge in her eyes. He was glad when Violet brought a platter of pancakes to the table and plopped a plastic bottle of syrup beside it.

"There's butter there." Violet nodded toward the butter dish and turned back to the stove.

"Forks." Paul jumped up, glad to escape Natalie's stare for a few seconds, and retrieved forks and knives from a drawer. He wouldn't ask her about the missing manuscript until she forced a conversation about publishing—which he was certain she would. As he distributed the flatware, Violet brought over a plate of bacon.

"This looks and smells terrific, Vi," Barney said. "Sit down and eat with us."

"Not yet," she said, patting her uncle's shoulder. "I've got a few more flapjacks cooking."

Besides which, Paul thought, she probably doesn't want to admit they didn't have another chair unless they wheeled in his desk chair.

Natalie sipped her coffee and grimaced, but quickly hid the expression. Did she usually take sweetener in her coffee? Or maybe she was used to gourmet brew, while Paul still used the same common brand he'd used for decades. He'd never asked Darrell to find him something fancier.

Barney dug into the pancakes and bacon. Paul took one pancake and two strips of bacon. Natalie hesitated, and then she forked a pancake onto her plate and added a modest squirt of syrup.

"Butter?" Paul asked.

She shook her head. After one bite, she focused on him. "Paul, tell me about your new books. You can't tell me you've been hiding away out here for ten years and haven't written anything."

"Did you take one of them last night?"

"I might have." She gave him a coy smile.

He took a large bite and chewed for several seconds. Swallowing seemed inevitable, but he had to respond. "You should have asked me first."

"I was afraid you wouldn't let me see anything, and I was excited about those piles of manuscripts. I had to check it out and see if I was right, that you'd composed several new books."

"Okay, so I did. But nothing's been published."

"That's not saying it's not publishable. The one I looked at certainly is."

"You read all the way through *Androscoggin Journey?*"

"Only a few chapters, I'm afraid. I was reading by flashlight. The batteries started to fade, so I gave up on it. But it's very good, and I intend to finish reading it."

Paul took a swallow of his coffee.

"Come on," Natalie cried. "Show me the rest! Your readers would be over the moon if we gave them a new Paul Scott thriller."

Paul sighed and looked away. "They're not ..."

Barney picked up his mug and drained it with a final glug. "Well, why don't I trek over to the shore and see how Asa and the others are doing?"

"Oh, would you?" Natalie gazed up at him, her brow furrowed. "I could go with you."

"No, stay here," Barney said. "It's probably still sopping wet out there, even if the rain's quit."

If only he *would* take Natalie with him. But Barney was right, she should stay in the house. "Take my raincoat," Paul said, nodding toward the row of pegs near the back door.

"And one of our walkie-talkies," Violet added.

"Good idea." Paul jumped up, thankful for another excuse to escape Natalie's piercing eyes, if only for a moment. He strode into the next room and retrieved two handsets from his desk. "Here. You know how it works?"

"Yeah. You keeping one on here?"

"We will." Paul hit the button on his unit and laid it on the table by his plate.

Meanwhile, Violet was taking her final batch of pancakes out of the large frying pan.

"Dad, why don't you and Ms. Wrenn go in the living room?" she asked. "I'm going to eat and clean up the dishes."

"Good idea." Natalie rose, leaving half her pancake and a third of a cup of coffee on the table. Paul wasn't surprised she didn't offer to help Violet. For a long time, she'd been paying people to clean up after her.

He didn't like her demands, but he didn't seem to have a choice. He took his mug to the counter and refilled his coffee, then followed Natalie into the next room, snagging the walkie-talkie on his way past the table.

Natalie had settled in the armchair he usually used. He placed the handset on the end table and lowered himself onto the couch, carefully balancing his mug.

"Look, Natalie, I may as well tell you. I'm not writing the same sort of stuff I used to. Anything I've done out here has a whole different slant."

She tipped her head and studied him keenly. "I didn't get that from the chapters I read last night. What are you writing? Some kind of spec? Paranormal?"

He let out a low laugh. "Hardly."

"Well, then? The one I started reading was great. It opened a little slower than most of your others, but ..."

He drew in a breath. "I've changed, Natalie. Since my wife died."

Her gaze sharpened. "Is it morbid, or what?"

"No, nothing like that. But I've ... I've come into a new relationship with God. I want to please Him. Everything I write now carries my faith entwined deeply in the story."

"Oh." She sat back and said nothing for a moment.

Paul felt the irrational urge to apologize, but he wouldn't. Not for this. "I don't believe Wrenn Publishing has a Christian imprint."

"No, we've never ..." She raised her chin. "Are they thrillers?"

"Not exactly. Suspenseful, some of them, but not in the same genre at all."

"I see."

But she didn't. No way could she understand the turn his writing had taken. Just for a moment, he wondered if he should let her read one. As if he could stop her, when she already had possession of one of the books. But if she finished it, maybe she'd grasp what he was talking about.

But no. She'd want the story, the plot, but not the spirituality. She'd want him to change it. He could imagine what she would do with it in her content editing.

"Have you submitted anything to other publishers?"

"No."

"Why not?"

That was a good question. He'd felt at first that he wasn't ready. People wouldn't understand his shift of perspective. Publishers wouldn't want to take a chance on him now. Lately, he'd felt the urge to get his work out there again. But was that God nudging him, or his old, insufferable ego?

Natalie eyed him keenly. "You could publish under a pen name, I suppose."

He shook his head. "I thought about that. What is the advantage?"

"None that I can see, except your established fan base wouldn't be disappointed."

"If you don't want them disappointed, you'd have to tell them it was me using a pen name, or they wouldn't know. Again, what's the advantage?"

"Paul, you write so well. If you can make a name for yourself in thrillers, you can do it again in another genre. True, it's a totally different market, but—"

"I don't want to hide behind a pseudonym."

"Fine." She nodded soberly. "I guess ... I need to think about this."

"What's to think about, Natalie? I don't fit the Wrenn model anymore. Let it go. If I decide to put it out there, I'll find an agent who'll submit it to Christian publishers."

With a sigh, she stood. "I think I'll lie down. You will tell me if there's any word about Kevin?" She glanced toward the window.

"Of course."

NINE

Violet put away the last of the clean dishes and dumped her dishwater. She was hanging up her damp towel when the back door crashed open and her uncle dashed in. She gasped.

"Uncle Barney? What is it?"

"Where's your father? Where's Ms. Wrenn?"

She pointed. "Dad's in there. I think Natalie went to her room—my room."

Barney strode into the living room, and Violet followed as far as the doorway. Her father had heard the commotion and stood from his desk chair.

"Have they found him?"

"No," Barney took a couple of labored breaths. He must have run all the way from the camp near the stranded yacht. "But they did find this."

He held out something, but Violet couldn't see it.

"It's Kevin's," Barney said.

Her father's face furrowed. "On land? But ... If he had it on him when he went overboard, it can't have fallen out of his pocket. It would have sunk."

Violet stepped forward and peered at the red Swiss Army knife in her uncle's hand.

"No way it would have washed up on shore," Paul said.

"It might have." Barney shook his head. "I don't know, but they all say it's his. Maybe he got it out and fiddled with it and dropped it."

"If he was that close to shore ..."

"I don't know," Barney yelled, sounding thoroughly frustrated. "They're looking for him now, down the shore from where they found it."

"All right, calm down, Barn." His younger brother was always easily upset. That hadn't changed over the years. "Where was it?"

A door opened overhead. Ms. Wrenn must have heard Barney shouting. She came down the stairs, her face pale and her hands shaking. She walked over to Barney and grabbed his arm.

"What's happened?"

Barney paused for a second and then held out his fist and opened it, disclosing the knife. "Is this Kevin's?"

Natalie's lips trembled. "Yes. His uncle gave it to him for Christmas several years ago."

"He'd have had it in his pocket last night?"

"No doubt."

Barney nodded grimly. "The crewmen found it on shore, a couple hundred yards beyond where the *Prospero* wrecked. But no sign of Kevin."

Natalie pulled in a shaky breath and reached toward the knife. She touched the red case with two fingers. "I don't understand. Did he make it to shore?"

"We don't know. The waves are still high, but the Coast Guard has a cutter out. They're patrolling on the west and south sides of the island."

"So, we do nothing?"

"We're not doing nothing. We're doing all we can."

"I want to go out there. If there's a chance he made it to shore ..."

"No." Barney laid a gentle hand on her shoulder. "Stay here with Paul. I'll go out with the men. If he's out there, we'll find him."

"I'll go too," Paul said.

Barney whirled on him. "No! This is your fault. You stay with Natalie."

"What? How is this my fault?" Paul stared at his brother.

"If you hadn't made such a stupid choice to live out here on this remote, isolated rockpile, this wouldn't have happened. Natalie could have called you or gone to you on dry ground, and Kevin would be alive."

A stunned silence hung over them.

Violet cleared her throat. "Let's calm down. I'm going to fill a Thermos with coffee and make a few sandwiches. I'll go out and comb the woods on the southeast part of the island, and if I meet up with the crewmen, I'll give them the food."

Barney wiped a shaking hand across his brow.

Violet pulled in a ragged breath and hurried into the kitchen.

TEN MINUTES LATER, Violet left the shore path and headed through the pines. The island was less than a mile long, and if she made her way through the woodsy interior, she'd either meet up with the boat crew or hit the shore beyond where they were searching.

The argument between her father and Barney had left her shaken. Her uncle had no right to accuse her dad of killing Kevin. No way was he responsible. Barney was too close to the tragedy. He'd been on board when Kevin was overwhelmed by the waves, and he was understandably upset. That didn't justify his explosion in front of the grieving mother.

Still, Violet had wanted to jump in and try to persuade her father that now was the time to move back to the mainland. Until that moment, she hadn't realized how badly she wanted it.

Had Uncle Barney felt this way the whole time? Why hadn't he ever discussed it with his brother? Maybe she could have allied herself with her uncle and reasoned with Paul.

She tried not to resent her father and the way he'd directed her life without giving her any options. They had no idea what was going on in the world, except what the outdated newspapers and magazines Darrell brought them said. For a long time, she'd wanted to take occasional trips ashore and see some other people. Have a chance to talk to others her own age.

Violet sighed. If she went to college now, she'd be older than most of the other students in her classes. But did that matter at the college level? Part of her still wanted to take on the challenge. Another part wanted to try for a job—any kind of job. She'd seen Dad's bank book. Yes, he'd made a lot on his books, but over the years, the royalties had trickled to a tiny rivulet. His savings wouldn't last forever.

A wet pine branch smacked her in the face, shedding water drops all over her. She ducked under it and plodded on, clutching her canvas bag to her side.

She wasn't going to find Kevin Wrenn way over here. If he'd made it to shore—and she had serious doubts about that—the sailors would find him way before she did. It didn't make sense to be looking in the island's interior. She paused and looked up. She couldn't see the sun through the thick evergreen branches, but it couldn't be past ten in the morning, and she was pretty sure generally which way was west. That was where the *Prospero* was beached on the rocks. But she wanted to check farther east, just to be sure.

Setting out again, she took a few steps through the trackless woods. This forest wasn't all that big. Even if she went the wrong way, she couldn't go too far without coming out of the trees, probably near the inhospitable southeastern shore.

"Hey!"

At the faint call, she whirled around and stared, trying to spot something between the trees that didn't belong.

"Where are you?" She called after a moment.

"Here." She spotted him then, or at least, his hand waving, near the base of a large pine. She hurried toward him, the wet brush and boughs swatting her, soaking her jeans and sweatshirt.

"Kevin?" She reached the tree and circled it until she could see him lying there on his side.

He was drenched and shivering. His hair was plastered against his skull, and he had an orange life vest buckled over his sweater.

"Are you okay?" Violet asked.

"Not really. I'm freezing."

"Of course. You've been out here all night."

"Who are you?"

"I'm Violet Scott. Do you remember me? We met a couple of times, back when we were kids."

"Violet ... Oh yeah, right."

"Here, I've got hot coffee."

"You're joking."

"No." She set down her bag and pulled out the vacuum bottle. She opened it, poured the cup that was the lid half full, and held it out to him.

Kevin took it and molded his hands around it with a thankful sigh.

"It's hot," she said.

"Right." He took a cautious sip then a larger one. "Mmm."

"Your mother thinks you're dead."

His eyes flew wide open. "My mother? You've spoken to her?"

"She spent last night at our house. She's worried sick."

"They made it to shore, then."

Violet scrunched up her face. "Yes, but the boat's damaged. Your man, Asa, thinks maybe they can fix it. But the radio was on the fritz last night. Asa shot off a flare, and I think the Coast Guard's out trolling the bay for you now."

"What?"

"Everyone's afraid you drowned. We should get back to the

house and tell them, so they can let everyone know you're alive. Can you walk?"

"I ... maybe."

"Wait." Violet reached into the bag. "I made these for the crew, but you should eat one now."

Kevin snatched the sandwich from her hand. "You're an angel. I can't believe you brought food."

"Sorry. I should have mentioned it earlier. Here, let me pour you some more coffee."

He wolfed the first sandwich and then ate another more slowly. Tipping up the cup, he finished the ration of coffee.

"More?" She held up the half-empty Thermos.

"No, I'm good. I think I can walk now. How far is it?"

Violet looked around. "Not sure exactly, but it's less than a mile. The island isn't all that big, but I came far enough from the house that I think it's shorter from here to go to where the *Prospero* wrecked. From there, a path leads to the house, and it's not too far."

"Sounds doable."

She pointed. "Let's go that way. If I miscalculate and we hit the shore in another spot, I'll know where we are, and we'll just follow the path to the house."

Steadying himself against the bole of the tree, Kevin rose shakily to his feet. "Let's go."

TEN

"I can't believe Kevin is gone," Natalie wailed. "I *won't* believe it until I have proof."

Paul swallowed hard and glanced at his brother, who was scowling at him. "Look, Natalie, everyone's doing what they can." His words sounded lame and inadequate.

Barney stepped close to Natalie and put his arm around her shoulders. "I'm sorry, Ms. Wrenn. I shouldn't have said what I did earlier. I know it's not Paul's fault. It's nobody's fault. Come sit down." He shot Paul a glare as he guided Natalie to the sofa.

Paul could tell the ramifications of his brother's outburst were far from over. "Where are the crewmen?" he asked.

"They went down the shore to see if they could find any more signs Kevin had been there," Barney said. "Well, I think one of them stayed near the boat to relay news if there was any."

"Did they get the radio going?" Natalie asked. Tears streaked down her cheeks, and Paul pulled a clean, folded handkerchief from his pocket and handed it to her. He'd quit buying paper products for the island house—except toilet tissue and printer paper—years ago.

"They did," Barney said. "The Coast Guard responded and

will touch base with them at their camp and patrol the island shore if there's no news."

Paul's brain was whirling. He turned to face Natalie. "That knife. Is it possible Kevin left it on board—say, in his cabin—and one of the men found it and took it ashore?"

"They would have said so," she faltered.

"Not if they were stealing it."

Barney shook his head. "The place where they found it was quite a ways down the shore—out of sight of their camp. They only found it when they started searching down that way this morning."

Paul sighed. "Okay, what can we do?"

"I think you should stay here with Ms. Wrenn," Barney said. "I can take your boat down there and help them look along the shore. I can get in closer with that than the Coast Guard boat can."

"It's still awfully choppy." Paul rose and looked out the window. "I don't think we should take small boats out yet."

"Well, Asa and the others left off fixing the yacht's hull to search." Barney shrugged. "I guess I can go help them search the shore. But you two stay here."

Paul hesitated. "All right, I guess." He darted a look at Natalie, and she didn't object. "Do you need anything?"

"An extra layer might help," Barney said. "Can I borrow a sweatshirt?"

"Sure."

The brothers went up to his room together. Paul pulled open a dresser drawer and pulled out a front-zip sweatshirt with a hood. "Here you go. This is nice and warm."

"Thanks." Barney pulled off his rain jacket and pulled the sweatshirt on. "I probably don't need the raincoat now."

"Everything will be dripping, even if the rain's stopped."

"You're right." Barney picked up the damp outerwear.

"Listen, Barn ..."

"Yeah?"

"Is there something you want to say to me?"

Barney looked down at the rug and shook his head. "I shouldn't have said that. It was—you know—heat of the moment."

"Yeah, but ..."

Raising his chin, Barney looked him in the eye. "Okay, I admit it. I've resented your moving out here and dropping out of my life. I've missed my big brother. And I felt helpless. I knew you were going through a lot, but there was nothing I could do to help. And then Violet."

"What about her?"

"I thought at first, you'd get over this in a year or two and come back to shore. But keeping her out here for ten years—isolating her like that. It's not right."

Paul pressed his lips together. After a long moment, he sighed. "You're right. I've been selfish."

"If you want to stay out here, bro, at least let her come back with me. Let her go to school if she wants to, or look for a job. Live a normal life. I'll look out for her, but you can't keep her in a box until you die."

Paul walked over to the closet and opened the door. He stood looking down at his manuscripts.

"What's that?"

Paul jumped. Barney was close behind him, peering over his shoulder.

"Books I've written since I've been out here."

Barney edged around so he could see Paul's face. "Natalie said you hadn't sent her anything since you came out here."

"That's right."

"Why don't you let her see those?"

"She stole one last night." Paul looked uncertainly at his brother. "I'm writing Christian stories now, Barn. Stories about faith."

Barney laughed, and Paul stared at him.

"What's so funny?"

"Stories about faith? In God?"

Paul nodded.

"Where's *your* faith, Paul? You're hiding out here, afraid to let anyone see what you wrote."

"Violet's read them." Paul realized the irony of never letting his daughter read his old books, but letting her devour the new stories.

"Let Natalie see them."

"She won't like the Christian parts. Wrenn doesn't have an inspirational line."

"Maybe she can recommend another publisher."

"No. She wouldn't. She'll say I should rewrite them as secular. Better yet, she'll want to edit them herself and take out all the parts about God."

Barney's lips skewed. "I don't know what to tell you."

Paul drew in a deep breath and exhaled slowly. "You believe in God, don't you, Barney?"

"Yes. I haven't been going to church lately, but yeah, I know He's still out there."

"That's good to know. I've been praying for Kevin ever since we heard what happened."

"You know what? I've sent up a prayer or two myself." Barney frowned. "I want the chance to be closer to you, but I guess what I really need is to be closer to God."

"We both need that. And, honest, I'll think about what you said. About going ashore."

Barney smiled. "If you did, we could see each other more often."

"Yeah. I'd like that."

Barney left the room, and Paul lurched to his bed and sank down on the edge. He heard the door to Violet's room open and close. Natalie must have come upstairs. Tears brimmed in Paul's eyes. *Was I wrong all this time, God? Please, let the boy live. I don't care about the books. I'll even give up the island. Just let him live, Lord.*

~

K EVIN FOLLOWED Violet as closely as he could through the forest. She looked back frequently and slowed if he fell behind more than a few steps. Once, he tripped over a tree root and bumped into her, but not so hard she fell.

She whipped around and grabbed his arm. "I got you."

He straightened and took a couple of deep breaths.

"Do you need to rest?"

Kevin shook his head. "No, I'm good."

"Okay." She nodded toward a white-barked tree a few yards away. "That's a birch tree, and they're mostly on the edge of the woods. We should hit a path soon that will take us to where the yacht wrecked. I think."

They plodded on, and she kept hold of his arm, letting go only if the trees and underbrush squeezed in on them. Surely they'd gone a mile by now. He was starting to imagine traipsing forever through an endless jungle of cone-laden pines and paper birch with Violet when they stepped into a break in the trees, and the sun shone down on them.

"This is the path," Violet said.

He looked in the direction she waved. Sure enough, a faint but definite trail led through the woods. They mustn't use it often—but then, there were only two people living out here, right?

The two of them could walk side by side now.

"Where's the *Prospero*?" he asked.

"Another quarter mile or so. Less. And it's not far from our place. Dad and I went out there last night and took Natalie and Uncle Barney home with us. The crew wanted to stay out there."

"On the boat?"

"I'm not sure. It was kind of up on the rocks. I think they were going to put up a tarp. They had a fire going. I was going to take them the sandwiches and coffee, but I took the long way, on the off chance I'd find you. I didn't think anyone had searched the woods yet."

"I didn't see anyone all night, and I thought the island was bigger. I don't know if I'd have made it without you. Thanks."

"No problem."

His breathing became more labored, and she paused. "Let's rest for a minute."

Kevin nodded. There was no place to sit—just soaking wet leaves and downed limbs. He made himself breathe deeply and slowly.

"It's not much farther," she said. "How are you doing?"

"I'm okay. Let's go."

Half a minute later, they broke out onto an open slope with bushes, grass, and even a few wildflowers growing between them and a boulder-strewn shore.

"Okay, we're just a little bit from the boat." Violet nodded to her right. "It's beyond that rocky outcropping. Come on."

As they came close to the big rock formation that blocked their view, Kevin jerked his head up.

"I hear voices."

Violet frowned. "Me too. Probably your crew."

They took a few more steps, and she held up a hand. Kevin stopped beside her.

"That sounds like—" She broke off and listened, and then she put a finger to her lips and tiptoed toward the rocks. A moment later, she beckoned to him.

Kevin hurried down the slope to her side, but she didn't lead him forward. She held him back, behind the big rock. He heard two men talking.

"So, ya think we could pull it off, do ya?" The man's New England accent was heavy, and Kevin didn't recognize the voice.

Violet leaned toward him and whispered, "That's Darrell, the guy who brings our supplies and mail from the shore. I've got a bad feeling."

Kevin frowned but waited, straining to hear the conversation.

"Where's the rest of your crew?" Darrell asked.

"They took the dinghy out to look for the kid. Should be back soon." That was Willy, one of their crewmen.

"Ayuh. Could we get this boat floatable before they come back?" Darrell asked.

"I'm thinking we can take it around the shore and anchor where they can't see us. That would buy us time to do anything else necessary. Then we can take off for parts south."

"Parts south?" Violet mouthed, her face a map of dismay. She whispered, close to Kevin's ear, "Sounds like they want to skip out on you."

Would Willy do that? Kevin frowned. His mother was paying the crew well. Maybe Violet had misunderstood. He leaned against the damp rock face and listened.

"Where can we sell it?" Darrell asked.

"There's a place in Connecticut. Unless you know someplace up here."

"Nah, everybody knows me. They'd report it. But maybe on Cape Cod."

Violet's jaw dropped, and she pulled Kevin close. "They're going to steal your mother's yacht and sell it."

"It sure sounds like it. What do we do?"

She pulled his sleeve and tugged him back up the incline and across the path, into the trees. When they were out of earshot of the duo near the shore, she said, "Let's hoof it for the house."

Kevin hurried after her as fast as he could. She led him through the woods for fifty yards and then veered back onto the path. His wet clothing chafed his legs, but he wasn't as cold as he'd been earlier.

On his left, the slope from the path down to the shore was steep and rocky. He hoped Violet knew what she was doing. He wouldn't want to take a tumble here.

She stopped a few yards ahead of him and waited for him to catch up.

"That's our boathouse." She pointed down the shore. "Our house is just a little farther."

Before he could take in the shingled building and the dock jutting into the water, she drew him uphill from the boathouse. The path became a well-worn trail.

"The water's still rough," he noted, puffing a little.

"Yes, but it's much calmer than last night."

Ahead, he saw a snug little house, half hidden in the trees—more of a cabin. He hoped it was warm in there, that she had more hot coffee, and that his mom was okay. So many things. He sent up a quick prayer. *Thank You, Heavenly Father. Thank You for sending Violet.*

"I ADMIT, this isn't what my company usually publishes," Natalie said, looking down at the manuscript she held. She looked up at Paul over her glasses. "However, if you'll let me take them with me—"

"I don't think so," Paul said.

Natalie drew in a breath and studied his face. "All right, maybe not all. How about this one and one other? Or the two you think are the best?"

Paul's brow wrinkled. "And what happens then?"

"I'll see what I think. If they're as good as I think they are, I'll speak to the editorial board."

"I don't know."

"Well, it's a bit unusual, but since you cut your agent loose ten years ago—"

"You want me to get another agent?"

Natalie shrugged. "It's the way we usually do business, as you know. But I'm sure any agent you could name would jump at the chance to represent you."

"I don't think I want to do that. They'd want me to have Internet and a phone and all that."

"Well, of course they'd have to be able to stay in touch with you."

Paul said nothing but wouldn't meet her eyes.

"What?" she asked. "Don't tell me you intend to stay out here the rest of your life and never let anyone read another of your books. Paul, you have published fifty novels, and they were well received. Just let me put a couple out there …"

"I need a whole new audience."

"That may be true, but we can find it. Don't hide here and deny your potential new readers the chance to enjoy your work." She paused, looking down at the typescript. After a moment she raised her chin. "I need to concentrate on Kevin right now. But whatever happens, I want to work with you, Paul. If we get bad news today, it may be a while before I'm ready to proceed, but—"

The front door crashed open, and Violet rushed in.

"Dad! You and Uncle Barney need to hurry. Darrell and one of the men are going to steal the yacht."

Paul leaped to his feet. Beyond Violet, a dripping wet young man stood in the doorway. One of the crew?

Natalie jumped up and ran toward him, shoving past Violet. "Kevin!"

ELEVEN

"I'm okay, Mom, really," Kevin said, holding his mother tightly. "I almost froze to death last night, but really, I'm all right."

"Where were you? Oh, come sit down and tell me what happened." Natalie tugged him toward the sofa.

"Dad!" Violet grabbed her father's sleeve. "Where's Uncle Barney? You have to come with me."

"Don't you think we should get Kevin some dry clothes?" Paul asked.

"But they're going to steal the boat."

Paul put his hands on her shoulders. "Calm down. Who is stealing the boat?"

"Darrell and one of the sailors from the *Prospero*. Kevin and I heard them talking about it. They think the hull is patched enough that they can sail it away and fix it completely somewhere else and then go sell it down the coast—Connecticut, maybe. I heard that guy Willy say so."

"What?" Natalie stared at her and then at Kevin. "Is this true?"

"I'm afraid so, Mom."

"Where was Asa when you heard this?" Natalie asked.

"We didn't see Asa and the other guy," Violet said.

"Jake," Kevin agreed, nodding. "They weren't there, but Willy was plotting with this Darrell guy Violet said brings them their mail."

"Is the rudder fixed?" Paul asked.

Violet and Kevin looked blankly at each other.

"The rudder was completely broken off," Natalie said. "They can't steer the yacht if that's not fixed."

"I don't know," Kevin said. "We're just telling you what we heard."

"They said Asa and Jake were out in the dinghy," Violet said. "We were hiding behind a big rock, and we couldn't see their camp. I did see the stern of the *Prospero*, though. It looked like they had it off the rocks now and floating. But we didn't stick around to hear any more."

"Okay," Paul said. "The first thing to do is to—"

At that moment, the door opened, and Barney walked in.

"Barney," Natalie cried, "Kevin is found!"

He gaped at the young man. "Well, what do you know! That's an answer to prayer." He walked over to Kevin and held out his hand. "Are you okay, son? You're upright, so you can't be hurt too bad."

"I'll be fine," Kevin said, "but we've got to go find Asa and save the boat."

"What's this?" Barney swung around to look at his brother.

Quickly, they filled him in on what the two young people had heard at the sailors' camp.

"We may be too late," Barney said.

"Could be. Do your men have weapons?" Paul looked hard at Natalie.

"Weapons?" she said. "I hardly think so."

"Asa had a shotgun in his cabin," Kevin said. "And I think Willy may have a pistol."

"What?" His mother cried. "Why didn't I know about this?"

Kevin shrugged. "You didn't ask."

"Be right back." Paul dashed up the stairs. A moment later, he was back with a holstered revolver on his hip. He handed Barney a semi-automatic pistol. "Here. Let's go."

"We'll come," Kevin said.

"No, you kids stay." Paul looked at Natalie. "Get him some dry clothes from my dresser and my closet. And leave the manuscripts alone!"

He ran out the door, with Barney right behind him. Violet hesitated.

"Ms. Wrenn, you can fix Kevin something to eat after you find him some clothes. You can use anything you find in the kitchen."

She hurried outside. As she shut the door, she heard Natalie saying, "Wait! Wait!"

Violet ran down the path.

PAUL ROUNDED the curve of the shore path and stopped in his tracks. Barney plowed into him from behind and nearly knocked him over.

"What is it?" Barney gasped.

Paul gazed out at the choppy bay. The *Prospero* was off the rocks now but anchored a little way out. Asa and his men must have taken advantage of the high tide to ease the yacht off the boulders.

What worried him most was the sight of Darrell Clipton's cabin cruiser moored inshore, close to the crew's camp. But where was Darrell?

"Where is everyone?" Barney muttered in his ear.

Paul took a few cautious steps closer to the camp, and then he saw them.

Darrell stood on the shore, a pistol in his hand. He was aiming at two men in the *Prospero*'s dinghy, which was nearly hidden beyond the cabin cruiser. Beside Darrell stood Willy, one of Natalie's crewmen, and he also held a gun.

"That's Darrell, our mailman," Paul whispered to his brother.

Violet puffed up behind them, and Paul put a finger to his lips. Violet slowed her steps at once and tiptoed to join them.

"What's going on?" she whispered.

"Darrell appears to be in league with Willy, as you said," Paul told her. "The yacht's dinghy is there, beyond his boat, and the two of them are holding whoever's in the dinghy at gunpoint."

Violet scowled. "That's got to be Asa and Jake in the dinghy. They were supposedly out looking for Kevin when we came by."

"If they'd been here when Darrell arrived, Asa could have asked for his help contacting the Coast Guard and getting reinforcements out here to search for Kevin," Barney said.

Violet nodded, her brow furrowed. She leaned to one side in an effort to see more of the dinghy and nearly lost her footing.

Paul reached a quick hand to steady her. "Easy now. Is the radio working, Barn?"

"Well, they did get a message to the Coast Guard. I'm not sure if it's completely fixed or not."

"We've got them outnumbered," Violet said.

Her father shook his head. "Two guns to two guns."

She glared at him. "What, I'm not worth anything? I can make a diversion."

"Too risky," Barney said.

Paul clamped his teeth shut. The last thing he wanted to do was endanger his daughter. He laid a hand on her shoulder. "Listen to me." Barney and Violet both leaned closer. "Can you get onto Darrell's boat without alerting him?"

Violet looked toward the cabin cruiser and then toward Darrell's imposing back, where he stood on the shore beside Willy.

"I—I think so. Might have to get wet, but—"

Paul hesitated.

"It's a good plan," Barney said. "Your dad and I will mosey on down there and act like we suspect nothing. You get in the cruiser and use his radio. He does have a radio, doesn't he?"

Paul nodded. "Ship to shore."

"Who do I call?" Violet asked. "Anyone I can raise?"

"Well, yes, but—"

"Try for the Coast Guard," Barney said. He quickly instructed her on exactly what to say.

"Get down below the rock, so they can't see you when we approach," Paul told her. "And Violet, be careful. I don't want you to drown or be shot trying to pull this off."

She gave him a peck on the cheek. "Don't worry, Dad." As silent as a cat out hunting, she slipped down to the water.

Paul looked toward the gunmen and nodded at Barney. "Let's go in like friends. Our presence alone may make them back off."

He pulled in a deep breath and strode toward Darrell and Jake before he could have second thoughts. When he was within ten yards of the men, Willy turned his head toward them.

"Hey," Paul shouted, mustering a big smile. "What's up?"

Darrell whirled to face him, the gun in his hand. Beyond him, Paul could see Asa and Jake in the yacht's dinghy. Jake's face was pale, and Asa's gaze flitted from Paul back to his wayward crewmate and Darrell.

"Mr. Scott," Darrell said uncertainly.

Paul gazed pointedly at the gun in Darrell's hand. Willy had lowered his and seemed to be trying to hide it at his side.

"Surely there's no need for weapons." Paul tried to give his voice a jovial lilt. "What's going on?"

Darrell's jaw tightened. "These men were going to climb aboard my boat, likely run off with it."

"Liar," Asa shouted. "We'd rowed down the shore, looking for Kevin Wrenn, and we came back to see if there was news. It seems Willy's made a scheme with this man to take the *Prospero*."

"Well, there *is* news," Paul said. "Kevin's found."

"Found?" Willy's voice shook.

"Yes," Barney said. "He's alive."

"Hallelujah!" Asa grinned. "Now if you can help sort these two out, Mr. Scott—"

"I don't think so." Darrell aimed his pistol squarely at Paul's chest.

"Here now, Darrell, think about this. There are four of us and two of you. There's no way you'll get away with it."

Barney stepped up beside him, the semi-automatic in his hand. "Especially not when we've got as many guns as you, mister."

Reluctantly, Paul pulled his revolver. "That's right, Darrell. You might take me out, but my brother will shoot you. I think Asa and Jake can take care of Willy."

Asa was already climbing out of the dinghy into the surf.

A faint voice reached them from the cabin of Darrell's cabin cruiser. "...Violet Scott aboard ME 7805. I need Coast Guard and law enforcement as soon as possible on Scott Island. Repeat ..."

"Hey!" Darrell yelled.

His glance toward his boat was enough. Paul shoved him, hard, into Willy. They both tumbled backward. Willy's gun flew from his hand into the weeds, and Darrell slid off the edge of the path and down to the rocky strand below. Barney stepped forward, retrieved Willy's gun, and stood covering the fallen man with his weapon.

Paul looked over the edge of the drop to the shore. Darrell lay on his back between two rocks, moaning.

"Permission to come ashore, Captain," Violet shouted from the cabin cruiser.

"Permission granted," Paul replied.

She hopped over the starboard rail and swam toward the dinghy. Asa met her in the shallows and gave her a hand up, so she could wade in and join them.

"Coast Guard will be here in fifteen minutes," she reported.

Paul was still keeping an eye on Darrell, over the brink. "Can't be too soon for me. Got anything to tie these two with?"

"Aye, there's a bit of rope in the dinghy," Asa said. "Fetch it, Jake."

By the time the Guardsmen arrived, they had Darrell and Willy tied up and sitting beside the path. Jake had retrieved Darrell's gun and transferred it to Asa.

"Do you think Darrell will be okay, Dad?" Violet asked, shivering. Clipton sat slumped over and bleary-eyed, his left hand clutching his right arm at the bicep.

"His humerus may be broken, and he's got a good bump on the head, but yeah, eventually."

Violet grinned up at him. "Make sure you put this in your next book. It'll make exciting reading."

Paul smiled, genuinely this time. "I think you should write that story, Violet. I'm sure you'd do it justice. And don't forget how you saved Kevin's life."

She looked down and kicked at a pebble. "That's a little dramatic."

"Not to hear him tell it."

"I can't wait to hear the tale," Asa said.

Paul nodded. "As soon as they take these two away, you and Jake come up to the house. We'll give you a proper meal and a good yarn."

"I'll need to check the *Prospero* first." Asa gazed soberly out at the yacht. "Our patching should hold if they haven't done anything to make it worse. I don't know about the rudder. It was a hobble job."

"We can take my motorboat in to the mainland later—or tomorrow, if the wind doesn't let up today," Paul said. "We can get someone there to come out and work on it."

"I can fix it," Barney said. "That's what I do all the time at the marina."

Paul smiled apologetically. "I forgot for the moment. Sorry. Of course you can. You might need some materials, though."

"I'll stay with Asa to check on it. If we need anything from shore, we'll make a list. Then we'll join you and the Wrenns for supper."

"Sounds good." His brother clapped him on the shoulder. "Thanks for all your help."

TWELVE

Back at the house, Violet ran upstairs to change into dry clothes. She and her father found Natalie lying back in Paul's recliner, a cup of tea at her elbow and one of his manuscripts in her lap.

"Well!" She raised the chair back to a straight position. "I saw the cutter go by. I take it all is in hand?"

"It sure is," Violet said, grinning. "The Coast Guard is taking Willy and our mailman, Darrell, to shore. Asa and Uncle Barney are checking out the yacht to see if she's fit to sail. Oh, and Jake stayed to help them."

"Marvelous," Natalie said.

"Where's Kevin?" Violet looked around eagerly.

"He's resting." Natalie sighed. "I can't tell you how much I appreciate what you did for him this morning, Violet. You brought him home safe. I opened a can of soup for him—hope you don't mind. He ate it, and now he's tucked up in your bed, Paul."

"Best thing for him," Paul said.

"The other guys will be here for supper." Violet turned toward the kitchen. "I think I'll start my preparations. They'll have big appetites."

"May I help you?" Natalie shifted in the chair, as if to rise.

"No, thanks. I know my way around, and it's not a big space. Stay here and talk to Dad."

As they spoke, she and her father had removed their jackets and hung them up.

"Dad, you want some coffee?" Violet asked from the doorway.

"Love some," he said.

"Coming right up."

She hastily made a fresh pot, and while it brewed, she mentally mapped out her supper menu and pulled out supplies. When she carried her dad his mug, Kevin was coming down the stairs.

"You shouldn't be up," she said.

"I had a nap, but if I keep sleeping now, I'll get all jet-laggy." Kevin stretched his arms.

He looked better—much better. Violet's stomach fluttered.

"How do you feel?" Natalie asked, rising.

"I'm fine, Mom. Just needed to get warm and rest these old bones for a few." He laughed. "I could take a cup of that coffee, though. The smell enticed me down here."

"Sure," Violet said. "Come on."

He followed her to the kitchen, and she poured him a cup. Instead of joining Paul and his mother in the living room, Kevin took a seat at the kitchen table. As Violet worked, he watched her from beneath lowered eyelids. When his coffee was half gone, he set down the mug.

Violet looked up from the cutting board, where she was chopping vegetables for a stew. "More?"

"No, I'm good, thanks. Violet?"

"Yes?"

"If we were ashore ..." His lips curved upward in a wistful smile.

"What if we were?"

"I'd ask you to go out with me."

Her hands stilled, and she met his gaze. "If we were ashore, I might say yes."

They were both silent for a moment, and Paul's testy voice came from the other room: "I asked you before we left, Natalie, not to look at—"

"Where would we go?" Violet asked.

Kevin made a wry face. "If it was up here in Maine, I haven't the slightest idea."

Violet sighed. "It's been ten years since I was on the mainland much, and back then, I didn't know where people would go for—for dates."

"We'd find a place. A nice place."

"Or something fun?"

Kevin nodded. "Definitely something fun. Something you haven't done for ten years, or maybe something you've never done before."

She smiled. "I'd like that. I think." What would he come up with that she'd never done before? Bowling, maybe? She'd never done that. Or roller skating. She *had* been ice skating and to the state fair, but that was so long ago, she barely remembered the Ferris wheel ride. Not bungee jumping, she hoped. She'd never agree to that.

"Maybe we can stay in touch anyway. If you're still out here, I mean." Kevin raised his eyebrows, hoping for a favorable reply.

"We'd have to write letters."

"No phone service at all?"

He looked so woeful, she laughed. "None, I'm afraid. But this situation might convince Dad to get a short-wave radio set."

"How does a writer survive without the Internet?"

She shrugged. "He's gotten used to it, I guess. He didn't want to be hounded, so he made it almost impossible to contact him. And me—well, I was so young when Mom died and we came here, I don't miss it, truthfully. I'd never had a cell phone or a computer of my own. But I'm never bored out here."

Kevin took a sip from his mug, and Violet went back to

chopping carrots. When she paused again, he said, "My mother wants him to go live on shore, you know."

Violet started to speak but closed her mouth. She didn't want to express anything that would sound disloyal to her father.

"Have you talked about it?" Kevin asked.

"Some. But not much, really. I don't think Dad's ready."

"Will he ever be ready to leave here?"

She frowned and reached for an onion.

Kevin stood with his mug in his hand. "I think I'll have more coffee."

"Help yourself."

He walked over to the counter and stood beside her. "Violet."

"Yes?" She looked into his eyes, disconcerted at his nearness.

"I really like you."

She swallowed hard. "It could just be the island. Some people think it's exotic to live on an island, and—well, I'm the only girl out here, you know. If there were others to pick from, you might feel otherwise."

"I doubt it. Anyway, I'd still like you."

Violet smiled. She scooped up handfuls of chopped vegetables and plopped them in the kettle. Then she got two packets of chicken out of the refrigerator. She'd taken them from the freezer that morning to begin thawing, suspecting they'd have company at least one more night. They kept a conservative supply of meats and other perishables in the freezer, but not enough so they'd lose a fortune if the generator ever failed them.

"Do you think your dad would let you go ashore without him?" Kevin asked. "I mean, he can't force you to stay here, can he?"

She thought about that as she cut up the chicken and added it to the pot. "I wouldn't say he can. I don't think he would. But I'd hate to leave him alone out here."

"Is he, like, really depressed?"

"Sometimes I think he is."

"For ten years?"

She washed her hands at the sink and turned to face him. "How long since your dad died?"

"Huh? He's not dead. He and Mom got divorced when I was fifteen."

"Oh. I'm sorry. Does she get depressed about it?"

"I don't know. She has her publishing house. She puts most of her energy into her work."

Violet nodded. "Dad's not very jolly, but he's nice to be around. I couldn't ask for a better father. He talks to me about important things."

"Except things like going ashore."

She said nothing but looked down at her hands and the towel she still clutched. From the other room, her father and Natalie seemed to be chatting amicably now.

"I guess you're right," Kevin said. "There are things Mom and I don't talk about much." He poured more coffee into his mug. "So, he's home-schooled you, right?"

Thankful for a neutral topic, Violet met his gaze. "Pretty much. I mean, I could read when we came here, and he made sure I had plenty of reading material. He did some math with me, and we walked through high school level science classes."

"Does he talk to you about your mom?"

"Yes. We talk about her a lot. Well, not every day, but it's a topic we're comfortable with."

Kevin nodded. "What do you think he'd say if I asked him if I could see you again?"

Violet swallowed hard. "I haven't got a clue."

PAUL LOOKED up as his daughter and Kevin entered the living room.

"Well, supper plans under control?"

Violet nodded. "I've got a chicken stew simmering, and I plan to make some biscuits a little later."

"Sounds delicious," Natalie said.

"Sit down, kids." Paul waved vaguely toward the unoccupied seating. Violet walked over and sank down beside him on the sofa. Kevin swiveled the desk chair to face them and took a seat.

"What's up, Dad?" Violet looked up at him, smiling, her blue eyes bright but tinged with concern.

Paul's heart squeezed. She was grown up now, but still so vulnerable. He'd thought he was protecting her out here, but how well had he prepared her for life—real life? Because Violet's world couldn't consist only of this island. He covered her hand with his.

"Natalie and I have been discussing letting her take a couple of my manuscripts back with her and showing them to her publishing committee."

"That's wonderful, Dad!" Violet turned eagerly to Natalie. "Be sure you take *The Arcane Mariner*."

Natalie laughed. "Sounds intriguing."

"Oh, that's not the best one," Paul said dismissively, even though he knew Violet loved it. True, it was action-filled, but had only a bit of romance in it, along with the mariner's cat, which had a major role in the climax of the story. Those were her favorite parts. "It's ... it's very light," he said. "And short."

"A novella, maybe?" Natalie asked.

"Well ..."

"Let me be the judge."

"Yes, Dad. Let her be the judge." Violet pressed his wrist. "She'll love it. I know she will."

She won't love the spiritual angle. Then again, he'd already told Natalie all twelve of the manuscripts he'd completed on the island had a Christian perspective.

"I'd love to take them on," Natalie said with a rueful smile. "However, Paul and I have agreed I'll take two, of his choosing. I rather like the one I started reading last night, but if he wants to pick two others, that's all right by me."

"What if Wrenn Publishing decides they're not a fit?" Kevin

asked. Violet had expressed her fears to him about the different genre her father was now writing.

"Well, I do own the company." Natalie frowned. "We shall see. If the writing is as strong as I expect it to be, we may have to overcome some reservations."

"You mean you'd print Christian books now?" Violet turned her eager face toward her father.

Paul pressed his lips together and remained silent. He didn't believe Natalie would change her policy. Or would she, to get him back? His older books had carried Wrenn Publishing for years. They outsold nearly all of Natalie's other clients. Would she radically change the structure of the company for this? And how would he feel if she promoted his new books beside others of a very different nature?

"I want my older books reverted to me." He'd wanted to say it earlier but hadn't dared. With the young people present, he took courage.

Natalie stared at him. "What do you mean? Revert all rights to you?"

"Yes. They're old books, Natalie. They're not selling like they used to."

"Well, a few of them I can see reverting. But most are still selling moderately, even after all this time. If we reissued them with new covers—"

"No." Paul held her gaze. "I'm making that a condition. My old contracts state that if a book doesn't sell a certain amount of copies within a pay period, all rights revert to me."

"And what would you do with them?"

"I want them off the market."

Natalie gasped. "Perhaps a few of the more gruesome ones." She watched his face and amended, "And maybe a couple of the really steamy ones, but Paul, those are actually our bestsellers."

"I know. Darrell delivers the royalty statements faithfully every six months, and I can see which books are still selling. I'm embarrassed by some of my own work now. If a reader buys one of my new books and then buys one of the older ones, thinking they'll have the same tone, he'll be mightily disappointed."

Natalie's face was red. "And if I refuse? Really, Paul, we sell enough e-books every period to keep most of your contracts in force."

He let out a big sigh. "Then we won't be doing business together any longer. I'm sorry, Natalie. Especially if Violet and I return to the mainland."

Violet let out a puff of air. "Wait! You're thinking of moving back?"

"Thinking of it. Haven't decided, by any means. But it seems I may need to find a new agent and approach some new publishers. That's hard to do without the Internet and the ability to interview."

Natalie held up both hands. "Let's slow down. Let me take two manuscripts—as you've already agreed—and I'll decide whether to go along with this latest plan of yours. But really, Paul, it would be a big financial blow to both of us to completely remove your backlist from the market."

"Not so big now as it would have been ten years ago, or even five. I stand by what I said."

Natalie's jaw clenched. "I wish you'd made this stipulation earlier."

"I should have."

She and Paul stared at each other. Finally, Natalie looked away.

"All right. Kevin and I will leave in the morning, provided the yacht is seaworthy. I will read the manuscripts and make my decision."

Paul frowned. He didn't want to be locked into something he would later regret. "Look, Natalie, maybe I should send them to a different publisher."

"You promised me I could look at two."

"Yes, but I didn't promise I'd let you buy the rights."

"That's true, and of course, you can always refuse any offer I make. Now, excuse me. I'd like to freshen up before supper." Natalie rose and went up the stairs.

"Dad," Violet said quietly, but he could sense her excitement. "Did you mean it about leaving the island?"

"I'm open to the idea." Paul reached for her hand. "I think maybe I've kept you here too long."

"No, you haven't. It's been a wonderful place to grow up. But … well, if you care about my opinion—"

"Of course I do!"

"Then I vote yes. Let's do it. If we hate it, we can always come back, right?"

"If these new books don't sell—and I don't just mean to Wrenn, but anywhere—well, I might have to sell the island."

Violet frowned. "I hope not. It would be wonderful to come back here summers. But I'd really like to see more of the world."

"And maybe get a cell phone?" Paul laughed.

"I wouldn't know what to do with it."

"I'll teach you," Kevin said.

Paul turned his attention to the young man, studying him pensively.

Kevin's cheeks flushed. "I—sir—well, Violet and I have been talking. If you do move ashore, I'd like to keep on seeing her."

"Yes," Violet chimed in, "Kevin and I definitely want to see each other again."

"With your permission, of course." Kevin looked suddenly frightened.

Paul smiled. "Violet is an adult, and a level-headed one at that. It's true, her social experience is extremely limited, but I think it would be a good idea for her to have friends."

"Thank you, Dad." Violet leaned in and hugged him.

"You're welcome, but as I said, I haven't decided for certain. Maybe you …" He eyed her cautiously. Would he ever be able to let Violet venture ashore alone? He rounded on Kevin. "Tell me, young man, do you believe in God?"

Kevin's eyebrows shot up. "Yes, sir, I certainly do."

Paul frowned, thinking of Natalie's attitude. "Your mother—"

"Oh, I know Mom's not—Well, she says she believes in God, but she doesn't think He's personal, that He's right here with us all the time. She thinks He's distant and ... Well, I can't claim to know exactly what she thinks. Perhaps you should ask her, Mr. Scott. But I definitely trust Christ as my Savior. And if I can continue to see Violet, you wouldn't have to worry about ... about anything inappropriate."

Paul gazed at him, wondering if this young man was too good to be true. Every young person faced temptation. He'd have to have some serious discussions with Violet about that if they were venturing into the world. He shuddered to think of the lifestyles some of his older fictional characters had led. How many people had he led astray with his secular books?

And what about Natalie? If he took his new work to a Christian publisher, would she find ways to keep the old books in print? Sales, promotions ... Maybe he should consider a pen name for his new work after all. He wished he hadn't let his old agent go, but there must be Christian agents out there. He'd never considered looking for one, because he'd hesitated so long to offer his new work for publication.

He drew in a deep breath. "I'll hold you to that, young man. Meanwhile, it seems I have a lot of work to do. Letters to write, and so on. Kevin, if I went ashore and bought a laptop computer, would I be able to use the Internet somewhere? I certainly can't out here."

"Why, yes," Kevin said. "In fact, a lot of public libraries have computer stations now. You can go in and use their computers. Sometimes you need to reserve a time, but—well, there are other places too. Some restaurants and coffee shops offer Wi-Fi service for free to their customers. You could take your laptop in with you and eat lunch and do business online."

Paul nodded slowly. He had so much to catch up on. "Kevin, what do you do? Are you employed?"

"I do tech stuff. I majored in computer science. Mom wants me to go to work at Wrenn, but I'm not so sure about that. I've started my own little independent business. I oversee people's websites."

"Writers?" Paul asked.

"Some. See, some of them don't want to be bothered with the marketing stuff—social media and all that. So I do it for them. It lets them just write. Oh, they have to do some things, of course, but there's a lot I can do for them to take the burden off."

"That sounds interesting. And very helpful. Of course, it's all done remotely?"

"Yes, sir. I'm a virtual assistant for clients all over the country. Well, not all over, just yet. But North Carolina, California, Ohio, Missouri ... other places."

Paul squinted his eyes nearly shut and tried to see into the future, but he couldn't. "I'll keep your services in mind."

"Thank you very much," Kevin said. "I have business cards, but I don't—There may be a couple in my duffel on the boat."

"If you have them, bring me one before you leave."

"I sure will."

Kevin looked at Violet, and the way she smiled at him wrenched Paul's heart. If they went ashore, would he lose Violet too? He supposed it was inevitable. And he wanted her to find someone, to fall in love, to have a family. He wouldn't begrudge those things to his beloved daughter.

But he didn't want her to fall too hard for literally the first man who came along, either.

Thirteen

The rain had stopped, and the wind had died to a stiff breeze. Violet was in the kitchen working on dinner for seven. Paul grabbed his jacket off its peg and went to the doorway. Kevin, to his surprise, scrubbed industriously at a pan in the sink and laughed as Violet tossed off a quip.

"Hey, kids, the wind's slacked off. I'm going down to check on the dock and the boathouse again."

Violet looked up. "Okay, Dad."

"Is my mother still upstairs?" Kevin asked.

"Yes." Probably speed reading, so she could get in an extra manuscript or two. Paul didn't like it, but he wasn't about to go up and confront her.

"May I go with you, sir?" Kevin had a hangdog look about him.

"Sure," Paul said. "You need anything, Vi?"

"No, I'm good. I'll have supper ready in"—She looked at the battery-operated clock—"one hour."

"Sounds good."

Paul found an extra coat for Kevin and pulled on his own jacket and a baseball cap.

As they strode down the path together, Kevin said, "It must be beautiful out here when the sun's shining."

Paul chuckled. "Maybe you'll get to see it that way tomorrow before you sail."

As they approached the dock, he eyed it critically but couldn't see any damage. He stepped out on the near end and jumped up and down a couple of times, testing the dock's strength.

"Feels solid." He walked out to the far end and checked it. Kevin followed, staying back a couple of paces. "I don't think we need any repairs here, which is good. I'll have to find someone to replace Darrell in bringing in our supplies if we stay. Maybe weekly, instead of monthly."

"Sir, if there's anything I can do to help you ..."

"For starters, you can quit calling me *sir*."

"Yes, s—Uh, Mr. Scott."

"Paul." He turned and met Kevin's gaze. "Let's avoid confusion between me and my brother."

"Sure." Kevin smiled, and Paul returned it.

"Now about my daughter."

Kevin caught his breath.

Paul looked over at the boathouse. A few shingles had been torn from the roof, and several large tree limbs lay on the ground around the shoreward end of the structure. "Guess I'll need to do a little work on the boathouse."

Kevin looked confused.

"Oh, yes, my daughter," Paul said. "I can see the need to visit the mainland. Whether I'll return to the island later remains to be seen. But I'll need to close things up here and pack up a lot of stuff."

"Where will you go?" Kevin asked softly.

"I'm not sure. Certainly not New York."

The young man nodded. "As I said, if I can help ..."

"Maybe you can. I'm from Maine, and I've lived here nearly all my life. Started out in Kennebec County and wouldn't mind returning there, but I don't really care which part, so long as I can get a decent communication setup."

"Right."

"Your mother would probably like me to move to New York, or at least southern New England, but that's not me." He eyed Kevin sharply.

"I understand. And you said it would be all right for me to communicate with Violet after you're set up? Phone, I mean. Texting, e-mail, whatever she's comfortable with?"

"That's up to her. I think she likes you."

Kevin's smile was a little goofy now. "I hope so."

"Yes, well, don't you ever do anything to make her like you less."

"I'll try, sir—Mr.—Paul. Thank you."

Paul gave him a nod and walked along the dock. Kevin kept pace.

"I'll need a house to rent, possibly with an option to buy. If I decide I like it and want to stay, that is. I know you're not in real estate—"

"No problem. I can locate some suitable properties online and, if you like the looks of them, set up appointments for you to view them. I'd need to know when you'll be available, of course."

As he ambled toward the boathouse, Paul thought about it. "We'll need at least a week. Did the Coast Guard take Darrell's boat?"

"I believe so."

Paul let out a sigh. "I'll have to line up someone to come out and carry a load or two of freight ashore for us. My boat's too small to carry much."

"I can arrange that."

"All right. But I assume you'll go back to New York with your mother tomorrow."

"I thought I might take a week up here, rent a cottage, or even stay at a hotel."

"That's expensive."

"True. Prices have gone up a lot in the last few years."

"I knew a couple who had a string of cottages about five miles from our landing spot in Pinecone Harbor. Burridge, their name was. You could check your computer and see if they're still in business. If they are, tell them you're a friend of mine and you're helping me out. It's the off-season now. They might give you a break."

Kevin grinned. "Thank you. That sounds great."

"Well, I can't guarantee anything. Haven't talked to them in years. But Rusty Burridge was an old school buddy of mine. You can trust him."

"I'll look into it as soon as I can get ashore."

Paul stopped and looked over the minor damage to the boathouse roof. Peering in through the one small window, he could see his motorboat riding easy in the water, and a rowboat he rarely used but kept on principle, on its rack as usual.

"Things look okay in there." He walked around the back of the building and checked the other side. Nodding in satisfaction, he turned and found Kevin close behind him. "Not much to do here. I'm thinking we might be wise to go ashore tomorrow for the day. We could leave you in Pinecone Harbor. I should visit the bank and a few other places."

"Can I rent a car there?"

"Last I knew. If it's changed, I'll scare up an old acquaintance who'll help you find a pickup you can borrow."

Kevin laughed. "Always wanted to drive a truck. It's not the thing in Manhattan, you know."

"Hmm. New adventure for you. And you can certainly rent a boat if you need to come back out here and communicate with us. I can help you set that up."

"I'm game."

"Do you have experience handling a motorboat by yourself?"

"Some."

Paul nodded slowly. "I don't want to put you in danger, son.

This is a totally different world for you, and you've got to realize it will be for Violet too, when she goes ashore. If we make that run into town for my errands, I'll take her along. She hasn't set foot on the mainland more than half a dozen times in ten years. That was remiss of me."

After a moment's silence, Kevin said, "I can tell she loves it out here."

"She does. But she also wants to leave. Wants to see what else is out there." Paul shook his head. "I don't blame her."

AFTER SUPPER, Barney Scott insisted on helping his niece with the cleanup. Asa and Jake had a short consultation with Ms. Wrenn and then went back to the yacht, where they would sleep in their berths.

Kevin waited until they'd left and then approached his mother.

"Mom, I've decided to stay in Maine for a bit. A week, maybe."

Natalie frowned. "What are you saying?"

"I'm saying I want to take in some of the sights of coastal Maine."

Paul stepped up to her and cleared his throat. "Kevin expressed a wish to stick around, and I've asked him to help me with a few things."

Her frown deepened. "Here on the island?"

"No, I'll take him ashore tomorrow. I need to run some errands in town myself, and I can help Kevin find a place to stay."

She looked from Paul to Kevin. "Can you keep up with your work up here?"

"Sure. Asa brought my laptop up from the boat. Paul says I should be able to get Internet service as soon as I'm ashore." Kevin deliberately kept his plans a little vague.

Natalie let out a slow breath. "I suppose you can work anywhere."

"I'll probably be back in a week or two. If that changes, I'll call you."

His mother held his gaze. Kevin stared back. He was an adult now, and she knew him better than anyone. Unless something totally unforeseen happened, he would keep his word.

"All right," she said at last. "Paul, I assume your brother is going back down the coast with me. We'll leave him off in his home port."

Paul chuckled. "I assume so too. Barney hasn't said otherwise to me."

Natalie nodded. "Good. Now, if you'll excuse me, I'd like to get some more reading done."

"You can read down here." Paul waved toward the comfortable seating in the living room.

"Thank you. And I do have a couple of questions about that first manuscript I read, if you don't mind discussing it. It's a powerful story, but ..."

Kevin edged toward the kitchen door. When he was sure his mother was deeply engaged in her conversation with Paul Scott, he slipped into Violet's domain.

"Hey," he said.

Violet looked up from the dish of leftovers she was covering, and Barney swung around from the sink.

"Can I help?" Kevin asked.

"We're nearly done." Violet smiled and looked around. "I guess you could take the trash out to the shed for me."

Barney grabbed a towel and dried his hands. "Let me do that, Violet. I know where you put it until your dad's ready for a bonfire."

"Oh, well ... Okay." Violet looked at Kevin and shrugged.

"I can wash dishes," Kevin offered.

She grinned. "I know you can. Thank you very much."

A minute later, Barney was out the back door with the full garbage bag, and Kevin cleared his throat.

"Did your dad tell you I'm going into Pinecone Harbor with you two tomorrow?"

"Yes, he did." Violet's smile was quieter now, and her eyes a bit somber. "He says you'll help us find a place to stay on shore."

"That's the plan. He thought you could move in a week or so. And—and he doesn't seem averse to my keeping in touch with you."

"Of course you can!"

Kevin smiled. "I'm really glad he's doing this, Violet. I'm not sure how much he's told Mom yet, but it sounds like he's considering staying on the mainland."

She nodded. "He told me. We talked for a few minutes before supper. I'm excited about it."

"I'll bet." Kevin took a step toward her, his chest tight. "Would you go out with me? I mean, would you—"

"Yes."

He relaxed and pulled in a deep breath, and Violet laughed.

"I've never been on a date before."

"I know," Kevin said. "And I promised your dad I'd be a gentleman."

"Really? I'm out of the loop, but that sounds a little old-fashioned."

"It is. Those weren't the exact words we spoke, but that's what we meant. You'll be safe with me, Violet."

"Of course I will."

He nodded. "I just wanted to say it because—well, because I think Paul felt he was keeping you safe by staying out here."

"Maybe." She picked up the dish of leftovers and took it to the refrigerator. "But I don't think that's why he stayed out here for ten years."

"It's not?"

She shook her head. "In the Bible, it says we should tell

others about Jesus." She shut the refrigerator door and turned to face him. "Do you read the Bible?"

"I do. Not as much as I probably should, but yes."

"Well, Dad's been struggling with that. He's been writing books with a Christian message for the past ten years, but he hasn't been sending them out."

"So ..." Kevin said slowly, "if he wants to obey God and tell other people, how can he do that if he stays out here and doesn't send out his books?"

"Exactly." Violet smiled. "We've talked about it some. I think God has put a burden on my dad. First, to change the way he wrote. And now, to put it in people's hands."

"Wow."

"Yeah, it's a lot." She picked up the dishcloth and wiped the counter.

"Maybe I shouldn't say this, but ..." Kevin eyed her speculatively and felt he could share his struggles with her. "My mom wants me to join her publishing company. I think I'm ready to give her a definite no on that."

Violet paused. "I thought your mom trained you to be an editor."

"She did, and I took classes in editing and publishing. But you know my mother and I don't see eye to eye on everything. Our faith, for example."

"Yeah. That must be rough."

"Sometimes. Anyway, I've set up a small business of my own. Some freelance editing, but more virtual assistant work. She wasn't happy about it. I think she figured after a year or so I'd give it up." He looked down at the floor for a moment and then met her gaze. "I can't go to work for her. I hate to see Wrenn Publishing promoting some of the stuff they do."

"But you haven't told her."

"Not in so many words. But I'm ready now. After hearing your dad stand up to her ... well, I think it's time."

"Whoa. Good for you."

"She won't like it."

Her lips quirked, but she didn't say anything. Maybe she wasn't sure how to respond.

Kevin smiled. "Anyway, I was pretty stoked when your dad asked if I could help him relocate."

"I'll bet. I can't wait to see how this all turns out. He may hire you to do some other stuff later on."

He nodded. "That would be nice. So, will you go to school? College, I mean?"

"I don't know. Maybe."

"Well, whatever you end up doing, I hope we can stay friends at least."

"At least." She walked over and touched his hand, and his pulse galloped. "Kevin, I think we're going to be friends for a long time."

"Me too."

"This can't be a coincidence, meeting up again after ten years," she said.

"You saved my life."

"Doubt it. But I did help you. I feel like you're helping me too. By helping Dad, you're helping me."

"I guess that's right." He folded his fingers around her hand and gave it a gentle squeeze.

Epilogue

Paul looked up from signing his name and grinned at the next two customers.

"Look at you!" He jumped up and hurried around the table to embrace Violet.

She pulled back and studied his face. "You look wonderful, Dad."

"Do I?" He self-consciously patted the front of his spanking-new shirt. "I feel overdressed." His publicist had suggested he wear a tie for the book signing, but Paul had assured him that "isn't me."

The table was set up in the middle of a large mall in Portland, and he'd been signing books for the last ninety minutes. Chatting with the readers had felt awkward at first, but after a few had told him sincerely how much they'd loved his first Christian book, and they couldn't wait to read this second one, he'd relaxed.

"Kevin, how are you?" He shook hands with the young man.

Kevin grinned. "Great."

"We're probably holding up the line," Violet said with a

glance over her shoulder at the waiting customers. "You'll be done in what—half an hour?"

Paul nodded. "Something like that."

"We'll shop a bit and come back then."

"Okay. Great to have you both here." He watched them amble away, rejoicing that Kevin had picked her up at her college dorm and driven her down here to see him. Violet paused in front of a jewelry shop to gaze at the window displays, and Paul resumed his seat smiling.

Twenty customers later, the assistant manager of the bookstore that had set up the event approached from the side. She leaned down and said softly in Paul's ear, "Our time's up, Mr. Scott. Great job."

Paul looked up at her in surprise. "Oh? There are still people waiting."

The woman shrugged.

Paul stood and cleared his throat. "Folks, thanks so much for coming out. I count—three, four—seven of you waiting for a signing. I'll take you seven, because I really want to meet you. After that, I'm afraid we'll have to cut it off."

The assistant manager stepped forward with a strained smile to the end of the line. Paul knew she'd make sure no latecomers joined in. Too bad they hadn't booked the space for an additional hour. To his surprise, he'd genuinely enjoyed this time with his readers.

He smiled, answered a few questions, signed his name, added the personalization when requested, and finally faced the assistant manager again.

"Thank you *so* much, Mr. Scott," she said. "We've got to close up now. This gentleman asked to see you, but I'd ask you to step away so our crew can break down the table and pack the books."

Paul looked beyond her and met his brother's sparkling eyes.

"Barn!" Gladly, he moved from behind the table and met Barney in a bear hug. "What are you doing up here?"

Barney shrugged. "Violet told me you were having a book

signing. I thought I'd come check it out. Didn't buy a book, though—sorry."

"That's because I sent you one already."

"Right. Any chance I can cadge supper with you?"

"Absolutely. Violet and Kevin are here somewhere." Paul glanced around but didn't see them. "Violet's working on a degree in creative writing, you know."

"I do. And she told me in an e-mail that she's started a novel."

Paul's eyes burned with tears, and he swiped a hand across them. "She has. It's really good."

"And things worked out with the new agent, I guess?"

"He's terrific. He set this up. And the new publisher's been great." Twenty yards away, Violet and Kevin approached, hands clasped. "There they are! I told the kids I'd take them to Hedge Castle for dinner. You're more than welcome to tag along, my treat."

"Sounds good." Barney stepped forward to greet his niece. He engulfed her in a big hug and then shook Kevin's hand. "Hey there, young fella."

"Hello, Mr. Scott. How's the boat business?"

"Busy, but I snagged a long weekend."

Paul sidled up to Barney. "Uncle Barn's joining us for dinner, if you two don't mind."

"Mind? Of course not!" Violet's smile stretched across her face. "It's so good to see you, Uncle Barney."

"Yeah? What's this?" Barney grabbed her outstretched hand and held it a little closer to inspect the ring twinkling on her finger.

Violet glanced up at Kevin.

"We, uh, found a jewelry store while we were waiting for Paul to finish," Kevin said.

"So it's official?" Paul asked.

"Uh-huh." Violet gazed up at him coyly from beneath her long lashes.

Everything inside him grew warm and mushy in a flash. "Come here, you!" Paul hugged her fiercely and then turned to Kevin and stuck out his hand. "Congratulations, son!"

"Thank you." Kevin blinked and smiled down at Violet.

"Well, come on," Barney said, clapping Kevin on the shoulder. "Let's get out of here. Paul, you all set?"

"I sure am. Let's go."

About the Author

Susan Page Davis is the author of more than one hundred books. Her books include Christian novels and novellas in the historical romance, mystery, and romantic suspense genres. Her work has won several awards, including the Carol Award, three Will Rogers Medallions, and two Faith, Hope, & Love Reader's Choice Awards. She has also been a finalist in the WILLA Literary Awards and Selah Awards, and a multi-time finalist in the Carol Awards. A Maine native, Susan has lived in Oregon and now resides in western Kentucky with her husband Jim, a retired news editor. They are the parents of six and grandparents of eleven.

Visit her website at: https://susanpagedavis.com.

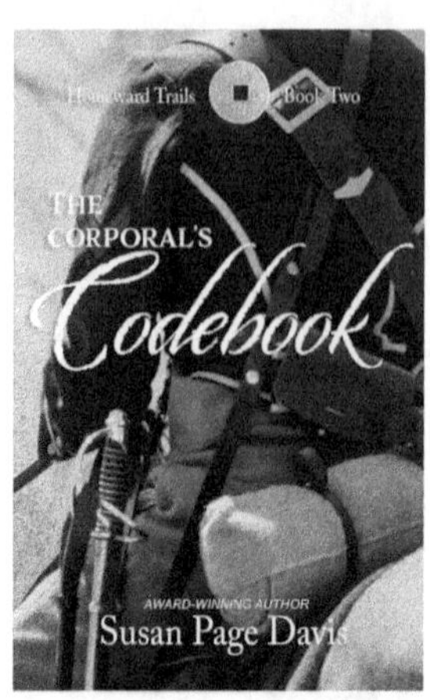

The Corporal's Codebook—Book Two

Get your copy here:

https://scrivenings.link/thecorporalscodebook

The Sister's Search—Book Three

Get your copy here:

https://scrivenings.link/thesisterssearch

Blue Plate Special—Book One

Get your copy here:

https://scrivenings.link/blueplatespecial

Ice Cold Blue—Book Two

Get your copy here:

https://scrivenings.link/icecoldblue

***Persian Blue Puzzle*—Book Three**

Get your copy here:

https://scrivenings.link/persianbluepuzzle

***Scream Blue Murder*—Book Four**

Get your copy here:

https://scrivenings.link/screambluemurder

***Scream Blue Murder*—Book Four**

Get your copy here:

https://scrivenings.link/truebluechristmas

≈

Sharktooth Island

A collection of Romantic Suspense novellas

Includes "Out of the Storm," a novella by Susan Page Davis, and three more stories set on Sharktooth Island, a fabled island that no one dares to tame.

Get your copy here:

https://scrivenings.link/sharktoothisland

Inspired by The Merry Wives of Windsor
by William Shakespeare

The Marry Wives of
SWEETHEART

a novella by
Shannon Sue Dunlap

ONE

"Better three hours too soon than a minute too late."
(Ford, Act 2, Scene 2, The Merry Wives of Windsor)

The tempo of Augusta Page's fingernails matched the second hand on her wristwatch. She drummed her red manicure on the windowsill. Frustration welled inside of her, along with a laundry list of questions.

Why was her daughter so late?

For the meeting?

For life?

For love?

She tuned out the wave of noise behind her. The community center echoed with the sound of thirty women talking at once. They passed their phones in an endless carousel of wedding photos and grandbabies. If Augusta was forced to admire one more picture of a toddler holding a sign marking how many months they'd been on the planet, she'd scream.

Her untapped potential to be the best doting Nana in Sweetheart, Texas, was going to waste. When would it be her turn? If she had anything to say about it, soon.

Augusta brightened as a familiar blue hatchback drove into

the parking lot. Time to get this happy ending on the road. She stuck her hand behind her back and beckoned her best friend.

"Ronnie! She's here."

Veronica "Ronnie" Ford hurried over and shoved her long-limbed frame beside Augusta. The two women peered out the glass. In the distance, a tall blonde in jeans and a long-sleeved coral top walked toward the entrance, carrying a large tray of finger sandwiches.

Ronnie whistled. "Are you sure Anne doesn't suspect anything?"

Augusta's lips quirked. "She has no inkling of the good news we're about to spring on her."

"Spring is right." Ronnie cringed. "I hope this announcement isn't four years overdue."

Augusta swatted her. "My baby has wasted more than enough time pining for her first love. Now that he's back in town, it's time to wrap the pair up and deliver them to the minister."

ANNE PAGE FROZE with her fingers around the doorknob. Balancing the sandwich tray on her hip, she gave herself a thirty-second pep talk. Any visit to the Sweetheart Ladies Auxiliary required a boost of mental fortitude. The members sported hearts the size of Texas, but their curiosity was continental.

"What are you afraid of?" Anne gnawed on her lower lip. "You've known these women since birth. Just drop off their order and leave."

Easier said than done. Did the by-laws contain a special clause declaring everyone who entered the auxiliary meetings must receive their fair share of meddling? Anne hated being meddled with. Her brain flicked through all the aspects of her life the members might try to improve. She'd better have a quick response ready.

"Yes, I'm still a waitress at the café. The flexible hours work well with my college schedule."

Uh-oh. Was it dangerous to mention her perpetual quest for a degree?

"I only changed my major twice. Now, I'm certain dental hygiene is the field I want."

Actually, there was still a smidgen of doubt. No need to bring that pesky detail up.

"I don't have a boyfriend. But I'm baking a cake for the Candy Hearts Festival auction. Who knows where the opportunity might lead?"

Anne knew exactly where it would lead. Nowhere. The town's annual Valentine's festival brought visitors from every corner of the state. And the big finale was the cake auction when hopeful gentlemen bid on the home-baked desserts of the women they fancied. But the man she wanted to purchase her cake wouldn't be in attendance.

The face of her high school boyfriend flashed through her mind, triggering bittersweet memories. The first time he'd bought her cake at the age of thirteen. Summer stargazing from their special perch in the corn fields. Him standing under the window serenading her with a guitar.

An unwelcome picture intruded in the happy montage—him driving toward the interstate without a backward glance. And not a word since then. He lived a mere one hundred and sixteen miles away in big city Dallas, but it might as well be a thousand.

She stomped her foot. "Stupid Connor Fenton."

No use wasting precious brain space on someone who was never coming back. She'd waited four long years. Time to move on. The cake auction was the first step.

Anne took a deep breath, turned the knob, and pushed the door open. The outdated wood panel walls of the community center encased a buzzing company of busybodies. A chorus of high-pitched voices greeted her.

"There you are!"

"Look who's here!"

"Food. Finally!"

Anne's own mother met her at the front, wearing a sleek aquamarine pantsuit, with her blonde hair and understated makeup done to perfection. "What took you so long, darlin'? I was starting to worry." She accepted the sandwich tray with the poise of a beauty pageant winner and slid it onto a table near the entrance.

A scan of the room revealed friendly, curious faces turned their way.

"It's a typical workday. Lots to do." She took a baby step to the door. "In fact, I'd better get back to the café. Susanna needs my help."

"Don't be silly." Her mom captured Anne's arm in a death grip and steered her to the table where her friends sat. "Your Aunt Ronnie was just asking about you. I'm sure you can spare two minutes to fill her in."

"On what?" Anne muttered. She followed her mother, sank into a metal folding chair, and nodded at the middle-aged women. "Hello, ladies. Did your meeting go well?"

"Excellent." The mayor's wife, Lanette Johnson, slapped her hands against the garish pattern of her leopard print pants.

The *former* mayor's wife, Anne reminded herself. It was still hard to believe her old babysitter, Katherine Bruno, was the new mayor. She was only in her thirties! And even bossy Katherine found a handsome New Yorker to fall in love with her. It seemed everyone was getting on with their lives.

Except for Anne.

Ronnie Ford rested her flannel-covered elbows on the table. She and Anne's mother were as different as night and day. Plaid and chintz. Oreos and escargot.

How had the two ever ended up being best friends? So close their children considered each other cousins, even though no real blood ties existed.

"Hi, sugar." She grinned. "Still baking a cake for the Candy Hearts Festival?"

"After you got on to me, I didn't dare skip it." Anne squirmed in her seat.

Lanette Johnson leaned into their conversation. "Are you participating in the auction? Good girl! It's been years since you entered."

"Guess so."

No guessing required. She knew exactly how long it had been. Four years. The last time Connor was in Sweetheart. She crossed her fingers under the table, praying Lanette wouldn't raise the subject.

Aunt Ronnie's eyes twinkled. "I bet you'll bring the highest bid. A pretty, young thing like you. No end of eligible men wanting to enjoy your company over a slice of cake."

Anne's mom patted her shoulder. "Sure as you're born. Two qualities our family is famous for are delicious cake and sparkling conversation."

"Sparkling?" Anne made a face. "I hope I can live up to the Page reputation."

"Don't fret." Lanette reached across the table to pat Anne's other shoulder. "There's one man who'll bid no matter how burnt the cake is. I imagine he spent all those years in stuffy, commercialized Dallas daydreaming about winning you back."

Dallas?

Her heart stopped. Was that physically possible? But it did. The muscle froze for half a second and restarted double-time.

Lanette couldn't mean ... him. Who else lived in Dallas who would relate to this conversation?

She cleared her throat. "I ... I'm not sure I understand you, Mrs. Johnson. Who are you certain will bid on my cake?"

"Why, didn't you hear?" Lanette's face lit with joy as it dawned on her she would be the first to deliver a tantalizing piece of news. "Connor Fenton is in town. Your old sweetheart came back to Sweetheart."

Two

Connor Fenton pulled his shiny, black food truck into a parking space across from the historic Sweetheart Memorial Bank. He was willing to bet his Bulgogi Burger Rig was the first of its kind in this sleepy town. He stepped from the truck, slammed the door, and stretched his arms over his head. Drawing in a cold breath of hometown oxygen, he let it seep all the way through to his soul.

Four years was a long time to be gone. Back then, he'd driven away from Sweetheart like an escaped prisoner on the run. Breaking free from his perfectionist father's suffocating expectations had been paramount. He hadn't planned to stay away forever. Just until he'd achieved his dreams of becoming a country singer. His brash, optimistic younger version never expected the insurmountable walls surrounding the music industry. Making a name for himself appeared more impossible with each passing year.

Yet here he was. Not quite the famous celebrity. But he couldn't stay away any longer. His soul ached for this beloved place.

Home, sweet, Sweetheart.

Connor soaked in the picturesque Main Street—wrought

iron lampposts lining the road, colorful stores with striped awnings, and a bevy of flags with the Texas lone star fluttering in the breeze. On the opposite side, two men in bright orange construction hats carried a load of lumber past the stone pillars, through the open door of the bank's carved wooden entrance. His mother had mentioned the ancient building was being renovated into the new town hall. What else had changed while he was gone?

A cherished face with a halo of golden hair crossed his mind. As it often did.

Please, God. Let Anne Page be unchanged.

Was she still as beautiful? As tenderhearted? As much in love with him as ever? It felt shameless to think that last arrogant question. But he really, really needed to know the answer.

Connor craved a chance to correct the biggest mistake of his life. Leaving her behind.

He strolled past Rosa's Taqueria, where they sold the best *elote* in the state. His appetite flared at the thought of the sweet, creamy corn dish. He drew near The Brunch Café with its retro-diner vibe on the opposite side of the street. His old classmate Susanna had launched it during his absence. Would she and Rosa mind new competition in the neighborhood?

The cell phone in his back pocket buzzed. He checked a text from his business partner, Yoon. Co-owning a fleet of food trucks was a far cry from becoming a famous singer, but he loved it. Their Bulgogi Burger Rig mixed the brisket-cooking know-how Connor inherited from his dad with the sweet-and-spicy sauces of Yoon's homeland of South Korea. The succulent fusion found great success catering to the ravenous student crowd at the University of Texas. So much success they'd bought a second truck to service the Arlington campus. When the time came for a third rig and another selling location, Connor didn't so much as consider downtown or the arts district. Sweetheart beckoned him with a tempting siren's song.

He hoped the move was temporary. It all depended on one

person. If she had to live here to be happy, he'd stay forever. Even if operating the truck in such a tiny town was a risk. Would the small population provide enough customers to earn a decent profit? Failing again wasn't an option. He had to make good. There were too many important things to do, like provide for his yet-to-be-created family.

With Anne.

As he neared the edge of the café, a glance through the squeaky-clean diner windows showed customers filling the vintage, cherry red booths. A woman ran around the corner of the building, plowing into him. Her soft body thudded against his own.

"Sorry." He caught her by the arms. "You're not hurt are—"

The words snagged in his throat as he looked into the face he'd spent his adolescence dreaming about. Anne Page stared up at him. Blue eyes wide. Brows raised. Her jaw sagging.

His brain stalled. He'd hoped to buy flowers and arrive at her door in his best clothes, not bump into her on the street. Too late now.

"Surprise!" He grinned. "Bet you didn't expect to see me here."

Anne didn't respond. Her body remained rigid, mouth still open. A chilly wind blew down Main Street, matching the temperature of her icy gaze.

He released her arms and took a small step back. "It's been a long time. I don't blame you if you're still angry. I should have never left. Believe it or not, I'm finally ready to admit you were right." He wrinkled his nose in the way that used to make her laugh.

She didn't laugh. Didn't speak. Didn't move.

Connor gulped. He'd been prepared for pushback, but groveling was hard to do with a statue.

"Hello-oooo." He waved a hand in front of her. "Is Anne Page home?"

Her lips shut tight. The first sign of movement. She swerved around him and marched into the café without a word. The bell jingled, and the door slammed behind her.

That could have gone better. He blew out a breath. Then again, it could have gone worse. Anne might have kicked him in the shins like she did when they were kids.

He pointed his face at the gray, overcast sky. "I may need divine intervention with this one. Send me a sign, God. Should I give her space or go after her?"

The clouds rumbled, and a drop of rain plopped onto his nose. Followed by another.

"Guess I better go inside." He smiled. "She can't begrudge a man the chance to get out of the storm."

The bell jingled again. Anne stomped out the door. She stopped in front of him. The soft raindrops dampened her silky, blonde hair and ran in little rivulets down her delicate skin. Connor lifted his hand without thinking, paused, and tucked it into his pocket. She might not welcome a tender caress so soon.

The street afforded them little privacy. At least no one was in sight. Connor waited as moisture drenched the front of his shirt. He'd listen to whatever she wanted to say. He deserved it, no matter how harsh.

When she still didn't speak, he raised both hands, palms up. "Go ahead. I can take it."

She opened her mouth. Slammed her lips shut again. Pivoted.

"Anne." He reached out to grab her elbow.

She spun and landed a swift kick to his left leg and then flounced back into the restaurant.

"Owwww." Connor crouched to rub the spot and cast a glance at the sky. "I asked for a sign, but I'm getting mixed messages here."

Augusta Page peeked around the corner of the old bank at the young man massaging his freshly kicked leg. Pulling back before

Connor spotted her, she heaved a disgusted sigh and shook her head. Raindrops sprayed from her carefully styled coiffure as she fumed.

What a mess. And she didn't just mean her hair.

Beside her, Ronnie clicked her tongue. "Our boy requires some lessons in sweet talking."

Augusta rubbed her fingers over her eyes. "Either that, or manners. We have our work cut out for us, Ronnie." A low rumble of thunder interrupted her. "Let's get out of this drizzle first."

The two exited the alley and hurried to Rosa's Taqueria. They entered and sat at a table by the window where they could keep an eye on the café. Augusta dabbed at her wet cheeks with a paper napkin while Ronnie swiped her blue flannel sleeve across her face and tucked short, flyaway hairs behind her ears.

"Just the ladies I wanted to see!" a boisterous voice boomed from behind them.

They observed John Falstaff rising from a spot in the back. His long, jean-clad legs ate up the distance between them in short order. As he walked, Falstaff tweaked the ends of his handlebar mustache and smoothed his graying goatee. He stopped at their table and shoved a thumb between his massive silver belt buckle and the stomach extending over it.

"Morning, John." Ronnie nodded at him. "What brings you to town? You normally stick to your ranch."

"Glad you asked me." He dragged a wooden chair to the end of their table and straddled it. "It's been mighty lonely out there of late. I've been wracking my brain, and I've come to an important decision."

Augusta's right eyebrow raised. What was the old reprobate nattering on about? Her attention wandered to the window. In the distance, Connor straightened his jacket, exhaled, and walked into the diner.

Good for him. He'd need a thick skin if he was going to win Anne back after all this time.

Falstaff pounded a fist on the table. "It hit me last night."

Augusta pressed her lips together, glaring at their noisy tablemate. "What hit you?"

"A revelation." He smoothed his hand over his paunchy belly. "I've only got a few youthful years left in me."

Ronnie eyed him from his mustache to his boots. "Where?"

He continued as if he hadn't heard her. "I decided to stop playing the field and settle down. My carousing days are done. It's high time I found a wife."

"Rosa!" Ronnie raised her finger. "Can we get a couple glasses of sweet tea here?"

"Good for you." Augusta patted his shoulder. "Why don't you start looking now?" She turned back to the window.

"No looking necessary. I already found her. The object of my affection is someone near and dear to us all."

"Oh? Bless her heart."

Augusta barely registered his words. Her brain spun with ways she could help Connor rekindle her daughter's slumbering affection. She'd always been partial to the boy. He was a little full of himself but not in a malicious way. More like a spoiled only child. In his high school days, he'd always treated her daughter with the best manners. And he made her laugh with his good-natured teasing. Anne hadn't laughed much since he left.

John Falstaff droned on, undeterred by the wandering attention of his audience. "Yes, sir. I've chosen Anne as the lucky girl."

Augusta's head snapped so hard her neck ached. She stared at the fifty-year-old man at her side with horrified eyes. "Anne who?"

He chortled. "You know very well which Anne I mean. Your Anne." He took Augusta by the hand. "My dear old friend. Will you do me the honor of becoming my mother-in-law?"

THREE

Anne crouched in a corner of the café kitchen. A towering stack of tomato paste cans provided temporary shelter. She blew into a paper sack, not even sure why. She'd seen a character in a movie use it as a calming technique, and she was desperate for any distraction from reality. Anne focused her attention on the bag clenched in her fingers. As she exhaled, it crackled and filled with air.

Connor was back.

Should she laugh or cry?

The love of her life reappeared after four years of radio silence. And what was the first thing out of his mouth?

"Surprise!"

Like he was throwing a birthday party instead of emotionally ambushing her on Main Street. Anne crumpled the sack and flung it across the room. Not a word of apology or explanation. Just Connor being his usual carefree, charming, infuriating self. This was why she'd refused to leave town with him four years ago. How could you trust your life to a guy who treated everything as if it were a joke?

The swinging door between the kitchen and dining room

squeaked as Susanna Sheppard entered. Undoubtedly wondering why her waitress was nowhere to be found. Her boss crossed the room and bent at the waist to look Anne in the eye.

"Would the reason you're hiding in the canned goods have anything to do with a certain gentleman who's back in town?"

Anne rose and brushed a strand of blonde hair from her forehead. "You heard the news?"

"I didn't have to. He's sitting at the front counter reading a menu."

She quivered.

Susanna placed a gentle hand on her shoulder. "Are you okay? I understand if you want a break. I'll take care of the café. You can slip out the back door and head home."

Anne's gaze darted to the exit. Oh, how she wanted to accept the offer. But Connor wasn't going anywhere.

She smoothed her ruffled apron. "No, thank you. I need to face him sometime. Might as well be now."

Anne walked to the swinging door, released one last calming breath, and entered the dining room. She grabbed a mug and a pot of hot coffee before heading to the counter.

Connor sat on a padded stool at the end, studying the menu. He looked up when she stopped in front of him. She set the mug down with a firm click and poured a pungent, black brew from the carafe.

"Welcome back."

Her voice sounded a tiny bit higher than normal. Anne figured that was pretty good when her heart was attempting to beat a hole through her rib cage. She grasped the mug handle. Her eyes concentrated on the coffee cup like it was the first time she'd ever filled one.

"Hello."

Connor's strong, lean fingers closed around the mug. Anne jerked her hand away before they made contact. She smoothed the front of her shirt.

His voice sounded the same as ever. Low and buttery. It melted over her and made her want to listen to anything he had to say.

But she wouldn't listen. Especially not in a roomful of ears tuned to their channel. She didn't have to scan the café to recognize they were the center of attention. All conversations ceased the moment she exited the kitchen. The gossipy citizens of Sweetheart knew their unhappy love story well. Some were probably even texting a play-by-play of this encounter to their significant others.

"Are you ready to order?" Anne squeezed the words out through gritted teeth. She set the carafe on the counter and pulled a small notebook and pencil from her apron pocket. She kept her gaze on the paper.

"I didn't find what I want on the menu."

Anne tapped the pointy end of the pencil on her pad. "What is it you're wanting?"

He folded his hands in front of him. "Please bring me a grande-sized forgiveness special with a slice of humble pie for dessert."

Her eyes jerked up. His blue gaze twinkled back at her. The corner of his mouth lifted in a chagrined smile.

Was it possible to hear air? The silence pounded through the room like a piledriver. Ten unending seconds ticked away. Her teeth ground from side to side.

A long finger tapped on the counter to their left.

"Good morning, Anne." Dr. Albert Caius leaned in from the neighboring stool. "Did you get over that head cold I treated you for last week?"

It took her a minute to process the man's words. He sat there in his tweed sport coat and khaki pants, his wire-rimmed glasses glinting in the fluorescent light. Dr. Caius had always been attractive in a distinguished, salt-and-pepper kind of way. But now he resembled an angel sent straight from Heaven. She'd never been so happy for an interruption in her life.

"Dr. Caius!" Anne dropped her pad and pencil in her pocket, stuck her hand out, and shook his. "I feel much better. Thank you."

He studied the desperate fingers clinging to his and offered her a caring smile. "So glad to hear it. I'd hate for you to miss the Candy Hearts Festival."

"Yes, the festival!" She shook his hand again. "I'll see you there."

Connor's stool squeaked as he swung in their direction. "Hello, Doc." He held out his own hand. "How have you been?"

The doctor tried to swivel his way, but his body jerked back. Anne held onto him with a tenacious grip. He turned his neck toward Connor.

"Fine, thank you." Dr. Caius looked at Anne. "Are you taking part in the cake auction?"

She zeroed in on him, ignoring the ex-boyfriend shifting in her peripheral vision. "I'd planned to."

"Wonderful. Please save me a piece. Or the whole cake, in fact. I'll make sure you win the prize for the highest bid."

Connor shifted his shoulders. "Excuse me. About my order—"

Anne dropped the doctor's hand and retrieved the coffee pot. "I'm sorry, sir. We don't serve what you want in The Brunch Café. You should try across the street." She beamed one more time at Dr. Caius before heading to the kitchen.

As the swinging door closed behind her, she slumped against the wall. Her body trembled. She slid the coffee onto the stainless-steel prep table and pressed her arms against the bass drum pounding in her chest.

First encounter finished. She hadn't weakened, she hadn't wavered, and she hadn't burst into tears.

A definite win in her book.

～

AUGUSTA PAGE TOWED John Falstaff from the cantina by his arm in a none-too-gentle manner. The light rain shower had stopped. Her heels swooshed through the tiny puddles surrounding the restaurant as she shoved him into a side alley where no one would spot them.

"What do you mean, your mother-in-law? You have the gall to cast your randy, old eyes on my baby?" She tossed his arm away. "Falstaff, we went to school together. You're old enough to be her father!"

He stroked his goatee. "There are plenty of couples with an age difference. Just look at Hollywood. Now, I can't deny I've dated my share of girlfriends in the past. But I've changed, Augusta. Love has made a new man of me."

Ronnie scampered to their sides, carrying an oversized purse under each arm. "What's going on? He can't really want to marry Anne. It's a bad joke, right?"

Falstaff raised his right hand like a witness on the stand. "I swear I'm in love with Anne Page. If I'm lying, you can spit in my face and call me a horse."

"I'd rather call you something else," Augusta muttered, "but you might tell the pastor." She rolled her lips inward and took a breath. "Listen, Falstaff. My daughter never got over her first love, Connor Fenton, and he's finally returned to claim her. I don't want anything or anyone getting in the way of their long-delayed reconciliation."

He settled his hands on his fat, leather belt and gave it a tug. "Augusta Page, mark my words. I've set my course. No amount of arguing will change my mind. Love is worth fighting for, and I'm ready to take on Connor Fenton and you and the whole town of Sweetheart if I have to."

Falstaff gave one last emphatic jerk of his chin. He shouldered past the two women. His boots stomped through the puddles, splashing muddy water on the leg of Augusta's pantsuit.

Ronnie clicked her tongue. "He's gonna make trouble. Mark my words."

Augusta raised her nose, her lower jaw jutting out. "Nobody makes bigger trouble than a mama bear." She grabbed her purse from her friend. "Come on, Ronnie. We've got work to do."

131

FOUR

Connor's rig coasted into the horseshoe driveway of the Page's two-story home. He killed the engine and stepped from the truck, tucking the keys into the pocket of his black dress pants. The English Tudor-style house with white stone and exposed wooden beams warmed his soul. He'd played with Anne in the front yard when they were kids and sang her love songs on the back porch as a teenager.

Were all the happy memories in the past? Not if he had any say about it. Straightening the cuffs of his white shirt and checking his tie in the side mirror, he whispered a silent prayer.

Help, God. That about sums it up. Help.

Mr. Page was old-fashioned. Anyone who married his daughter would have to obtain her father's approval first. Connor paused. Considering the fact Anne refused to talk to him, this visit might be a tad premature. But he'd wasted enough time. He needed people on his side, and Mr. Page had always favored him.

Connor walked to the front door and knocked. Footsteps sounded inside, along with muttering. The door swung open to reveal Mr. Page with his glasses shoved on top of his head.

He squinted. "Hang on. Can't see a thing without—" He pulled the glasses down and froze. "Connor. Fenton."

Connor swallowed. The man's tone was far from friendly.

"Good morning, sir ... Good to talk to you again ..." He paused between each sentence, giving Mr. Page a chance to respond. The man stood silent, eying him with pursed lips. "It's been a long time."

"A *very* long time." He took his glasses off, withdrew a handkerchief from his pocket, and polished the lenses. "Is there something I can help you with before you leave?"

Connor swallowed again. He'd imagined being invited in, sitting down with Anne's father, and explaining the motivation behind his long absence. Then perhaps he could give Mr. Page a tour of the rig, show him his profits spreadsheet, and impress the man with his business acumen.

Instead, he stood on the front porch like an uninvited salesman.

"Sir." Connor drew in a deep breath and blurted, "I've come to ask for your daughter's hand in marriage."

Mr. Page stared. His chest shook, and a low rumble escaped from his mouth. It grew in magnitude. The small chuckles multiplied. He leaned one hand against the wall as deep belly laughs overtook him.

Connor rubbed the back of his neck. Was laughter better or worse than stony silence?

He gave a tentative smile. "I realize this is out of the blue, but I assure you my intentions are serious. There hasn't been one day in the four years I've been gone I haven't thought of Anne. My future plans always included her, even when we were apart."

Mr. Page snorted and dabbed his eyes with the handkerchief. He replaced his glasses on the bridge of his wide nose and took a disdainful survey of Connor. Turning his back and crossing the threshold, he shut the door with a decisive thump.

Connor's shoulders slumped. He'd been in town less than

forty-eight hours, and the score was zero for two. He rubbed both hands over his face. Wasn't there anyone on his side?

An irritated, female voice rang from the side of the house. "You're not serious, Ronnie! He wrote you one too?"

Mrs. Augusta Page stalked around the corner in sequin-studded jeans with a matching jacket. She waved a red envelope, her cell phone pressed to her ear. "The nerve! He thinks he actually has a chance with—" She spotted Connor. The anger on her face evaporated, and a smile appeared. "Ronnie, I've got a visitor. Why don't you meet me at my house? Ok. Bye."

She tucked the phone and envelope in her pocket and marched toward Connor.

He spread his feet apart, bracing himself. "Good morning, Mrs. Page. I confess I'm a brazen idiot for being here—"

The woman threw her arms around his torso and crushed him to her. "Save the apologies for later, honey. We've got four years' worth of hugging to catch up on."

His body relaxed in the comfort of her welcome. He slipped his arms from under hers and tucked her closer, blinking over and over. Mrs. Page was a second mother to him, but it wouldn't do to break down in their front yard. What if her husband saw?

"I missed your hugs," he said.

"Of course, you did." She patted his back. "I'm famous for them." Pulling away, she held him at arm's length and cocked her eyebrow. "You admit you've been a fool?"

He nodded like a bobble-head doll. "The biggest one who ever lived."

"Good enough for me." She sniffled and rubbed a finger under her eyelid. "Wish I'd skipped the mascara today. Come inside, while I repair the damage."

He cast a wary glance at the house. "Maybe I shouldn't. Your husband wasn't exactly happy to see me."

"Oh, pooh." She pushed him to the front door. "He takes a little longer to warm up than some people, but he'll come around."

She steered him into the house, through the entry hall, and into the living room on the left. Pushing him onto the floral damask couch, she opened a drawer on the end table and took out a small bag. While she fixed her makeup in the mirror above the fireplace, Connor took in the well-known room. He hadn't spent much time in it as a child since it was reserved for company. But he'd passed it more times than he could count. They'd added floor-length, olive-green curtains to the windows, and a few new pictures sat on the mantle.

He rose to study one of Anne in a pink chiffon dress. Her hair curled around her cheeks in soft waves. A gentle yet restrained expression graced her face. She looked older. Not in a wrinkled way. In a mature way. How had the girl he left behind changed into a woman while he was absent?

Mrs. Page joined him. "I took that picture a few weeks ago at Katherine Bruno's wedding. Even though the whole town was there, my baby was the prettiest."

Connor smiled. "Always."

Her lips thinned. "Why did you stay away from such a beautiful angel for four years? I can make allowances for a man following his dreams. But no calls? No email? No message by carrier pigeon?" She slapped him on the chest. "What's wrong with you?"

Here it was. The chance to explain himself. As his list of practiced excuses flashed through his mind, they all sounded so paltry.

Connor sank to the couch and clasped his hands between his knees. "At first, I was angry. We were so much in love, I assumed Anne would follow me anywhere. When she didn't, it hurt. Like she didn't believe I could make something of myself."

Mrs. Page sat beside him. "I understand that particular reason keeping you away for one year. But four?" She smacked him again.

"If you hit me twenty times, I deserve it and more." He ran a hand through his hair. "I spent two years in Nashville working part time as a waiter while I tried to make it as a singer. I was playing a tiny gig one night when it hit me. My songs held no meaning. Without Anne to sing them to, I didn't want to do it anymore. I packed that night and drove as far as Dallas."

"You couldn't have made it just two hours further?" Mrs. Page crossed her arms.

"No." Connor laughed. "I really couldn't. I tried more than once. Each time I pointed my car toward Sweetheart, I heard my father's voice in my head saying, 'I told you so.' Welcoming me back to the family business."

She nodded. "He always did want you to take over his ranch someday."

"The trouble is I hate cows." Connor shuddered. "I needed to return to Sweetheart with some measure of success. To show my father, and Anne, and everybody else I made my own way in the world."

"Is this success related to the big, black monstrosity you've got blocking my driveway?" Mrs. Page flicked a finger at the window.

"Hey, don't hate on the rig." Connor grinned. "I met my business partner Yoon Lee at church. We both played guitar on the worship team, trying to figure out what to do with our lives. One night, at a barbeque, I was manning the grill when he brought me a bottle of his mother's homemade bulgogi sauce. We added it to the burgers and almost had to chase people away with a stick." He pretended to straighten an invisible tie. "I think you can guess the rest. That's our third food truck parked out there. We've gained so much business we've even hired employees."

"The glamorous world of payroll taxes." Mrs. Page grimaced. "You *have* grown up."

He nodded and took her by the hand. "If you help me convince—"

The front door slammed, and Anne's voice rang out.

"Mom, did you buy the pecans? You promised to help me bake—"

She rounded the corner and halted. Her gaze jerked from Connor, to her mother, and back.

A silence so awkward it could be whacked with a flyswatter filled the room. The two stood in unison.

"Look who's here, dear." Mrs. Page withdrew her fingers, placed them behind Connor's shoulder, and nudged him forward. "He came to talk to you about—"

"Sorry, I'm busy." Anne took a step back. "I promised to bake a cake for the auction." She whirled on her heel and disappeared.

Connor raised his eyebrows at Mrs. Page.

She glared at him. "Why are you still standing there?"

The front door knocker pounded.

"That might be Ronnie." Her nose scrunched. "But she usually walks right in." Mrs. Page propped both hands on Connor's back and propelled him toward the kitchen. "Stop wasting time making excuses to me, and let Anne hear them instead. I'll see who's at the door."

AUGUSTA WAITED until Connor was out of sight before she headed for the entrance. The knocker echoed through the house like the visitor was hammering a nail. She grabbed the handle and yanked the door open. John Falstaff stood on the other side, dressed in a brown suit he must have bought when he was two sizes smaller.

"'Bout time someone answered." He slipped a meaty finger under his bolo tie strap, loosened it, and undid the top button of his checkered shirt. "Did you get my card, Augusta?"

She bared her teeth and picked the crinkled, red envelope from her pocket. "You mean this thing?" With two fingers, she held it in front of her.

"That's the one." He propped a hand on the doorjamb. "I wanted to make my case for why I'll be such a great son-in-law."

Augusta crumpled the paper and tossed it at him. "Forget it. The best lawyer in the world couldn't make that case for you."

Falstaff straightened. His bushy eyebrows lowered. "I heard Connor Fenton is back in town. That's his truck in the driveway, isn't it? Has he poisoned you against me?"

A brisk wind rattled the tree branches, and irritation rattled Augusta's nerves. The unneighborly desire to toss the man off her property swelled. She rubbed her temple.

"If you were the last man on God's green earth, I still wouldn't let you date my daughter. This has nothing to do with Connor Fenton."

"So you say." Falstaff's gaze flicked to the hallway behind her. "Is he here? Maybe I should have a little chat with that boy. Don't you worry, Augusta. I'll send the runt packing."

A mud-splashed Jeep careened into the driveway and screeched to a halt behind Connor's rig. Ronnie Ford climbed out, slammed the door, and hurried to Augusta's side.

"What is this old hound dog saying?" She brandished a matching red envelope. "Did he write you the same kind of unholy valentine?"

Ronnie shoved the paper at John's chest, let go, and pulled back like it was contagious. "If I never read such a mess of self-aggrandizing fripperies again, it'll be too soon."

"Hold on, now." John clutched the envelope in his hand. "I can comprehend how you ladies might feel a little jealous of my—"

"Jealous!" The women shrieked together.

"It's only natural." He stroked his goatee. "You both harbored crushes on me in high school, but you're married women. It's time to let go. Allow Anne to have a chance at love."

Augusta clutched her head. "John Falstaff, leave my house and my daughter alone."

"No can do." He smoothed the red envelope and tucked it in

his checkered shirt pocket. "If I have to camp on your front stoop, I refuse to leave until I've plighted my troth and you've accepted me as Anne's suitor."

Falstaff plopped on the ground and crossed his arms. The already-taut fabric of the outdated jacket pulled at its seams. His mulish look declared he would stay on her doorstep for as long as it took. Even until his suit fit again.

She eyed him a second and kept her voice level. "Could you give us a moment, please?"

Pulling Ronnie inside the house, she shut the door in the obsequious man's mug. "He's gone too far."

"I'll say. Thinking we'd ever be jealous of him." Ronnie shivered.

"There's a bigger problem." Augusta bit her lip. "Anne and Connor are in the kitchen. I'm afraid if I throw John out, he'll raise a ruckus and disturb them. Connor deserves a chance to explain himself without interruption."

Ronnie's eyes grew large. She glanced down the hallway and lowered her voice. "What do we do?"

Augusta scanned right and left as she tapped a finger against her leg. The ghost of a smile crossed her face. "Follow my lead."

She opened the door and squinted in disgust at John Falstaff. He lounged on the top step with his legs stretched out, ankles crossed, and cowboy boot heel tapping the concrete.

"You win, John. Anne dropped by to make a cake for the Candy Hearts Festival. I'll permit you to speak to her on one condition. You can't disturb her until she's finished."

Falstaff hefted to his feet. Audible pops sounded from his belabored joints. "Why do you make me a villain? I'll let her do her baking. After all, I'm the one who's gonna eat the thing."

Augusta picked at one of the sequins on the padded shoulder of her jacket. "Do you suppose you could help me with a little project while you wait? Our washing machine is acting strange. I remember you were pretty handy with machinery." She bumped Ronnie with her elbow.

"Huh?" She started. "*Oh!* Right. You could always fix anything in high school."

Falstaff puffed up. He tugged his bolo tie from his neck and stuffed it in his pocket. "Just lead me to it. I'll get that thing working in no time."

Augusta moved aside and allowed him to enter. She directed him down the opposite hallway from the kitchen where she hoped Connor was making progress with Anne. Murmuring soothing words and complimenting Falstaff's unique choice of neckwear, she distracted him all the way to the laundry room and shut the door behind them.

Anne gathered her ingredients on the marble-topped island in the middle of the kitchen. She sifted the flour for her Italian cream cake and cracked the eggs into the stainless-steel bowl. Dusting her hands against her black apron, she raised on her toes and opened the cabinet door in search of the vanilla extract.

No matter how many times she told herself she was alone, it didn't change the fact Connor sat at the table, watching her like a chastened puppy. He hadn't said a word since following her to the kitchen. Was he waiting for her to speak first? He'd be waiting a long time. Until death or the Rapture. Whichever came first.

She grabbed a small brown bottle and slammed the cabinet door. Measuring exactly one teaspoon full of vanilla, she dumped it into the cake batter and tossed the spoon into the sink.

The man disappeared for four years and didn't offer a word of explanation. Was he a moron? Of course, he was. Why else would he be sitting there in silence?

Anne snuck a glance at Conner. He leaned forward with a hopeful expression. She looked away and picked up the handheld electric mixer.

The legs of Connor's chair squeaked as he stood. "You might be wondering—"

Whirrrrrrrrrr.

The mixer clattered against the metal bowl as it combined the ingredients for her cake. Anne trained her gaze on the swirling, creamy concoction. Her thoughts spun with the batter. She willed herself to stay focused on the task. What did she need for the icing? Butter, cream cheese, pecans.

A large hand settled on her shoulder. She yelped. Jerking away, the wire whisks of the mixer spun from the batter. Off-white goop flew, covering them both in a sugary shower.

Anne scrambled for the off switch. The mixer stilled. She sighed and dropped it on the counter, glaring at Connor.

His cheeks stiffened in apology. "Sorry."

"You should be."

"I am. For everything."

She crossed her arms and raised her eyebrows. "I'm very busy. Why are you so desperate to talk to me? After four years of silence, you could wait one more day."

He started to respond. Hesitated. Closed his eyes and began again.

"You told me never to speak to you again."

"What?"

His blue eyes met hers. "The day I left for Nashville. I begged you to come with me. Marry me. Share the adventure. You wouldn't budge. Wouldn't listen. Wouldn't consider it."

Anne's teeth ached from clenching them. "Are you saying this is my fault?"

"No!" Connor reached for her, but she skittered away. He lowered his hands. "I'm just trying to explain why I didn't contact you. The last words you shouted as I walked out the door were, 'Give up the fantasy.' You said becoming a singer was impossible. And even if I did make it, you never wanted to hear my voice again."

Anne flinched at the ugly sentiments. Had she really said

those things? She remembered the night well. The setting. The look on his face. The gut-wrenching pain and disappointment she felt. But she couldn't remember her exact words.

He'd told her to expect a surprise. She'd thought it was an engagement ring. When he broke the news he was relocating to Tennessee, with or without her, the hurt, anger, and fear had blinded her.

The memory made her stomach swirl.

Connor mussed his hair and scratched the back of his head. "Seeing how life panned out, I guess you were right. I regret causing you pain. I regret not calling to say I was sorry. I regret staying away for so many years." His lips firmed, and he stood straighter. "But I don't regret leaving. I've made something of myself while I was gone, far away from my father's influence or help. I did it on my own, with hard work and the grace of God to get me through."

Anne's breath left her in a disgusted gasp. Was he apologizing or bragging?

"Good for you." She spun away and braced her hands on the kitchen island. "Can you please leave? I have a mess to clean up."

In her peripheral vision, she saw him grab a dishtowel from the counter. He moved behind her and gave a gentle tug to her arm. She inched around, her lips pressed tight together, determined not to say anything else she'd regret in a few years.

Connor stood over her, close enough she could smell the scent of his shampoo. The same one he'd used for a decade. It brought back memories of high school dances and sitting in the bleachers with her head on his shoulder. He studied her, his gaze swerving from her forehead to her chin and settling on her mouth. His head bent to the side.

Anne's insides squeezed like a lemon. Connor leaned forward the slightest bit. She held still, not allowing even a breath as his face drew near her own. He raised the towel and dabbed at the corner of her lips. Running the soft material over her skin, he cleaned the sticky remnants of batter from her cheeks.

"You're more beautiful than I remember." After the last swipe, he tossed it on the island. "I've spent the last two years striving to become someone you would be proud to call your husband. I'm still not worthy of you, but I'm better than I was. A man instead of a careless boy. I hope you give me a chance to prove it."

He tapped a finger to her chin and put some distance between them. "I'll let you finish your cake. Fair warning, I plan to be the highest bidder."

Five more seconds of agonizing perusal and then he left.

Anne stared at his back as he exited the kitchen. A frustrated squeal escaped her. She grabbed the dishtowel, wringing it between her hands.

Now what?

~

"THIS WASHER SEEMS ALL RIGHT to me." John Falstaff shut the metal lid with a clang.

"Shhhhh!" Augusta darted a worried glance at the closed door. "We don't want to disturb ... anyone."

Ronnie herded him back. "Anne's baking her cake. I'm sure you want to bid on her best work. Right?"

His bushy eyebrows waggled. "I hope it's chocolate. That's my favorite."

"It's Italian Cream." Augusta picked up a full laundry basket and shoved it in his arms. "An old family recipe."

Ronnie grabbed a pile of dirty towels from the floor and heaped them on top. "Take these too."

The stack towered past Falstaff's nose, his eyes barely visible above the terry cloth.

"I came for courting, not cleaning. If you two will let me through that door, I'll commence to wooing."

"Today's not a good day." Augusta pulled a clean load from

the drier and added it to the burden in his arms. "But you might as well make yourself useful while you're here."

"What is this?" Falstaff staggered under the weight. "Is the green-eyed monster rearing its ugly head again? You women need to curb those jealous tendencies."

The jaws of Augusta and Ronnie drooped in tandem. How delusional was this man?

The laundry room door opened, and Anne stood there. "Mom, you were going to help me with this ca—"

She stared at the mountain of towels with two pudgy legs poking from the bottom. "Who's that?"

"Nobody important!" Augusta stepped in front of the tottering load bearer.

An outraged grunt sounded behind her. "Nobody? Anne Page, I've come to you on a special mission."

Ronnie grabbed a folded bedsheet from the side table and plopped it on his head. "It can wait, John."

"Love waits for no man or woman!" Falstaff dropped the basket. An avalanche of laundry spilled onto the floor. He glared at the two older women and whipped the sheet off. "Anne, would you do me the honor of, mmphhhh—"

Augusta supposed stuffing a washcloth in a guest's mouth wasn't exactly Southern hospitality. At least it was clean. More than the old letch deserved. She took firm hold of her daughter's arm and backed her out of the room.

"Yes, dear. I'll help you now. Ronnie, can you please show our visitor out?"

Her best friend snapped the door shut behind them.

"Mom, what's going on?" Anne tried to wriggle away, but her mother steered her along the hallway and up the stairs. "Are we baking a cake in the bedroom?"

"Trust me, dear. You'll thank me when you find out the reason."

They clomped through the second story until they reached the furthest point in the house from the laundry room. Augusta released her daughter and pressed a hand to her heaving chest. All she wanted was Anne's happiness and a few adorable grandchildren. Was this chaos the price she had to pay to accomplish it?

Arguing echoed from downstairs. John Falstaff's cranky baritone was shushed by Ronnie's insistent voice. The front door slammed behind them.

Her husband poked his head from their room. "What's all the racket?"

Augusta rushed to him and leaned on his arm. "Honey, you have no idea the sorry excuse for a son-in-law wannabe who came calling."

He wrapped an arm around her. "Oh, don't I? Did you let that lazy, good-for-nothing Connor Fenton in?"

Augusta shrugged his arm off her shoulders. "I'm not talking about sweet Connor. I mean that delusional crackpot, John Falstaff."

"John?" Her husband cocked his head. "How did he get on your bad side?"

"Mister Falstaff decided he wants to marry our daughter."

"He what?" Mr. Page bellowed.

"What!" Anne staggered back. "Mr. Falstaff is the same age as you and Dad. Do I really look so desperate?"

"Of course not." Augusta rubbed her back. "He's a doddering old fool."

Mr. Page glowered as if he wanted to burn a hole through the carpet. "He was always pretentious when it came to women. Remember in high school he thought the entire cheerleading squad was in love with him?"

She grimaced. "I remember it well. I was *on* the cheerleading squad. Now he's set his sights on the next generation."

Mr. Page clasped a hand to his forehead. "Has the whole world gone mad?" He spun in his daughter's direction. "Stay away from that old womanizer."

She nodded. "Don't worry."

"And stay away from Connor Fenton too. I won't allow our family to be saddled with a careless loafer."

Anne's forehead crinkled. "That's a little harsh, Dad. Connor may have had some crazy schemes, but he always worked hard for them."

A smile crept across Augusta's lips as her husband railed about the inefficiency of daydreamers. If Anne was ready to defend Connor, her daughter was halfway to the altar, whether she realized it or not. Someone should inform the boy one more good push might do it.

Where did she leave her phone?

SIX

Connor checked his phone but still no response. An encouraging call from Mrs. Page had bolstered his courage enough to text Anne, asking her to meet him. He glanced at the hundred-foot tower beside him. It glistened under the full moon and starry sky.

The Miller Lighthouse was one of the more whimsical spots in Sweetheart. Five hundred miles from any major body of water, it was built in the early-1900s by an imaginative farmer who'd always hankered to be a sailor. When Old Miller saw a picture of the Cape Lookout Lighthouse in North Carolina, he was captivated. The man cleared a spot in his fields and spent ten years recreating a smaller replica of the tall, white spire with black, diamond patterns lining the side. His grandson still switched the light on at sunset. Its beam swung through the unlit darkness of a small-town night, providing a welcoming beacon of warmth and hope.

Connor tried the door—unlocked, as always. After a century, the entire town of Sweetheart considered the lighthouse their own personal property. Anyone and everyone could climb the tower to enjoy the view from the top.

He made his way up the curved, concrete stairs and exited

onto the outer platform. The revolving light blinded him, and he turned his back. His eyes adjusted to the darkness. He scanned the nearby road for any sign of a car.

Would Anne come?

Connor waited in the stillness, anticipating the luxury of listening to her voice again. It had been four long years without its musical cadence. He longed to drink it down like a glass of his mother's sweet tea.

Each time he stood near her, he felt the hunger of a starving man staring at the world's most lavish buffet. He had to use caution so as not to scare away the tentative heart inching toward him with the tremulous steps of a baby deer. His own heart raced faster than a lion. Not that Anne was prey, but the magnitude of his emotions scared even him. How much more might they worry his resentful beloved?

He must be patient. Must give her time. No matter how hard it was.

What would he say after she arrived? When she stared at him with eyes awash in hurt and anger, any justification sounded pathetic. He would trade the lyrics of every song he'd ever written for the one word that could wash away her resentment.

Connor checked his phone for the tenth time.

She hadn't responded to his text.

Perhaps he should have said more than, *Meet me at our special place.*

For a songwriter, he'd chosen a decidedly unpoetic invitation.

Idiot.

ANNE PULLED her hatchback to the side of the road and killed the engine. She read the text one last time and chucked her phone on the passenger seat.

Meet me at our special place.

Did he think they were two teenagers slipping off for a secret date?

She leaned her forehead against the steering wheel and moaned. What was she doing here?

Answers.

She wanted them.

Craved them.

Their earlier conversation in the kitchen put a different perspective on the resentment she'd harbored for four years. All this time, she'd blamed Connor. But it appeared she'd also played a part in their breakup however unintentional.

If she stopped retreating and said more than ten words to him, she might learn more.

Anne took a bolstering breath, climbed from the car, and slammed the door. Miller's Lighthouse stood proud against the spangled night sky. She wandered beside the winter wheat fields that wouldn't ripen until the warmth of spring awakened them. A golden beam of light swooped above the short sea of green stalks. It cut through the darkness like a sparkling angel's wing, beckoning her to come find relief from the storm inside her soul. She walked along the dirt path, tugging her jean jacket closed against the brisk night air. Another shaft of light illuminated the crops.

She reached the bottom of the tower and paused. Tapping a foot against the cold, hard dirt, she looked back at the car. It wasn't too late to leave.

A deep voice floated from the top of the lighthouse. "Thinking of making a break for it?"

She chuckled. He still knew her well.

"It crossed my mind," she hollered.

"Understandable." His tone held that cheeky, playful quality she'd missed. "I hope you fight the urge."

The door to the tower stood open, inviting her to discover the answers she sought. Anne bit her lip and entered. Even as she climbed the stairs, a host of reasons for turning around flooded her brain, but she kept going.

When she reached the end of the staircase, Connor stood at the rail, a grin on his face.

"Thanks for not running away."

She scrunched her mouth to the side. "I admit it was a struggle."

He waved a hand to the floor where he'd spread a blanket over the weathered wooden planks. "Would you consider having a seat?"

Anne lowered herself to a sitting position. She pushed her feet through the gap between the lowest bar of the guardrail and the floor. It was a familiar setting. They'd swung their legs from this high perch since childhood, counting the stars in the endless Texas sky above them.

Connor joined her. He sat close without any part of his body touching hers, but she sensed the heat of his presence like a blazing furnace.

They remained silent for several moments before he spoke.

"Go ahead. Let me have it."

She pretended she didn't understand him. "Have what?"

"Anything you're angry about. You've had four years to bottle your emotions. I imagine there are a lot of things you want to say." He gave a short laugh. "Are dying to say."

Anne hesitated. She'd spent many nights rehearsing her speech. Yet all the anger and frustration really boiled down to one simple question.

"Why didn't you come home sooner?" she whispered.

Defeat traced the edges of her words. Would hearing the reason make any difference? Yet, he was right about one thing. She *needed* to know.

Connor didn't answer.

She asked again. "Why did you stay away so long? You said you gave up on the singing career after two years. You could have come home then."

He rubbed a hand against his leg and cleared his throat. "I couldn't come home a nobody." He lifted his face to the sky, releasing a long, slow breath. "Everyone told me it would never work. You. My father. Everyone who mattered. I couldn't come home the loser they predicted I'd be. I had to prove myself first."

She recognized the validity of his reasoning. She didn't like it. But she understood it.

Still ...

She sighed. "Why didn't you at least call?"

"And tell you what?" A bitter laugh escaped his lips. "How I was an unemployed washout with nothing to offer?" He thumped a soft, insistent beat against the wooden floor with his fist. "I missed you so much I ached inside." His voice lowered to a murmur. "Like I was walking around without a heart in my chest."

Anne recognized the feeling. Her own heart had been absent for four years as she went through the motions of life without any joy. She trained her gaze on the field below. Every fifteen seconds, the light passed across the burgeoning crop. The gentle breeze ruffled the stalks in slow, hypnotic waves.

Connor pointed at the wheat. "It resembles moonlight on the ocean, doesn't it?"

Anne murmured her agreement.

He propped his arms on the bar in front of them and leaned his chin on top. "I bet old Miller took a lot of ribbing from his neighbors for building this place. A landlocked farmer who longed for the sea."

"You have to admit," Anne mirrored his posture, leaning her own chin on the bar, "a lighthouse in the middle of a wheat field must have seemed crazy."

He kicked a foot in the air. "I relate to the old guy. An aspiring sailor who couldn't bear to leave his family. In the end, he relinquished one dream for another."

Anne resented the guilt rising inside her. She'd never asked Connor to give up his dreams. Not really. She'd merely wanted him to stay here in Sweetheart. With her. Where it was safe.

She dropped her arms from the bars and crossed them in front of her. "You make it sound tragic."

He laughed. "Bittersweet, yes. Hardly tragic. I admire him. He found a way to make his desire a reality here in Sweetheart. Just because things don't always work out the way we plan doesn't mean we give up our dreams entirely. We have to tweak them a little."

Connor drew one of his legs under him. "It's funny. I thought I knew exactly what I wanted to be. How wrong I was. My singing may not grace the airwaves, but I can pull out my guitar and serenade the customers who visit my food truck. And leading worship at my church brought me more joy than any gig I ever played in Nashville. I still get to do what I love, but now—"

He paused as if weighing his words. Anne kept her eyes pointed at the ground far below. She felt him study her.

"Now," he continued, "I can do what I love near the people I love. Mainly you."

She braced her hands against the floor. "You loved me four years ago and left anyway."

"I'm sorry." He reached out and covered her fingers with his. "I'll say it a hundred times."

She withdrew her hand with a snort. "Only a hundred?"

He grinned. "A million then."

A tiny, hot needle pricked her conscience. More than one person needed to apologize, but the admission stuck in her throat. She stood and moved around the circular platform.

Standing with her back to him, she whispered the words. "I'm sorry too."

She heard him scrambling up behind her. He drew close but kept a foot of space between them. He'd always been good at reading her moods. That was one of the reasons she loved him so much.

"What did you say?" he asked.

"I'm sorry too," she ground out. "All these years, I've been blaming you for our breakup, while I conveniently forgot the harsh, unforgivable things I said to you on the day you left." Tears welled. She swiped them away, hoping he hadn't noticed. "I didn't want to be a dream killer."

"Anne, I didn't mean it that way." He closed the gap between them, reached for her arm, and pulled her to face him. "I wasn't blaming you."

"I know." Her shoulders sagged. "But I acted spiteful and cowardly." She finally looked at him. "I'm truly sorry, Connor."

The lighthouse beam swerved over their heads, highlighting the gold of his hair. In the dark, his blue eyes sparkled down at her like twin stars.

He smiled. "I'll offer you a deal. How about we both make this our final apologies? I'll forgive you for stepping on my singing dreams if you'll forgive me for being the biggest idiot in the whole Lone Star State."

She returned his smile with a tentative one of her own. "Deal."

Even as she agreed, Anne silently wondered if she could let go of the bitterness with a simple declaration. But it was a start.

Connor held out his hand. She eyed it for a second and then placed her fingers in his. He shook them once and didn't let go. They stood with their hands clasped for the length of time it took the light to make one revolution. As the blinding beam cut between them, Connor looked at the ground.

"I brought you something." Releasing her, he grabbed a shoebox from the floor by the blanket. "I may have never called, but I wrote you often. Whenever I missed you. If you wonder what I was thinking while I was away, it's recorded in here." He held the box out to her.

She took it and lifted the lid. A pile of papers filled the container to the brim—envelopes, sticky notes, handwritten scrawls on the back of receipts. It appeared he'd missed her a lot.

A wave of anticipation rose inside. The strength of it frightened her.

She snapped the lid shut. "We agreed to forgive and forget. Maybe it's better I don't read these."

His smile drooped.

Anne pushed on. "Just because we've reached a truce doesn't mean we can go back to the way things were." She faked a cheery attitude. "You know the old cliché: Once bitten, twice shy."

His head tilted slightly, his lips lifting in that familiar grin. "I prefer, 'All's fair in love and war.'"

Anne's jaw tightened. "'Fool me once, shame on you. Fool me twice, shame on me.'"

He advanced until only the box separated their bodies. His gaze dropped to her mouth. "How about, 'Let's kiss and make up?'"

He stepped so close his toes bumped hers. She tensed. His head lowered. His mouth drew near her own. Her chin automatically rose to shorten the distance. His warm breath brushed her lips a split-second before she backed away.

The beam of light swooped across their bodies, highlighting the space that gaped between them. A mockingbird whistled in the darkness.

"I—" Anne fussed with the zipper on her jacket. "I think that's enough reminiscing for tonight. I have a cake to finish icing for the festival."

Connor stuffed his hands in his pockets and nodded. "I still plan to be the highest bidder." He reached out and tipped her chin with the crook of a gentle finger, studying her expression. "Is that okay with you?"

Anne wished she knew. Everything was happening too quickly. After four years of hurt and resentment, it was hard to let it all go in two days. They'd talked things out, admitted their mutual guilt, and agreed to put it in the past. She wanted to start fresh, but her heart trembled like a child at the top of a roller coaster. Perhaps they should stay on the friends' side of the line this time.

It was safer.

Less painful.

She shrugged one shoulder. "Suit yourself."

Seven

Anne stopped at the kitchen counter and took one last, proud peek at her Italian Cream cake. Artful swirls of rich, velvety icing coated the layered creation. A ring of harmonious pecan halves dotted the top. She'd spent an hour picking out the unbroken nuts and matching the sizes so the garnish looked uniform.

It was perfect.

Placing the cake in a pink, cardboard bakery box, Anne scurried around her apartment, grabbing car keys and purse. She cringed at the mountain of unfolded laundry on the couch. Her neat freak mother would faint at such a public display of messiness. She wavered toward the pile and then shook her head. It could wait. She'd been living away from her parents for a few months, and she might as well take advantage of the freedom to leave her place however she chose.

The shoebox on the coffee table made her pause. After returning home from the lighthouse, she'd been unable to resist peeking inside. It took her half the night to read his messages. He'd dated everything he wrote. One thing became obvious as she'd lined the notes in chronological order. Hardly a day went by when he didn't write her. Sometimes twice a day.

She ran a finger over the battered shoebox lid. The mismatched slips of paper beckoned her. Even the hardest heart would be moved by such a gesture.

Anne noted the time on the wall clock and squealed. She was supposed to be at the park five minutes ago to help with the auction setup. Racing for the door, she shifted the items in her hands to open it and almost ran into a man on the porch, a bouquet of red roses blocking his identity.

Had Connor decided to launch another romantic confession?

But she hated roses, and he knew that.

The flowers lowered, and a grizzled face with a handlebar mustache, graying goatee, and a confident smirk appeared.

"Mr. Falstaff!" Anne gasped.

"Good morning, my dear." He stood in his wrinkled brown suit. Bending at the waist, he extended the bouquet, placing it on top of her cake box. "I've brought roses for the fairest flower in all of Texas."

She barely stopped herself from gagging. Scooting out the front door, she forced the man back with the pile in her arms, hooking her foot around the bottom of the door and shutting it behind her.

"Now isn't a good time, Mr. Falstaff—"

"Please, call me John." He hooked his thumbs in his belt loops. "No need to stand on formality. You're a grown woman now." He took a slow, appreciative glance from her head to her toes.

"As I said, now isn't a good time. I'm on the auction decorating committee, and I'm running late."

She teetered to the porch steps with her arms full, her unwelcome visitor on her heels.

His sausage-fingered hands reached for the box. "Let me help lighten your load, little lady. I might as well carry that cake since I'll be the one to buy it."

Anne tamped down her annoyance and kept moving. Perhaps

it was a case of early-onset dementia. She couldn't be unkind to one of her parents' friends. No matter how delusional he was.

"Thank you, Mr. Falstaff—"

"John."

"I can manage fine on my own. I was due at the park ten minutes ago. I promised Lanette Johnson I'd help decorate the gazebo for the auction. She'll probably give me an earful for being late."

Anne made it to the passenger side of her small, blue car before he halted her with a hand on top of the cake box.

"Lanette drafted an army of her cronies to help. She can spare you for another ten minutes. What I have to say is of the utmost importance."

Air snorted from Anne's nose. She squeezed her eyes shut, drew a calming breath, and turned.

"Yes?"

John Falstaff straightened his spine and rearranged his face into a solemn expression. "I've come to make my intentions known. Out of all the fair ladies in Sweetheart, you captured my attention." He offered his tanned, oversized hand. "Would you do me the honor of joining with me in the act of courtship?"

Anne restrained a shudder with effort. "No." She rattled her keys. "Was there anything else?"

His hairy eyebrows dipped in a confused crinkle. "Perhaps you didn't understand me. I, John Falstaff, one of the most well-respected, set-for-life ranchers in the county, desire you to be my wife."

"I understood you perfectly, Mr. Falstaff, and my answer is no."

He froze. His gaze wandered to the side as he processed her rejection. His lips moved in a silent mutter.

Anne seized the opportunity to open the car, place her things on the passenger seat, and grab the roses. She slammed the door and thrust the flowers into his limp arms.

"Thank you for the bouquet, but I can't accept it. It wouldn't be right after refusing your suit. Please excuse me."

"Confound it!" He threw the roses to the ground and jabbed his fists on his hips. "Does this have to do with that no-good layabout Connor Fenton?"

Anne ignored him and walked around the front of her car. Falstaff followed so close the pointy tips of his cowboy boots clipped the back of her heels. His breaths came in short, angry puffs. He stormed in front of her.

"You had the good sense to turn that boy down once. Don't let him fool you into thinking he's changed. He's always been the idle, aimless, dreamer type. You can't depend on him. What you need is security. A man who's steady. Like me."

Anne opened the driver's side and held the car door between their bodies. "Thank you for your advice, Mr. Falstaff. I'll make my own decisions about Connor. Regardless of my feelings for him, my decision about a courtship with you won't change. My answer is and will always be a definite no."

She climbed inside, slammed the door, and inserted her key in the ignition with a trembling hand. The dust kicked up as she sped away. Her fingers clenched around the steering wheel. A slight tremor rocked her torso.

What a joke! A man older than her father wanted to marry her. As her stomach catapulted like a tilt-a-whirl, she tried in vain to settle her emotions.

John Falstaff was a pompous fool to assume she'd want to marry him. But something bothered her more than his declarations of romance.

His words about Connor.

Ugly as they'd been, they were a direct reflection of the worries in her own mind.

Dependability. Security. Home.

She hungered for those things. There was nothing wrong with that. But was she sacrificing her opportunity for true happiness by being unwilling to take a chance?

AUGUSTA SLIPPED an Earl Grey teabag into her favorite flowered cup and lifted the delicate porcelain to her lips. The pungent odor tickled her nostrils as she anticipated the first rich gulp. A lowing sound interrupted her afternoon reverie. Had a cow wandered in the yard?

"What on earth?" She left her steeping tea in the kitchen and hurried to the front.

Wrenching the door open, she found John Falstaff standing on the lawn, wearing the same brown suit with a different checkered shirt, a crooked cowboy hat on his head, and a bunch of half-wilted flowers grasped in his hand.

"Augusta Page!" he bellowed at her second-story windows. "Show yourself."

"I'm right here, you old coot." She shut the door behind her and stepped onto the porch. "What is it now?"

He stalked to her side, flower petals trailing in his wake. "You've poisoned your daughter against me!"

"I beg your pardon?" She raised her nose. "I haven't the foggiest idea to what you are referring."

"I stopped by Anne's apartment this morning to declare my intentions. Even brought a dozen long-stemmed roses." He waved the bouquet under Augusta's tilted nose. "She couldn't spare me the time of day. Just shoved the flowers back and said she had to be at the park to help decorate for the cake auction."

Augusta sniffed. "What makes you think I had anything to do with it? My daughter is a clever girl. She can count to twenty-six. That's the difference in your ages, in case you forgot."

Falstaff paced in front of her. "The world is full of May-December romances. Why should a few years bother her?" More petals floated from the roses onto the lawn, and his muddy boots trampled them underfoot.

Augusta pointed at the sorry-looking mess. "Fine. Putting

aside the question of your age, you know absolutely nothing about my daughter. Anne hates roses with a passion."

He stopped. "She does?"

Augusta nodded. "She says they're cliché."

"What's wrong with that girl? All women love roses." Falstaff muttered as he dumped the stalks in the flower bed. "How does Anne feel about chocolate?"

"She can take it or leave it."

"No chocolate. No roses. What kind of strange girl is she?" He scratched his head. "That leaves me in a quandary. How am I supposed to impress her? I'm gonna need insider information. You have to help me."

"There'll be icebergs in the Sahara first."

"Aww, don't be that way, Augusta. Take pity on a lovesick friend for old times' sake. You used to be right fond of me back in your cheerleading days, remember?"

"For the last time, I didn't—"

Augusta pressed her hands to her face. What was the use of arguing? John Falstaff believed what he pleased, and no amount of logic would sway him. Someone ought to teach the simpleton a lesson.

An idea popped from her brain like a sprouting seed. It curled into vines and stretched long, spindly arms until they tickled her funny bone. But she hesitated. He could never fall for such an outrageous suggestion. Could he?

She lowered her hands. "Should I give you the scoop on what Anne truly loves?"

"Now you're talking." He tipped his Stetson back and propped his fists on his hips. "Lay it on me."

Augusta bent forward and said in a stage whisper, "There's one thing that makes my daughter giddy as a schoolgirl. She can't get enough."

Falstaff leaned in with a matching air of secrecy. "What is it?"

"Christmas."

"What!" He reared back. "It's February. You want me to wait until December to court her?"

"That's not what I meant." Augusta flapped her hand. "Stores hold Christmas in July sales. And TV channels run those holiday movie marathons in the summertime, right?"

He grunted. "I guess."

"You can bring a little early yuletide cheer to Anne. Deck yourself out in red and green. Maybe a little tinsel. Or better yet, reindeer!" Augusta held her hands up to her head, splaying her fingers. "If you found yourself some antlers and wore them to the auction, I'm sure she would take notice."

"Reindeer antlers." He stroked his goatee. "Sounds a little farfetched. Are you sure this will work?"

Augusta's lips twitched. "Trust me. If you arrive at the festival in your Christmas best, it will make an unforgettable impression."

He sucked his teeth as he thought. "I do have an old hunting trophy in the barn. What if I take the antlers off and spray paint 'em?"

Augusta widened her eyes and pressed her trembling lips together. She nodded. It took a few seconds to compose herself before she answered. "Th-that's ... that's a sure-fire plan. She can hardly ignore you in such an outfit."

"But is it enough?" Falstaff's brow crinkled. "I don't want to repeat the same mistake I did with the roses. How do I make Anne recognize this gesture is tailor-made for her? Does she have a favorite reindeer?"

Augusta barely kept from crowing in delight. Not only had he swallowed the outlandish idea, he was asking for more.

"Must I even say it?" She pointed a red-tipped fingernail at her nose. "Who's everyone's favorite?"

Falstaff twirled the end of his handlebar mustache and smirked. "Augusta, it appears you're warming to the idea of welcoming me into the family. Rest assured, I won't let you down."

"I'm counting on it, John." She shooed him away. "You better hurry home and get ready. You don't want to be late for the show. I mean the auction."

He started to leave and paused. "Will you be there in case I need help with the getup?"

Augusta smiled. "I wouldn't miss it for all the cows in Texas."

Anne clutched her cardboard box and raced across the dry, winter grass of the Sweetheart Memorial Park. A slight February chill left her wishing she'd grabbed more than a thin jacket before she left. People scurried around, tacking vibrant red and pink streamers to the tables and tying balloons to the booths.

Lanette Johnson stood in the middle of the swarm in her purple jean ensemble with matching cowboy boots, shouting orders. The Ladies Auxiliary President's booming voice echoed through the air as she coordinated the chaos.

"Elise! That garland on the gazebo is crooked. Raise it an inch."

Anne took a circular detour around the crowd. She loved Lanette, but the do-it-my-way woman was best taken in small doses during festival time. Anne cut through the kiddie playground, ducking under the jungle gym. Her body doubled over as she crept along, face pointed at the brown, rubber mulch at her feet.

"Anne!"

Lanette had spotted her.

Anne cringed and straightened.

Clang!

Her head whacked an overhanging bar. She staggered to the side, tripped on the sandbox, and catapulted forward. Her hands full of cake box, there was no way to catch herself. She hit the ground with a sickening crunch.

"Oh, no." Anne whimpered. "No, no, no!"

She raised her body off the crumpled remains of the pink box and sat back on her heels. Eyeing the crushed container, she tried to work up the courage to open the wrinkled lid.

Footsteps hurried. A pair of men's brown leather oxfords appeared in her peripheral vision.

Connor's worried voice called out to her. "Anne, are you hurt?"

He reached the playground and crouched beside her. She ignored him as she reached shaky fingers toward her bakery box and lifted the crinkled flap.

Anne gasped. Her beautiful cake slouched like an angsty teenager. The right half smooshed lower than the left, and most of the matched pecans stuck to the sides of the box in renegade tufts of escaped icing.

"Nooooooo," she wailed. "All that work gone."

Connor reached out, hesitated, and gave her shoulder blade a gentle pat. "It's not so bad. You can get a plastic fork from the refreshments table and fix it."

"How do I fix this catastrophe?" She shot to her feet, longing to kick the destroyed cake past the tree line. "I can't enter it in the auction. The very idea makes me shrivel with embarrassment."

Connor gathered the box in careful hands, brushed a few pieces of rubber mulch from the sides, and rose. He held it out to her. "I guarantee you'll have at least one bidder." He poked his thumb at his chest.

"Don't bother." Anne slid her finger along the cardboard edge where a particularly large glob of smooshed icing protruded. She held the creamy evidence in front of his nose. "Just five minutes ago, it was perfect. Now, it's a mess."

A mischievous twinkle entered Connor's blue eyes. He bent and licked the dollop from her fingertip. "Tastes pretty perfect to me."

Her inner thermostat skyrocketed. She jerked her hand away and stuck it in her jacket pocket. The heat jumped to her cheeks. Her face must be the color of the festival decorations.

Anne spotted The Bulgogi Burger Rig in a parking spot by the curb.

"Are you opening your truck for the festival?"

Connor shook his head. "I still require a local county health department permit." He chuckled. "I doubt anyone in town would report me to the authorities if I opened for business, but I try to do things by the book."

"How mature of you," Anne deadpanned.

"Yes." His expression grew serious. "I'm quite the dependable fellow."

She got the feeling they weren't talking about food trucks anymore. "Are you really going to set up your business here?"

"That's the plan. Sweetheart has the one thing I can't get anywhere else."

She didn't ask him what the one thing was, but he told her anyway.

"You. Anne—" He stepped closer, and the pink box he was holding tapped her stomach. "Four years ago, I made the biggest mistake of my life. Leaving town alone. I won't do that again. If you need to stay in Sweetheart to be happy, I'll take my rig and introduce this town to the best bulgogi burgers they've ever tasted." He scratched his eyebrow. "I have to be honest. Someday, I plan to return to Dallas. But not without you. Whether it takes five months or five years, I'll wait until you're ready."

He passed her the mangled box. "Life gets a little lopsided.

Like your cake. It may not be perfect, but it still tastes delicious."

She scowled and swiped the box from him.

Connor winked. "Until the auction."

Anne looked down at the crumpled, pink cardboard and chewed on her lower lip. He still had that thirst for adventure in him. It was one of the reasons she'd fallen in love with him in the first place. The question was, did she possess enough courage to go with him this time? Wherever the adventure might lead?

CONNOR SCANNED the teeming crowd of Candy Hearts Festival goers. Attendance had grown in the last four years. They must be advertising it to the neighboring cities to bring in this many out-of-town visitors. Colorful booths lined the sidewalks of Main Street, selling home-baked goodies, signature barbecue sauces, and painted knickknacks. Pink paper mâché lanterns swung from the wrought iron lampposts, and cheerful fifties pop music played from the loudspeakers.

He resisted the pull to soak in the joyful atmosphere and revel in the delight of his cherished hometown. That could come later. Right now, he was on a mission. He must find the person he sought before Anne's turn arrived to take the stage. The cake auction was set to begin in ten minutes.

Connor spotted the man he was looking for in the crowd. Mr. Page's stocky body towered over the other festival-goers by several inches. The grizzly bear quality of his stature was mimicked in his expression as Connor approached. He'd seen more welcoming faces on Mt. Rushmore.

Mr. Page stood at the entrance to Sweetheart Memorial Park, holding his wife's magenta purse. The feminine bag did nothing to soften his surly demeanor. Connor stopped in front of him, unwilling to hold out his hand and risk rejection. Instead, he stood at attention with a deferential nod of his head. One thing he knew about Anne's father, the man was old-fashioned as a rotary phone.

"Good evening, sir."

Mr. Page grunted.

Connor gulped. He held out a large manila envelope.

The man eyed it with suspicion. "What's this?"

"It's my five-year business plan, sir." Connor passed him the envelope. "I currently co-own three food trucks with my partner in Dallas, but our aspirations don't stop there. I've also included my tax returns for the past two years. Please be sure to note the growth in my income. I've reached the level where I can provide for a family."

Mr. Page's expression remained stoic. It showed neither delight nor disbelief. Anne must have inherited her poker face from his side of the family.

Connor straightened his shoulders an inch. "I've also included a recommendation letter from my pastor in Dallas. I want to assure you I was leading a clean, honorable life while absent. If I had achieved success sooner, I wouldn't have been gone so long. But I refused to return an unemployed loser."

Mr. Page didn't respond. He shifted his wife's purse under his arm. Slipping a finger under the envelope flap, he eyed its contents but made no move to take them out. His nostrils scrunched like he smelled something foul.

Connor managed a smile. "I plan to bid on your daughter's cake at the auction tonight. I hope this won't be disagreeable to either you or her."

Still no response.

"Thank you for your time, sir." Connor nodded.

Giving himself a mental pat on the back, he raised his chin and walked away. He'd tried his best. It was out of his hands.

Mr. Page and Anne favored each other in many ways. Tall, proud, and stubborn. With both father and daughter, he had no idea where he stood.

Nine

Connor wandered to the side of the crowd when auction time was announced. People gathered and sat in the plastic folding chairs by the white gazebo. After a rousing rendition of "Texas, Our Texas" by an elementary school choir, the auctioneer Willy Walker took the stage wearing a black silk top hat and tuxedo. Instead of a gavel, Willy held a large mallet with a poofy plastic heart on the end. He slapped it against the railing. Whistly squeaks filled the air.

The festivities were far from quiet as a petite blonde ascended the steps with a lemon cake that matched the yellow accents on her vintage, navy-blue outfit. Hoots and hollers abounded. Whoever won had the pleasure of enjoying the baker's company while they ate their delicious dessert. Good-natured ribbing followed as the locals cast fervent bids on their favorite lady's sugary creations.

Connor stood at the periphery of the merriment. Changes had been made since the last time he was home. It used to be only women who entered the auction, but tonight's event turned into an equal opportunity free-for-all when a good-looking, male school teacher offered himself up with an apple pie.

Connor envied him. Should he have baked a dessert to prove

his sincerity to Anne? There's no telling if she would have placed a bid. There was less risk in competing for her cake.

He checked his wallet. Three hundred dollars was more than enough. No one had bid over two hundred, even for the popular male teacher.

Connor spotted Anne grabbing her warped Italian Cream cake from a side table and heading for the gazebo. She must be next. He scooted around the crowd and sat in an empty chair on the front row. Their gazes met as she passed. Anne flushed and lowered her eyes. He'd made progress in the past few days. If her not retreating at the sight of him was considered progress. But she never truly looked glad to see him.

He gripped his wallet and murmured a silent prayer. Even if he won the cake, the possibility of public humiliation loomed. She might spurn the chance to eat with him. They'd been on friendlier terms since their chat at the lighthouse.

But friends wasn't what he wanted to be.

ANNE TWISTED the plate and surveyed her ruined culinary masterpiece. What a mess! Would the crowd burst out laughing when they saw it?

The auctioneer called her name, and she blanched. Might as well get it over with. She advanced up the gazebo steps and spun.

Willy Walker eyed the cake, pushed the brim of his top hat back, and cocked his head. He opened his mouth but stopped at one glare from her. Clearing his throat, he gestured to the crowd.

"Ladies and gentlemen, we have a unique entry. An ultra-modern interpretation of an Italian Cream cake. It may lean a little sideways, however, I can vouch for Anne's cooking ability. Who'll bid ten—"

"Ten dollars," Connor said from the front row.

Anne wasn't sure if she wanted to smack him or ... something else. He balanced on the front of the chair with his head tilted forward. She had to admit, his eagerness was endearing.

"Well, I declare." Willy chuckled. "Let me finish, boy. You're gonna bid me out of a job. I have ten dollars. Do I hear twenty?"

A rancher Anne knew by sight raised his hand from the back.

"There's twenty. Do I hear thirty?" Willy's tone took on that droning, nasal quality TV auctioneers used. "Thirty. Thirty. Who'll give me thirty? I spy thirty from the front row. How about forty?"

"Forty." Dr. Caius called from the middle.

"Fifty!" The rancher hopped to his feet.

Anne sighed with relief. The danger had passed. She wouldn't suffer the shame of being a one-bid wonder. Maybe the men in this town preferred their cakes crooked.

"One hundred dollars!" Connor glared at the other bidders.

With a serene smile, Dr. Caius raised an index finger. "Two hundred."

The rancher shook his head and sat down. "Too high for me."

Anne blinked. Dr. Caius had been more than kind at the diner when he played the buffer between her and Connor. Could he really be interested in her? Or was this about two male egos dueling it out?

Connor stood. "Three hundred dollars."

A collective gasp sounded from the crowd. People elbowed each other. A few started catcalling and egging the men on.

Anne grasped the plate tight in her hand. How mortifying! She'd been reduced to a piece of livestock being auctioned off.

"Woo-hoo." Willy rolled his head. "We may break a record tonight." He pointed his heart-shaped mallet at Anne. "Who are you hoping will make the winning bid, young lady?"

She hesitated. Her gaze flitted between Connor and the doctor. A cool breeze kicked into gear. It rattled the branches of the oak trees and sent the leaves flying.

"Ummmmm."

She glanced at Connor. He raised his brows—a question in his eyes.

"I ... feel ... perhaps ..." Anne wasn't sure how to end the sentence since she had no clue what she felt. That was the problem.

"Five hundred dollars!" a gruff voice bellowed from the edge of the crowd.

Everyone in the audience spun in their chairs to see the new bidder. John Falstaff stepped forward in jeans and a brown plaid shirt, sporting a humongous pair of sparkly green antlers on his head. A bulbous, rubber red nose any clown would have been proud to wear adorned his snout. The pointy horns tilted precariously as he moved. He reached up to shove them back in place.

Laughter rippled through the crowd. People pulled out their phones, and lights flashed as they snapped pictures. A few called out teasing remarks.

Falstaff struck a pose. "What can I say? Love has made a beast of me."

He clomped halfway down the aisle, stopped, and eyed the swarm as if he was enjoying the spectacle he made. "You all heard me. My bid is five hundred big ones."

Anne shrank. No question how she felt this time. Horror careened through her. It shot from her heart, bounced around her rib cage, and catapulted to her brain. She looked at Connor.

He stared back, the same horror painted across his own face.

Oh no. Had he run out of money?

TEN

Front row. Aisle seat. Left side.

Augusta Page had chosen her spot with care—not wanting to miss a moment of the spectacle Falstaff was sure to create. When he came closer to the stage with his bedazzled antlers, she elbowed Ronnie sitting beside her.

"Can you believe he went through with it?" she murmured with a chuckle. "I was half-afraid he'd get home and common sense might reassert itself."

"Common sense?" Ronnie said. "John Falstaff? I don't suppose the two ever met."

The women leaned their heads together. They giggled as a few townsfolk hustled into the aisle to take selfies with the out-of-season Rudolph the red-nosed reindeer. Augusta pointed her attention at the stage to see how her daughter was enjoying the show. Anne held her cake slightly askew, her eyes wide, mouth ajar.

Was she overwhelmed with her unexpected bidder? Her daughter should relax and enjoy the joke. There was no way the old rogue would win. Connor would make sure of it.

Augusta followed her gaze to where Connor Fenton stood at

the edge of the crowd, scrambling in his pockets with an alarmed look on his face.

Why was the boy so panicky?

It couldn't be that he—

"Oh, you must be kidding!" Augusta shifted in her chair.

"What is it?" Ronnie bent her way. "What's the matter?"

"I think we've encountered an unexpected problem." Augusta stood. "Wait here. I've got to get my purse."

CONNOR TUGGED his wallet from his jacket and opened it. He thumbed through the bills, already knowing what he'd find.

Three hundred dollars.

And randy old Falstaff just bet five hundred.

Connor dug in his jeans pockets but found a handful of change. That wouldn't help. Why hadn't he brought more cash?

Anne begged him with her eyes to say it wasn't so.

"Uhhhhhhh." He stepped closer to the gazebo and whispered. "Mr. Walker, could I have five minutes to run to the ATM?"

Willy Walker snorted. "Sorry, son. Ain't happening. You bid with the money you brought. And it's a cash-only event. We can't put the whole auction on hold for you."

Connor rubbed a hand against his jaw. Folks leaned forward in their seats as if watching a play.

Falstaff stomped to the end of the aisle and shoved his tilted antlers into place once again.

"You tell him, Willy! My bid's the highest. If he can't beat it, that means I win the fair lady's cake." He sidled Anne's direction. "Don't worry, girl. I won't let this slacker pester you anymore."

Anne's knuckles whitened against her plate.

The auctioneer pointed his mallet at Dr. Caius. "What about you, doc? Can't let this charming, young lady and her"—he eyed the slanted Italian cream cake—"her unique creation go for a mere five hundred dollars. Would you care to up the bid?"

Dr. Caius shook his head with a smile and waved away the suggestion.

Connor blew out a breath. One competitor eliminated. It looked like he was going to pitch every last shred of pride out the window before this was finished. He faced the crowd.

"Ladies and gentlemen, I'm afraid I've been a fool. Of course, it costs more than three hundred dollars to win the cake of someone as beautiful as Anne. But that's the amount I brought with me. Would anyone be willing to make me a temporary loan? I'll pay you back directly after the auction, with interest."

"Hold on, darlin'!" Mrs. Page waved from the side. She tugged her purse from her husband's reluctant hands and hurried over. "Help is on the way."

"Augusta Page"—Falstaff planted his feet in a territorial stance—"you aren't bidding against me, are you?"

"Course not, John." She smiled. "I'm giving money to Connor, so he can do it."

"If that don't beat—" Falstaff stopped mid-complaint as the antlers drooped to his nose.

Mrs. Page dug in her giant bag and pulled two hundred-dollar bills from inside. She slipped them to Connor and whispered, "Sorry. This is all I got."

"Thank you, ma'am." He added the money to his stash. "My bid is"—he paused to count the coins he'd found in his pocket—"five hundred dollars and fifty-three cents."

Willy Walker slapped his heart mallet on the gazebo railing. "Five hundred and fifty-three in change. Do I hear fifty-four cents?"

Falstaff scoffed. "Why did you even bother? Six hundred bucks!"

"Oh, John." Mrs. Page slapped his brown flannel-covered back. "Why do you have to be so stubborn?"

She grabbed a ballcap from the balding head of a man on the

second row. "Let me borrow this, Abe. I'll bring it back." She thrust it high. "I'm about to take an offering. Who here will support the cause of true love?"

Laughter erupted. A few arms waved, and the hat passed up and down the aisle. When it made its way to the front, Augusta dumped the money on a chair, counted, and passed the money to Connor.

He held the donations with both hands and strode to the stage. "My bid, thanks to the lovely citizens of Sweetheart, is eight hundred and five dollars." Laying the money on the railing, he grinned at Anne. "And fifty-three cents."

"Oh, you do remember I exist?" she muttered.

His grin faded. Did she think he wasn't serious? He was fighting for his life. For their very future.

Together.

He leaned over and spoke low for her ears alone. "As far as I'm concerned, you're the only one here who matters."

Her eyes met his. A soft smile settled on her lips. She took a step toward him.

"Hold your horses!" roared Falstaff.

The two turned to the forgotten rival. He stood with sparkly green antlers askew, two sweat stains in the armpits of his shirt, and a scowl on his face. He snatched the red ball from his nose and chucked it to the ground.

"It's my turn to bid."

Mrs. Page stomped to his side and grabbed his sleeve. "Can't you bow out gracefully, John? It's obvious you don't stand a chance with my Anne."

He yanked his arm away and pointed a thick finger at Connor. "You may have sweet-talked your way back into this little girl's affections, but I remember how you left her high and dry. And she will too when she comes to her senses. I'm doing her a favor." He took out his wallet, snatched all the bills from the back section, and nodded at the auctioneer. "One thousand big ones."

The crowd gasped.

Connor winced. They'd already taken an offering from the spectators. There was no one left to ask for a loan.

He squared his shoulders and faced John Falstaff.

"I don't blame you for desiring Anne's company. She's worth any price. I may be out of money, but this won't end with the auction. Whether I win her cake or not, I've returned to Sweetheart for one reason. This time, I won't leave town without her."

Mrs. Page pressed a hand to her chest and whimpered. "Son, I hope my grandchildren get their daddy's way with words."

"Mom!" Anne hissed from the gazebo.

"Don't be embarrassed, honey. We all know it's a done deal."

Anne's eyes cut to Connor—her cheeks the color of Falstaff's discarded fake nose. He resisted the urge to wink at her and kept a straight face. She was embarrassed enough as it was.

A deep cough echoed behind Connor. He turned to see Mr. Page rise from his folding chair in the front. The older man raised weary eyes to the darkened sky and crooked a finger at him—just once. Connor scooted to the end of the row and stood beside him. Mr. Page reached into his back pocket and extracted a money clip. He slipped the metal prong off, counted every bill, and passed them over.

"Consider this an investment in your five-year plan. Two hundred dollars. I expect you to pay me back tomorrow."

He took the money, stood taller, and stuck out his hand. "Yes, sir. I'll be at your house first thing in the morning. Thank you, sir."

The money meant more than a simple loan. It was tacit acknowledgment Mr. Page accepted him.

Connor hurried back to the stage, added the bills to the pile sitting on the railing, and nodded. "One thousand and five dollars and fifty-three cents."

Cheers erupted. A few tossed their cowboy hats in the air. People left their seats to pat Connor on the back.

Willy Walker danced in a circle with the mallet raised over his head. "And the winning bid is—"

"Woah! Woah! Woah!" John Falstaff bulldozed through the well-wishers and glowered at the crowd. "Why are y'all celebrating like it's a done deal?" He waved his wallet and withdrew one remaining bill from behind the credit card dividers. "Good thing I always keep my emergency gas money in here." He slapped the wad of bills on the gazebo railing next to Connor's pile. "My bid is one thousand twenty dollars."

The right side of his mustache quirked at Connor. "Who you got left to beg for a handout now?"

ELEVEN

Thick, heavy silence settled on the crowd at the Sweetheart Memorial Park. Not a person stirred. The high-pitched chorus of crickets and katydids buzzed from the surrounding oak trees.

Anne stood alone on the gazebo stage. Forgotten. It was her cake they were bidding on. Her company. Her life!

She took in Connor and his shell-shocked expression. Mr. Falstaff in his ridiculous antlers. The entire town of Sweetheart sitting with mouths open, waiting for the next act to unfold. She pinched her tongue between her teeth. Did her whole romantic future depend on whether or not someone took enough cash out of the ATM?

Not hardly.

Anne rolled her eyes and descended the steps. With lifted chin, she thrust her cake into the auctioneer's hand. "Hold this, please."

She marched through the crowd and met her father on the front row. "Dad, do you still have my purse?"

Her father found the small, black crossbody bag under his chair. Anne unzipped it and fished through the inside. She located her wallet and dropped the purse on the grass. Skirting through the rows of chairs, she approached Connor on the side and stopped in front of him.

"I admit I'm still a little mad at you. Staying away for four years to save your pride was the dumbest thing you ever did. Even worse than leaving."

He squirmed. "No argument here."

"Me refusing to forgive you to save my pride would be dumber." Anne unsnapped her wallet and pulled a twenty-dollar bill from the pocket. "I think we need to spend more time together and find out if we can find a compromise that suits us both." She held the money out to him. "How about we start tonight?"

Connor drew near, took the bill from Anne, and kept her hand wrapped tight in his own. "Sounds good to me."

He waved the crumpled bill in the air at the auctioneer. "My bid is one thousand twenty-five dollars," he smiled at Anne, "and fifty-three cents."

Anne laced her fingers through his and returned the smile.

"Going once." The auctioneer called.

Every eye in the audience focused on Falstaff.

He huffed and stuffed his stack of bills into his plaid shirt pocket. "I might be a little slow on the uptake, but I can see the lady's made her choice."

Ronnie Ford stood from her aisle seat and whacked him on the shoulder blade. "Good for you, John."

The auctioneer skipped the rest of the ceremony and hollered. "Sold!"

People whistled. They hopped to their feet and applauded as Connor made his way to the gazebo, still holding on to Anne. He took the asymmetrical cake from the auctioneer and held it high.

The audience cheered louder, and a few rambunctious souls hollered, "Kiss her!"

Panic shot through Anne, spinning her heart like a hamster

on a wheel. This wasn't a wedding ceremony. She really didn't want their first kiss after reconciling to be in front of the entire town. She cast a wary look at Connor. He'd never been stage shy? Would he take advantage of the situation?

His blue eyes softened in understanding. Shifting the cake to his left hand, he placed his right behind her back and leaned low to whisper in her ear.

"I don't want to share that moment with anyone but you." He raised his mouth and pressed a quick peck to her forehead.

A few disappointed moans were drowned out by the calls of congratulations. The town of Sweetheart was overjoyed to witness two of their own find the happy ending for their love story.

Anne's cheeks blazed. She laughed and hid her face behind Connor. They left the stage, and a crowd of well-wishers surrounded them.

AUGUSTA PAGE STOOD AT A DISTANCE, allowing her friends and neighbors to congratulate her daughter and Connor. She was content to watch. She would have many occasions in the future to celebrate with the happy couple.

Pictures still to be taken filled her brain.

Wedding. Thanksgiving. Babies. Anniversaries.

Moisture stuck to her lashes, and her breath rumbled in disgust. "I've got to buy some waterproof mascara."

A white handkerchief waved in front of her nose. She found her ever-faithful husband at her side. Augusta took the cloth and dabbed at her makeup before elbowing him.

"I approve of the sweet gesture you made—giving Connor money."

"It's the first and last time." He grunted. "He better not ask me for a loan again."

"Don't fret, darlin'." She wrapped an arm around his sturdy

waist. "Our new son-in-law is more than capable of providing for his own family."

Ronnie loped over to join them. "I can't remember a more exciting Candy Hearts Festival. How will they ever top it?"

John Falstaff ambled to their side, his mouth screwed down in a pout. "It's hard to make any romantic headway when the whole town's against you."

"Don't worry, John." Mr. Page thumped his back. "There's plenty of fish in the sea."

"Not as pretty as Anne." He moaned. "My heart will never love the same way again after—"

He paused as a stylish, raven-haired beauty walked their way. The woman wore a soft, fuzzy pink sweater and tailored gray dress slacks. Her neck stretched like she was looking for someone.

"Who's that?" Falstaff's head turned as she passed.

"Not in a million years." Ronnie waggled a finger. "That's Victoria Park. The new elementary school principal. She's filling in while Mrs. Kilgallen is on maternity leave. She's way out of your league."

He cleared his throat. "I don't recall making her acquaintance yet. Perhaps I'll go introduce myself."

Augusta caught his arm. "When you're finished, come to our place. We'll light up the barbecue. Eating a good charcoal-grilled steak should soothe your hurt feelings."

"Well ... I'll think about it." He sauntered off but threw over his shoulder. "Be sure to make mine rare."

Ronnie surveyed the crowd. "Where did the two youngsters sneak away to?"

"Wherever it is, I hope they stay there," Augusta said. "Be at my house tomorrow, bright and early. We can start planning the wedding decorations. I've collected a whole folder of pictures and ideas I've been saving."

"Are you sure about this?" Ronnie shook her head. "Anne

agreed to give Connor another chance, not marry him. Besides, I get the sneaky suspicion she thinks we've interfered enough."

"Don't worry." Augusta poked her friend. "Even if takes my daughter a while to work through her emotions, we all know how this story ends."

EPILOGUE

Six Months Later

"And do you, Anne, take this man to be your lawfully wedded husband, to have and to hold, from this day forward, for better, for worse ..."

Anne's attention faded as Pastor Thibodeaux read the vows from his leather-bound book. Her wedding day. She should be floating out of her rhinestone-studded high heels. But that one phrase jerked her from the white satin euphoria back into cold, hard reality.

For worse.

Why did they include those words in the ceremony?

She gripped her Texas bluebell bouquet. A twinge of panic hit her. She loved Connor. And he loved her. There was no doubt about it. In the past six months, he'd proven to be a trustworthy, patient suitor who would court her until she was ready. And she thought she was ready.

Until now.

What if something happened?

People who truly loved each other still separated when the

romance wore off. Or they couldn't handle the pressures of life. Or so many other reasons.

She and Connor had broken up once before. Who's to say they wouldn't do it again? She wanted a guarantee.

"Anne?" Pastor Thibodeaux's deep voice broke through her musings.

Her head jerked. "Huh?"

The minister's kind eyes were a little wider than usual. "Do you?" He nodded the groom's direction. "Take this man?"

Anne's gaze darted around the sanctuary. The garlands along the altar rail. The tulle and flowers and feathers and every other minute detail Augusta Page had pulled from her voluminous folder of wedding plans. Her mother sat on the front row, her father on one side, and Aunt Ronnie on the other. Would the whole town hate her if she backed out?

She glanced at Connor. He studied her, his eyebrows puckered. He took her by the hand. His thumb stroked the back.

"Anne"—he bent close and whispered—"do you need a minute? We can wait."

Her panic faded. His simple acknowledgment of her feelings reassured her. When Connor had left town the first time, he declared he was going with or without her. This older and wiser Connor Fenton was willing to wait. Give her space.

Marriage didn't come with a guarantee. But she was prepared to take the chance. With God's help, she and Connor would do just fine.

She smiled. "I do."

Pastor Thibodeaux shifted. "You do what? Need a minute?"

"No." She laughed. "I do take this man, for better, or worse."

Connor blew a long, quivery breath from his lips. "That's a relief."

The guests broke into laughter, and the ceremony continued. A soul-stirring kiss sealed their union. Audience members punctuated the sweet moment with whistles and applause.

A riot of red and yellow autumn glory met Anne's eyes when she exited the white clapboard chapel, holding the hand of her brand-new husband. Flower petals rained as she and Connor dashed from the front door. Friends lined the sidewalk, calling their congratulations and goodbyes. The Bulgogi Burger Rig stood on the street with blue and silver streamers adorning its black paint job.

They ran down the front steps. Anne's heel caught the hem of her silky, white gown, and she tripped on the last stair. Connor caught her around the waist. Pulling her close, he whispered in her ear.

"You almost gave me a heart attack during the ceremony."

She played dumb. "Whatever do you mean?"

"I mean the endless ten seconds you waited before saying, 'I do.'" He cocked an eyebrow at her. "I was afraid you'd changed your mind."

She slipped her hands around his body and moved closer. "Nope. My doubts are dead and buried. I trust you." She took a wavery breath. "I admit I still get scared about moving. Scared, and exhilarated, and a million other emotions all jumbled into one."

He searched her face. "We can stay in Sweetheart until you're ready."

Anne smiled. "There's a difference between ready and nervous. It's possible to be both at the same time." She stood on tiptoe, kissing his cheek. "The nicest thing about being married is I don't have to be brave alone."

He planted a quick smooch on her lips and led her to the rig. Anne stopped at the curb to give her waiting parents a hug. Her father gave Connor a fist bump.

"You two were smart to hold the reception last night. Helps you get on the road at a decent time."

Her mother's eyes welled. "Are you sure you don't want to take a honeymoon before heading to Dallas?"

Anne embraced her. "Relocating to the big city is adventure

enough for me. Besides the new semester starts in a few weeks. It'll take me a while to adjust to the bigger college campus."

Her mom sniffled. "I can't believe you're a married woman moving far away. I never realized I could be this happy and this miserable at the same time."

Connor patted her shoulder. "It's only two hours away, Mom. You can visit whenever you like."

He bear-hugged his new mother-in-law and hustled Anne into the rig. A group of eager young women crowded around the window as she tossed her bouquet. Well-wishers cheered them as they drove away with strings of tin cans rattling from the bumper.

❧

AUGUSTA PAGE STOOD in the middle of the street, waving until the food truck was out of sight. Her husband rattled his keys, motioned toward the parking lot, and walked away. Ronnie joined her on the road and gave her a one-armed side hug. They stood gazing into the distance where the happy couple had disappeared.

Ronnie nudged her. "You gonna be okay?"

Augusta raised her nose and blinked away the remaining tears. "My baby girl found the right man and finally cut the apron strings. I'm right as rain. And I take comfort in knowing what an important role I played in the proceedings." She bumped her friend with her hip. "*We* played."

"You got that right. Those youngsters might have dilly-dallied forever if it weren't for us."

"Just the ladies I wanted to see!" a grumpy voice called.

John Falstaff stomped over in his outdated three-piece brown suit.

"Hello, John." Augusta chuckled. "Why didn't you wear your antlers to the wedding?"

"Very funny." He stopped in front of them. "I'm glad you

mentioned the subject. You two owe me for the humiliation I suffered at the Candy Hearts Festival. People are still calling me Rudolph."

The two ladies covered their mouths and snickered.

He frowned. "Don't you think you should make it up to me for sabotaging my relationship with Anne?"

"Your relationship with—" Augusta rubbed the spot between her eyebrows. "I'm sorry, John. I can't even justify that mess of nonsense with a proper reply."

"Do you deny you opposed my marrying your daughter?"

"Of course, I opposed it. Anne opposed it. Everyone opposed it!"

"You admit it." He pointed his finger at her nose. "That means you owe me."

"Fine." She sighed. "Come on over to the house for dinner. You and my husband can talk fishing while you eat."

"I don't want dinner. I want a wife." He crossed his arms. "And it's y'all's responsibility to find me one."

"Have you lost your senses?" Augusta gaped. "How can we find you a wife?"

"You're smart women. Something'll come to you. How about I accept your generous offer for dinner? We can make a list of candidates who are interested in me."

Ronnie snorted. "Talk about a short list."

"No need to be jealous, Ronnie girl. Just cause you and Augusta missed the boat, doesn't mean another woman shouldn't sample the marital happiness of being Mrs. John Falstaff. How about that pretty school principal I saw at the festival?"

"I hear she's already taken. Besides, she's half your age. Again." Augusta poked him in the extended stomach. "How about we set some ground rules? The first rule is, I'm not going to match you with anyone more than ten years younger than you."

He scowled. "How about fifteen years?"

Augusta rolled her eyes. "Twelve. I won't go any higher."

"Deal." He stuck out a meaty hand.

Augusta shook it and linked her arm with her best friend's.

"Come on, Ronnie. Let's see if we can find a woman willing to be this old goat's wife. There's a lid for every pot, no matter how tarnished it may be."

"Tarnished?" John grumbled. "That's a bit harsh."

Mrs. Page and Mrs. Ford ignored him. The women listed their options as they walked away from the church with John Falstaff trailing behind, complaining all the way.

-The End-

About the Author

Shannon Sue Dunlap completed an M.A. in Journalism from Regent University in Virginia Beach, VA. She has indie-published a clean and wholesome romance novella and sequel novel (*Flower Boy Tour Guide* and *Reality Show Romance*) and Christian romantic suspense (*Decoy Valentine*). Her new rom-com, Love Overboard: A Novel, will be released in May 2024.

Shannon loves traveling and draws from her many experiences around the world. From New York City and Seoul, South Korea, to Gaborone, Botswana, these beautiful places have provided inspiration for her stories. When at home in Houston, Texas, she teaches music to an adorable bunch of students at a local school and writes in her free time. You can sign up for her newsletter at shannonsuedunlap.com.

Coming Soon:

If you'd like to know more about the good-looking, male school teacher who baked an apple pie for the auction, be sure to check out the next book in this series, *Substitute Sweetheart*, coming in October.

~

Lone Star Sweetheart—Sweetheart Series Book One

Katherine Bruno's passionate, unfiltered temper makes her the shrew of small-town Sweetheart, Texas. When she's drafted to help the mayor's wife run against her own husband, Katherine meets opposing big city political consultant Ryan Park. The good-looking, flirtatious campaign manager gets under her skin, but fraternizing with the enemy is off-limits.

Katherine must battle her lack of experience, campaign sabotage, and her growing feelings for Ryan as she strives to succeed. His unprejudiced acceptance of her strong-willed character beckons her heart, but his jaded rejection of God is an insurmountable barrier. Will Ryan return to his faith and stay with her in Sweetheart or leave when the election ends?

Get your copy here:

https://scrivenings.link/lonestarsweetheart

Inspired by Much Ado about Nothing
by William Shakespeare

Much Ado about
MATRIMONY

a novella by
Linda Fulkerson

"You got it?"

Tricia Waters patted a lump in her cross-body bag and grinned at Halle Holt, her younger cousin and best friend. "Yep. Let's do this!" She clicked the lock button on her SUV's key fob.

Linking arms, the two skipped toward the entrance of Ed's Bridal Emporium. When they reached the double-glass doors, Tricia grasped the handle and paused. She grinned at the bride-to-be and said in a sing-song voice, "If you're gonna get wed ..."

"You're gonna need Ed!" Halle finished the store's hokey jingle.

The pair burst into a fit of giggles as they crossed the threshold and entered the wonderful world of satin and sequins. Tricia stopped and took it all in. Had it been six years since she'd last been here? It seemed like a lifetime ago. And yet, it seemed like yesterday.

A larger-than-life cardboard cutout of Ed Stephens, the franchise's founder, stood near the reception area. Consultants scurried about the sales floor, assisting other soon-to-be brides and their entourages. Racks of gowns, organized by color palettes, lined the left half of the building. To the right, an assortment of all-things-wedding, from flowers and photographers to cakes and catering—even a travel agency— were arranged in neat stations, each attended by a set of specialists, ready to serve—a veritable one-stop bridal shop.

Nothing in the store had changed. But everything in Tricia's life had. Not wanting to spoil the mood for her cousin's special day, Tricia forced the memories from her mind. She grinned at Halle, who gave her a tentative smile. "You ready?"

Her cousin nodded. "Yeah. You gonna be okay with this?"

"Sure. Come on!" Tricia nudged her bestie forward and moved alongside her to the counter.

Within a few moments, a young woman with stylishly coiffed platinum-blonde hair wearing a shimmering turquoise bodycon dress and matching stilettos strode toward them. A trio of aides, each with an armful of gowns, tottered behind their leader.

"Hi. I'm Fallon. Welcome to Ed's Bridal Emporium. I'll be helping you select the gown of your dreams." She reached her hand to Tricia, who nodded toward Halle.

"She's the bride."

Fallon's mouth transformed into a perfectly shaped *O*. "Of course." She immediately shifted her full attention to Halle.

The helpers busied about, hanging various-styled gowns on a nearby rack. Halle beelined toward a gown that shimmered with sequins and pearls.

"It's like something out of a fairy tale!" Halle traced the translucent bow at the back with her finger. She flipped the tag around and gasped.

"It's gorgeous! Is it your size?" Tricia reached for the tag.

"Yes." The bride-to-be spun toward Fallon and glared. "But it's *way* out of my price range." She pointed to the paper in the consultant's hand. "Did you read my responses to the questionnaire?"

Fallon's face contorted, and she resembled one of those shamed-dog memes. "Why, yes. I read what you *put*, but I also noted you're a nurse practitioner, which means you're practically a doctor—" The words spilled quickly from her mouth.

"Which means I'm smart enough not to spend a fortune on a dress I'll only wear once." Halle cut her off. "This gown costs over four thousand dollars. My budget is three *hundred*."

Tricia struggled not to laugh. Halle might be petite, but the family feistiness filled her small frame.

Fallon stiffened. "You were serious?" Noting the unwavering expression on Halle's face, she turned toward the trio. "You heard her," she snapped. "Check the budget and clearance racks!"

After an uncomfortable space of several minutes, the harried helpers returned with a fresh set of gowns for Halle to consider. Tricia found a chair and pulled her phone from her bag. A slip of paper fell to the floor. She picked up the tattered piece, slowly unfolded it, and read the scribbled word for probably the thousandth time. "Arkansas."

Halle twirled in front of a nearby mirror. "What about this one?"

Her question disrupted Tricia's musing. "Oh. *Um*, that's lovely." She hadn't lied. The simple dress featured a slim-cut bodice that flowed into a loose A-line skirt. "How much?"

"Two eight-nine. But I'll need a slip, which'll be a bit more."

Tricia stuffed the paper back into her bag.

"What's that?" Halle didn't miss much. Her gaze met Tricia's, and she knew she was busted. "I ... *uh* ..."

"You *kept* it?"

Tricia lowered her eyes toward her feet. A corner of polish had chipped off her left big toe. Time for a pedicure. "Yeah. I kept it. For all the good it did me."

Halle slipped into the seat next to Tricia, ignoring the scowl Fallon sent her way. If the woman worked on commission, she was likely counting the minutes until the end of this half-hour so she could move on to a more lucrative session.

"Hey." Halle tipped Tricia's chin upward with a finger. "It

brought you home. To me. And to your dream house." She smiled.

Tricia brushed away a tear. "Yeah. It did." She cleared the raspiness from her throat. "I threw away everything else—even all the pictures."

Halle looked thoughtful for a moment. "You'd already broken up before I moved here. I never even met him."

"Some days, I wish I hadn't." Tricia faced Halle and forced a smile. "So, what about this dress? Is it a winner?"

Halle stood and spun one more time. "It's comfy. Like a nightgown."

"Comfy is good. You ready to say 'yes' to your dress?"

She nodded. "I'll take this one."

Fallon pointed a finger at one of her followers and then toward the dressing room. "Candace, please help our bride-to-be out of the gown and zip it into a bag." She glanced at her smartwatch. The high-tech gadget did nothing to accessorize her chic ensemble.

"Thank you for your time," Tricia offered. Her curt tone was harsher than she intended, but she didn't apologize. "Of course," Fallon responded. She peeked at the bulky timepiece again and added, "Gotta run. Best wishes to your friend." And she was gone.

Halle emerged from the dressing room, a soft glow radiating from her face.

Tricia smiled. "You look happy."

"I am! I can't wait until CJ sees me walking down the aisle." She paused, and her expression softened. Taking Tricia's face in her hands, she said, "God's got the right guy out there for you. You'll find him."

"I thought Ned *was* the right guy. Until he wasn't." Tricia sighed. "But today isn't about me. Come on, let's check out, then we can splurge on some sundaes. You have plenty of room in that dress for a few more pounds." She winked.

A slight panicked look flashed across Halle's face.

"What's wrong?"

"My purse! I don't have it."

"I don't remember you bringing it in with you. Did you leave it in my vehicle?"

Halle shrugged. "I don't know. I wonder if I left it at CJ's." She reached into her jeans pocket for her phone. After punching in a text, she glanced up. "But you've got the goods, right?"

Tricia laughed, patting her lumpy bag.

When they reached the checkout counter, the clerk wore a well-practiced smile as she rang up the order. "Congratulations on your upcoming nuptials. Your total today will be three hundred forty-two dollars and seventy cents. Will this be cash or card?"

"Cash." Halle winked at Tricia, who pulled out a Pringles can and handed it to her cousin.

They both giggled as Halle peeled the lid back and shook out a wad of five-dollar bills. She counted them toward the clerk. "Five, ten, fifteen, twenty."

The young woman stared at the mound of bills and sputtered, "Are you seriously going to pay with *that*?"

"It's legal tender, right?"

"Yes, but … I'm afraid I'll need to call a manager."

Halle put a finger to her lips. "*Shh*. I'm counting."

Tricia laughed out loud. May as well enjoy this experience as the maid of honor because she knew she'd never be the bride.

BEN MCINTYRE TOOK the steps two at a time until he reached the stoop of his best friend's apartment. Anxious to see CJ again, Ben banged on the door.

When the door opened, CJ pulled Ben into a man hug. "Wow. The mighty doctor, returned from war. Or wherever you've been hiding since we left Ole Miss."

"It's been a minute, right?" Ben chuckled and held up an envelope. "I brought pics and a brochure."

"Of the venue?"

"Yep." He took three long strides and reached the dining table. "You ready to move out of this matchbox into a real house?"

CJ ran his hand through his straw-colored hair. "Definitely. It'll be a stretch with both of us just starting our careers. We're saddled with student loans."

"True. But an endodontist and a nurse practitioner should make it just fine." Ben sighed and looked down. "Trust me, I'd rather have the debt and have my parents back."

CJ put a hand on his shoulder. "Sorry, man. I can't imagine. How you making it?"

Ben sucked in a deep breath. "It's tough, I'm not gonna lie. Hopefully, things will work out for me to move here. Still waiting to find out about the clinic, but it's all good."

"I'll be glad to have you here." CJ moved toward the table and leaned over the spread of photos. He faced Ben and furrowed his brow. "Where are you staying? You get a place yet?"

"I have an accepted offer. I should hear something back any day. Oh, and I'm meeting with a lawyer in Little Rock later this week. Apparently, Mom's family had property here. Not sure of the details yet, but I'll know more about it soon. I found a room to rent in the meantime." He pointed to the table. "Well, what do you think?"

"Wow." He looked up at his best man. "You sure about this?"

"Am I sure of giving my best friend the wedding his bride has always dreamed of?" Ben laughed. "Yeah. I'm positive."

"Halle's wanted a beach wedding ever since she went to one when she was a little girl." He looked Ben in the eye. "No way could I afford this. And no way can I pay you back. Not for a long time, anyway."

"*Pfft.*" He waved his hand in a dismissive gesture. "It's a gift. Your wedding gift. I'm glad to do it. But I need to know now if you're sure you want a 'destination' wedding. Too bad there aren't any beaches in Arkansas."

"Well, at least the Mississippi Gulf isn't too far away. Yeah, I'm sure. Thanks." He laughed. "It still feels weird calling you Ben. Why'd you change your name?"

He shrugged. "Some of my classmates said Ned was too stuffy. Asked if I had a nickname. So, I switched to using Ben."

"Well, it suits you. It's ... friendly."

Friendly. Maybe too friendly. That's what got him in trouble in the past. He shook off the memory. "Speaking of names, what's the story behind yours? I never heard it."

"*Ah*, that. My dad was a huge Jean-Claude Van Damme fan. I was born while he was deployed, and Mom got the names mixed up. My birth certificate says 'Claudio Jean.' When my dad returned stateside, he started calling me CJ."

"Which is way better, *Claudio*." Ben punched him in the arm. "Okay. Back to the brochure. There are some villas along the beach here for the wedding party. And here's a pavilion for the reception." He pointed to one of the photos.

CJ shook his head. "Halle's going to be thrilled. I can't wait to tell her." He brushed a tear from his eye. "Sorry. Got a little emotional."

"Nothing wrong with that." Ben gave him a light slap on the back. "The venue is Halle's present. Now, for yours."

"Mine?"

"Your official engagement announcement."

"Yeah? It's tonight. You made reservations for the wedding party at Joe's Place, right?"

"Yep. And I stopped by there on my way over here. It's all taken care of."

"*What?* I was supposed to handle that."

"No sense in you running up a credit card. My parents may be gone, but they ensured I'd be well taken care of should anything happen." He'd known his mother's family had money, but he was shocked at the amount he received following their fatal car accident. "And if I can't use their blessing to bless my friends, what kind of schmuck would that make me, *hmm*?"

"It's just …"

Ben shook his head. "Forget about it. You've found the girl of your dreams." He sucked in a deep breath. "Besides, it's not like I'm ever going to get married."

"You don't know that."

A sigh passed through his lips. "Yeah, I do. There was only one girl for me, and that ship has sailed."

Both of their phones dinged with texts.

CJ laughed and pointed at Ben. "You first."

He glimpsed at his phone. "I'm glad you said you were sure about the beach venue because they just slam-dunked my debit card for the non-refundable deposit."

"Already?"

"The deposit is due thirty days before the wedding, which is today. Haven't you been counting?"

"Wow. It's coming up fast."

"Yep. What's your text say?"

CJ swiped his screen, and the text appeared. "It's from Halle." He blushed a little. "She wants me to swing by her apartment and see if she left her purse there. She can't find it."

"Didn't you say she's out shopping for the big dress today?"

He nodded. "Yeah. But she told me her cousin was holding the cash for her. Probably so she wouldn't spend it." CJ grinned.

"I'm parked behind you. Let's help your damsel in distress and get her purse. Then we can go grab a burger."

"Sounds good. I'll text her back while you drive and tell her about your generosity."

Fifteen minutes later, Ben pulled his truck alongside the curb in front of Halle's house. He nodded toward another vehicle parked there. "Looks like she has company."

CJ scratched his beard. "I doubt she's home yet. I don't see her cousin's rig." He hurried up the sidewalk and dug in his pocket for the key.

Ben raised his eyebrows.

CJ laughed and shook his head. "Don't get any wild ideas. This is for emergencies."

Before he could insert the key, the door swung open. A man a couple of inches taller than Ben grinned at them. White teeth contrasted against his well-tanned complexion. "Well, looky here. The bridegroom has arrived."

"Jonathan. What are you doing here?"

Ben noticed the disdain in CJ's voice.

"I came to return your blushing bride's purse." Jonathan held up the bag, then leaned in and whispered, "She left it in my car when we were … well … when she was in my car." He winked.

CJ grabbed the purse from Jonathan's hands. "Give me that!"

"How'd you get in?" Ben asked, his voice terse.

Jonathan held up a keyring and dangled it. "I know it's rude to look inside a lady's purse, but when I arrived, and she was gone, I had no choice."

"Get out!" CJ demanded.

"You forgot to add, 'or else.'" Jonathan smirked as he stepped past them. "And I may have been stretching things when I used the word *lady*." He skipped toward his car and sped off. Ben had to physically restrain CJ from chasing after him.

"Nothing but trouble there, buddy. Let's go find Halle and hear her side of the story."

"Her side? You heard what he said. She was making out with him in his car and forgot her purse."

"That's *not* what he said. There are two sides to every story." Ben paused, thinking back. "And it's not fair to not hear both of them."

"You know what's not fair? My 'blushing bride' hanging out with that no-good—"

Ben released his hold on CJ. "Look. Take some time to cool off, and then tonight, you can give Halle her purse and listen to her side. That's all I'm asking."

"I'll give her her purse, all right. And I'll give her her

freedom, too, because she obviously values that more than our so-called engagement."

"Come on, CJ. Try to be reasonable."

"Reasonable?" he scoffed. "I mean, she's always been a flirt. It was cute when it was with me, but she promised she was done with Jonathan."

"They have a history? Is that why your anger went from zero to off-the-scale so fast?"

"I guess." CJ sucked in a breath. "Looks like their so-called 'history' has made its way from the past to the present."

"All the more reason to get Halle's take."

"Are you worried about me, or are you worried about the nonrefundable deposit you just spent for nothing?"

Ben took a step back. "That's not fair, and you know it."

"Well, I'm sorry you're out that money. But you can have a party on the beach or find yourself a woman and get married there yourself, for all I care. I'm done."

"Will you at least show up tonight for the dinner? Talk to Halle. See what she has to say?"

CJ blew out a long breath and shook his head. "You missed your calling. You should've been a salesman. You could always convince people to do things, even when they know it's against their better judgment."

"I don't think going tonight and giving Halle her purse is against your better judgment. And it's not about the money. I'm asking as your friend."

After a long pause, CJ looked Ben in the eye. "Fine. I'll go tonight and give Halle her purse."

Two

The *maître d'* gave a slight bow to Tricia and Halle. "Good evening, *mademoiselles*. How may I assist you?" A thin smile graced the man's lips.

Tricia tried not to gape at his impeccable suit jacket and starched white shirt. She cleared her throat. "We're with the engagement party."

"*Ah*, yes. Welcome. Our hostess will show you to the private dining room."

A light wisp of pale smoke filtered from the posh eatery's kitchen as Tricia followed the young woman. Aromas of grilled meat and freshly baked bread blended, prompting a grumble from her stomach.

Halle gently elbowed her in the ribs. "Hungry?"

"Yeah. I guess more than I realized."

"Here we are, ladies. You may sit wherever you like." The hostess held an arm toward the dimly lit room. Mellow jazz emanated from the corner piano, mingling with murmurs of light conversations.

When the hostess was out of earshot, Tricia scanned around and whispered, "Fancy."

"Yeah. Ben booked it."

Tricia paused before entering the back room. "Ben?"

"The best man. You'll meet him tonight. He's footing the bill for our engagement reception. And, get this, he's gifting us the beach venue in Mississippi as a wedding present."

"Wow."

"Well, he's a doctor. And he inherited a bundle when his parents got killed a couple of years ago."

"That's sad."

Halle linked her arm through Tricia's and led her toward the table reserved for the wedding party. "It is. But let's not think sad thoughts tonight, okay?"

"Of course."

"Besides, lucky you get to walk down the aisle with him during the recessional."

"Lucky me?"

"He's drop-dead gorgeous." Halle winked.

Tricia felt a scowl forming. "Halle ..."

The bride-to-be shrugged. "Flirt, but don't touch. That's my motto."

"Does CJ know what he's getting himself into?"

"Probably. I mean, if I hadn't been flirting with him, we would have never gotten together." Halle pointed across the room. "There he is now."

Tricia spotted her bestie's fiancé. His face turned somber when he saw Halle. What was *that* about?

Halle slowed her pace as she eased toward her betrothed. Tricia sat near the stage, hoping to stay clear of whatever storm was brewing between the "happy" couple.

"Hi, babe," Halle said, leaning her cheek toward CJ.

He planted the expected kiss, but Tricia could feel the chill coming off him twenty feet away.

"CJ?" Halle's voice quivered. "Is everything okay?"

The man should be giddy over how gorgeous Halle looked.

Her short, dark curls formed a perfect frame around her heart-shaped face. Instead, he shrugged. "You tell me."

Uh-oh. Had Halle's habits finally caught up with her? Tricia wondered how long CJ would tolerate his fiancée's flirtations.

Heavy footsteps creaked across the small stage, and Tricia turned to watch her worst nightmare sidle up to the groom. "Hey, buddy. Sorry, I'm late."

CJ offered a fist bump. "Hey, Ben."

Ben? That was Ben?

The drop-dead gorgeous best man. The wealthy doctor. The man who had ruined her life. Benedict McIntyre. His last name should have been *Arnold*.

All the feels struck at once. Tricia couldn't breathe. She scooted her chair away from the table so fast that it fell backward, and she stumbled, nearly toppling onto the overturned seat. "Excuse me," she muttered to the man who stood to right her chair. She pushed past him as her tears morphed beyond the welling-up stage to falling full speed down her cheeks.

She made her way to the ladies' room, heaving sobs as she leaned against the counter. Ned was Ben. Ben was Ned. What difference did it make which name the scoundrel chose to use? She couldn't bear to be in the same room with him. At least Halle was right about the drop-dead part. Well, a girl could wish …

Tricia rubbed her tear-filled eyes with a balled fist. Less than a second later, excruciating pain shot through her right eye. Her subsequent yowl caught the attention of a young woman, who had apparently followed her from the engagement party.

"Are you okay?"

"My eye! My eye!" Tricia tried to blink a few times, which only exacerbated the agony. "It hurts, and I can't see! Everything is blurry." She bounced around in circles like Tigger from the Winnie the Pooh cartoons, holding her hand over the offending eyeball.

"I'll get some help," the poor girl stated, gripping the door handle.

Tricia put the hand not covering her eye on her shoulder. "Get Halle. The bride. She's a nurse."

A moment later, Tricia's rescuer returned from her quest, followed closely by Ned/Ben.

As if her eye wasn't painful enough. "Wh-what are *you* doing here?" She pointed at Ben. "I told her to get the nurse."

"He's an eye doctor," the girl explained.

Ugh. Of course, he was. He'd just been accepted to optometry school when their engagement imploded.

"Hi, Tricia. I know this is awkward—"

"Awkward?" She backed away. "*Awkward* is witnessing your fiancé snuggled in the arms of another woman."

The girl who fetched Ben inched toward the door. "If you won't be needing me—"

He spun toward her. "Actually, I will. Please stay."

At this point, Tricia wasn't sure if the tears stemmed from the pain in her eye or her heart, but they spilled softly, regardless. And her nose started running. If she hadn't been afraid of ruining her dress, she'd blow snot on him. Instead, she eased open a stall door and rolled off about a foot of toilet paper, fending off the embarrassment of dripping the slime.

Ben/Ned followed her into the stall and motioned for the onlooker to join them. At least it was the handicapped stall, allowing all three of them to squish into the cramped area. He placed the toilet lid down. "Have a seat. I'm going to wash my hands."

"What?"

"I need to look at your eye. Are you wearing contact lenses?"

"*Um*, yes." She sniffed and dabbed at her nose. Thankfully, the tears had let up.

He re-entered the stall and looked at the poor woman who'd been roped into assisting him with whatever he was about to do. "Do you have a flashlight app on your phone?"

"Sure." The girl dug a phone out of her minuscule clutch purse.

"Thanks. I need you to hold it where I can see, please." He turned to Tricia. "I suspect your contact lens is under your eyelid. It may even be torn. I'm going to flip your lid and—"

"Flip my lid? *Ha!* I flipped my lid on the day—"

"On the day you stormed off without giving me a chance to explain?"

"Explain? Or make up an excuse?"

The sound of a throat clearing caught Tricia's attention.

"Are we going to be done here soon?" the flashlight girl asked.

"I'm so sorry. Thanks for helping. I didn't even ask your name." Tricia tried to focus on the young woman with her good eye.

"I'm Claire. One of the bridesmaids. I went to nursing school with Halle." Her face formed what Tricia thought was a smile. "I know I'm just the lamppost here, but if you two need a moment." Claire turned her head back and forth between them like someone watching a tennis match.

"No," Tricia answered, quicker than she meant to. "I mean, I want to get my eye fixed. It really hurts." She paused, then added, "Hey. You're a nurse. Why don't you get the contact out for me?"

Claire shook her head. "The doc here is the most qualified person to help you."

Tricia huffed. "Fine, then." She crossed her arms across her chest.

"Okay. Let's get this contact out of your eye so we can get back to the party. We can discuss the past later. Ready?" Ben asked.

Tricia nodded.

"Hold still. This will only take a few seconds."

Claire followed his instructions on where to aim the light, and Tricia held her breath. She hoped the bridesmaid hadn't activated her phone's video app, although who could blame her if she had? A minor eye procedure conducted by one's ex in the ladies' room of a posh restaurant would make some excellent social media footage.

Ben pulled his hand away within a few seconds, and Tricia felt instant relief.

"Here's your culprit." He held up a torn contact lens. "Do you have a spare?"

She shook her head. "Nope. Guess I'll have to Cyclops it for the rest of the night."

He gave her that grin that used to make her go all gooey inside. *Used to?* Who was she kidding? Tricia felt her innards going mush. He took her by the hand and helped her up. "Ready to go back?"

Tricia's body tensed as tingles shimmied up her arm at his touch. Probably just residual nerves from the whole my-eyeball-tried-to-kill-me incident. *Right?*

He placed his hand at the small of her back as if it belonged there. The prickling intensified. This sensation was definitely *not* left over from the contact lens attack.

"Not so fast, mister," Claire butted in. "Look at her face. It's a mess. She can't go back in there looking like that. But you go on. I'll get her fixed up." She pushed Ben toward the door and dumped a pile of cosmetics onto the counter.

Tricia wasn't sure how someone could cram so much stuff into such a small purse. Mary Poppins would be proud.

A scream pierced through elevator music, wafting through the bathroom speakers. *Halle.*

Tricia turned from the mirror and gripped the door handle.

"Wait!" Claire's voice held a panicked tone. "Your face is still tear-streaked!"

Ignoring her, Tricia raced toward the back room just in time to see Halle fleeing out the side door, wailing.

Ben hopped on the stage, grabbed CJ by the shoulder, and spun him around so they stood face to face. "Dude, what happened?"

CJ shrugged off Ben's hold and twirled an engagement ring between his fingers. "I gave her her purse."

THREE

Tricia did an about-face and rushed toward the restaurant's front entrance. Right eye closed, she wound her way through the tables full of diners, teetering as she swung wide to avoid a server hoisting a meal-laden tray. "Sorry," she muttered.

Just as she reached the door, a hand put slight pressure on her shoulder.

"Where are you going?"

Ned. Ben. Whoever. *Ugh!*

"I'm going to find Halle." She pushed through the doorway and stopped long enough to rummage through her purse. She pulled out her vehicle fob and headed toward the parking lot.

"You can't drive with one contact lens."

She stopped and turned to face him. "Really?"

He nodded. "It's not safe."

"Okay. But is it illegal? Like, can you pull my license?"

Ben expelled a huff. "I want to look at your eye with real equipment. Make sure you don't have a corneal abrasion."

"As in *now*?"

"Yeah. Let me drive you to the clinic."

"Wait. What clinic?"

"Doc Ballard's."

"What about Dr. Kent? Is he going to meet you there and let you in?"

Ben rubbed his hand through his wavy black hair and sighed. "I have a key. Kent is out of town. Gone to see his wife's parents. Her mother isn't well."

"And you're—"

"I'm filling in. I took some time off after my parents ... Well, I'm between jobs. Kent knew I always wanted to move to Arkansas, so he gave me this opportunity."

"So, you're not just here for the wedding?"

He shrugged. "I'm waiting to see how things play out. But I will run Kent's clinic for him for a bit. Maybe longer. His wife wants to live closer to her folks."

Panic welled up inside her. It was bad enough enduring his company for the best man/maid of honor roles—that is, *if* the wedding would still take place. But Ned—er, Ben—working *here*? Maybe permanently? Her heart couldn't take that. She shuddered.

Before she could protest, he shed his dinner jacket and slipped it over her shoulders. "*Um*, I appreciate the chivalry, but I'm not cold."

"You were shivering."

Admit the shiver was from her mixed feelings about him setting up camp in her hometown or let him go on thinking she was chilled. *Hmm.* But she had to admit, the evening air and her little black dress didn't mix well. She pulled the jacket tighter and murmured a quick "Thanks." Let him think what he wanted.

"Now, let's get you to the clinic."

She let herself look him in the eye. "You weren't joking?"

"Yep. As much pain as you were in, your eye may need a drop. You don't want to risk an infection."

Her bangs whooshed upward as she blew out a breath. "Fine. Let's get this over with. And then I need to find Halle."

Ben returned his hand to the small of her back and steered

her toward a sleek sportscar. Figures he'd have a sweet ride when she could barely make ends meet. He continued past the car and clicked his key fob. The lights on a late-model pickup flickered on. "Your chariot, m'lady." He gave a mock bow and opened the passenger door for her.

Do not fall for his charm again. There. She considered herself warned.

He pulled into the lot at old Doc Ballard's clinic within a few minutes.

"I heard you considered buying this clinic when Doc Ballard retired a few years ago."

Ben nodded as he unlocked the door and flipped on the lights. "I wanted to. But I didn't think you'd want me living here then, so I stayed in Mississippi."

"You think I want you living here now?"

He shrugged. "I don't guess it matters. I needed a change after my parents ..." He turned on the lights in the exam room. "Hop up in the chair."

Tricia suddenly felt like a heel. "I'm so sorry. Halle told me about their accident. I didn't know because, well ... They were wonderful people."

"Thanks." He sucked in a breath. "Anyway. I'd taken a job at a clinic near the church where Dad was preaching."

"They moved there after ... after we—"

"Yeah. By the gulf. One of the church members owns the beach property where the wedding venue is. When I first visited this town years ago ... well, I understand why you love it here so much. The people. The church. I like it here. So, when this opportunity came, I took it."

She gave a slight gasp. "The wedding. We have to talk to Halle."

"Yes. I want to hear her side of the story."

Whether the jab was intentional or not, Tricia felt it. "I—*um*—I never let you tell your side of the story back in college, even when you begged me to listen."

He turned on the slit lamp. "Put your chin here and look over my right shoulder."

"Ned? I mean Ben ..." She blinked as the bright light caused her eye to water. He handed her a tissue. "I mean, what's up with that? You're *Ben* now? That'll take some getting used to."

"Long story. I suppose I could use my full name."

She shook her head. "No. Not Benedict." A giggle escaped her lips, and she mentally replayed the pep-talk/warning about resisting his charms, even though less than ten minutes had passed since her last internal heart-to-heart.

"Hold still." After a moment, he switched off the lamp and swung it away from her. "I didn't see any damage."

Not to my eye, at least. "Thanks."

Ben cleared his throat. "Can we call a truce? Just long enough to help Halle and CJ reconcile?"

Tricia waited a moment before responding, then sighed. No sense in both couples being miserable. *Couple?* Where had that thought come from? She and Ben/Ned were *not* a couple. "Okay. We can help them get back together. But after that ..."

An expression Tricia couldn't describe crossed his face. Shock? Sadness? Guilt twinged her conscience.

She slid off the chair, doing her best to ignore his hand on her arm, steadying her as she eased to the floor. "I'm sorry. About not letting you explain what happened back then. You can tell me now if you want."

He shrugged. "It doesn't matter. We've both moved on. And I promise, after we finish Mission Reconciliation, I won't bother you again." After an awkward pause, he finally spoke. "Let's get you home. It's dark, so I'd feel better about things if I drove you. We can get your SUV tomorrow." His tone was decisive but not demanding.

"What about Halle?"

"You want to change first before we start the search?"

"Sure." The scene of Ned/Ben embracing another girl played in her head for the millionth time. Why had she been so judgmental and not listened to his explanation? Would that have made a difference? Another voice reminded her of the little things he did that annoyed her. Like deciding she couldn't drive one-eyed. Why was life so complicated? The sudden wisp of brisk air brought her back into the present. She hadn't even realized they were outside. She shook her head, hoping to either rattle some sense into her brain or shake the memories loose.

He opened the truck door, waited until she was in, and buckled before closing it and walking to the driver's side. A sigh escaped from his lips, and Tricia suddenly realized he was probably exhausted. "Where to?" His tone was somber. The grin gone.

"There's this old Victorian bed and breakfast on the edge of town—"

"Just past the vet clinic?"

"You know where it is?"

"Might need a little TLC, but it's quaint. Are you staying there?"

"*Um*, yeah. I live there."

Tricia tucked her clutch under her chin and reached to unlock the front door. As soon as she stuck her key in the lock, a hand reached around her and turned the knob. She called over her shoulder. "Thanks for the ride. I've got this."

She marched across the parlor and waved to Lauren, the desk clerk.

"Hey, Trish. You've been gone a while."

"Anything exciting happen while I was out?"

Lauren shrugged. "Sink in the common area kitchen is wonky again. I put up a sign. I suppose guests will have to use the employee kitchen in the meantime." She took a sip of her coffee. "Oh, and a new guy checked in. Well, he phoned in a reservation. I haven't seen him yet, but he should be here tonight."

"Good." Tricia dropped her purse on the counter and slipped off her heels. "Did you call Red about the sink?"

"Flu."

"Great. What about Nick?"

"Went to see their grandkids in Texas."

"*Ugh!*"

"You want me to call someone out of Little Rock?"

Tricia shook her head. "I doubt I can afford a big-city plumber. I'll get on YouTube and watch some videos. I mean, how hard can it be to fix it?"

She felt a presence at her back and spun around. Ben was right behind her. *Stalker.* "Is everything okay?"

His mouth twitched into that grin that did her in every time. "New guy." He pointed to his chest.

"*You're* the new guy? *This* is where you're staying?" Her voice squeaked a little louder and higher pitched than she intended.

"Yep. Of course, I didn't realize you were the ..." He paused as if searching for the correct word.

"Owner." She filled in his blank. "Well, soon-to-be owner. I signed a lease-to-own agreement a couple of years ago. We're open but still in fixer-up mode."

"It's an amazing property."

"McIntyre, right?" Lauren flipped through a handful of envelopes on her desk. "*Ah*, here you are." She opened one and handed Ben a skeleton key.

He held it up and examined it, chuckling. "Thanks." He stuffed the key in his pocket and thumbed behind him. "I'm gonna run out to the truck and grab my things."

"Wait." Tricia shook her head. "You staying here—isn't going to work for me."

"Why not? I paid two weeks in advance. And besides, I need to help you with the ... *um* ... you know ... quest."

"The quest?"

"The mission. Remember our agreement? The one we made not twenty minutes ago?"

Great. "Yeah. But I didn't know it would mean being stuck with you day in and day out." She quickly sent up a Lord-we-need-to-talk prayer. "Fine. But you're not staying here one day past what you paid for. Agreed?"

Ben shook his head and marched out the door.

He had barely cleared the threshold when Lauren nodded toward the front door. "What's up with *that?*"

"You ever hear the old folk song, 'The Cat Came Back'?" Tricia asked, not leaving enough time for a response before continuing, "Well, *that,*" she pointed toward the parking area, "is the cat."

A moment later, Ben returned, hauling an armload of clothes on hangers and dragging a spinner suitcase behind him. "Which way?"

Lauren pointed to the right wing. "Second door on the left."

"But he will be right next to my—"

"Got it. Thanks." He turned to Tricia. "You want to resume the search party now or in the morning?"

"No need to call a posse. I know where she is."

He plopped his pile on top of the roller. "What? How could you know?"

"I figure she's in her old hiding place."

This time, the expression on Ben's face was clear. Anger. Perhaps mingled with a bit of confusion and frustration, but anger topped the list. "You hold a grudge against me for years for 'keeping secrets'?" He formed air quotes with his fingers. "Yet now, you withheld this information? Half the wedding party is out there looking for her!"

"Well, I haven't confirmed it yet." Tricia bit her lip.

Lauren raised an eyebrow. "If you're talking about your cousin, she dashed through here less than an hour ago."

Tricia met Ben's eyes and immediately regretted looking into them. She averted her gaze and muttered, "Meet me here in ten."

He gave a huff and rounded the corner.

She turned toward the front desk and faced her receptionist, who had a Cheshire cat grin plastered across her face. "What?"

Lauren moved her right index finger back and forth between Tricia and the hallway where Ben had disappeared. "You're gonna tell me what's going on, that's what."

A sigh blew through Tricia's lips. "History."

"History was my favorite subject in school."

Tricia picked up her shoes and bag. She let out a long breath. "Well, it wasn't mine."

FOUR

Ten minutes later, Tricia led Ben up the back staircase to the third floor. She reached the top and opened what appeared to be a closet door, but he realized it was a short set of stairs to another door.

"A hidden staircase? Nice!"

"Attic," she explained.

When she turned the knob, he could hear muffled sobs. In an instant, Tricia was across the room. She plopped onto a couch that had seen better days and pulled Halle into her arms. The sobs mingled with wailing as Tricia attempted to console the inconsolable. She lifted her cousin's chin and brushed the tear-matted hair away from her face. "Hey, baby girl. You doing okay?"

Halle shook her head. "It's too late. He hates me. He won't answer my texts or calls."

"No. It's never too late. And he doesn't hate you. I promise." She brushed a tear from her eye.

"I wish Uncle Roger was here. He always knows what to do. When are they coming back from their trip?"

Tricia shrugged. "They planned to be gone another four or five weeks.

Ben swallowed hard as he witnessed the pain flowing from the two women before him.

Tricia turned toward the slight sound. She must have forgotten he was here. "Guess what? I brought backup." She gestured for him to join them. "I don't think you've met Ned yet."

Halle's head swung back and forth between them. "Wait—Ben is Ned? The guy from college?"

Tricia whooshed out a sigh. "Yeah. The guy from college." She faced Ben as she gave him some background. "Halle's parents split up a few years ago, and my mom and dad took her in until she could get her own place. Mom has always wanted to tour Europe, so when Dad got a chance to teach abroad this semester, they packed up and left. Halle's right. My dad would know what to do."

"I don't blame them. I just miss them." Halle sniffled.

"Yeah. Me too. But even without Dad's help, we will fix this."

Ben knelt before Halle and took her hands in his. "Tricia is right. We're going to fix this. CJ and I had already planned to meet for coffee tomorrow morning. But I need to know your side of the story so I can tell him what's going on."

"Don't worry about it," Halle sniffed. "If he's going to embarrass me in front of our closest friends without even bothering to ask me what happened, then I'm done with him."

"Oh, honey," Tricia soothed. "Don't say such things." She paused for a minute. "*Um* ... what actually did happen?"

"That's the rub—I don't even know." Halle grabbed a tissue from the box she must have brought with her. "I couldn't find my purse, so I asked CJ to look for it. He never even texted me back. And then, when we got to the dinner, you saw how he glared at me."

"When was the last time you saw your purse?" Ben asked.

Halle shrugged. "Oh, yeah. Margo asked me to borrow some hand lotion, and I handed it to her. I was running late to meet

Tricia, so I rushed out the door when Trish pulled up. I never thought about it again. Until ..." she didn't finish.

"Margo?"

Both women looked at Ben. "Halle's roommate," Tricia explained. "Margo is a slime and a mooch. She only lives with Halle because she would have otherwise been homeless, and Halle is too sweet to let her live on the street."

"Well, that clears up how Jonathan got into your house. And got your purse. Margo must have given it to him."

"Jonathan? What are you talking about?" Tricia's tone turned accusatory.

Halle spoke up. "Jonathan. *Ugh.*" She shuddered. "He wanted to date me back in high school, but I thought he was a jerk and started dating CJ. He hates CJ. They barely speak. Why would he have my purse?"

Ben shared the details of their earlier encounter.

"And you're just now sharing this info?" Tricia stood and brushed the attic dust off her clothes. "Now, who's withholding information? This whole situation could ruin Halle's future, yet you still hold it against me for not allowing you to explain something that happened *six years* ago?" She poked a finger in his chest. "You fix this, Ned. Ben. Whatever your name is. Fix it with CJ." She spun on her heel and took two steps toward the exit, then turned around and added, "Or else!"

ABOUT TWENTY MINUTES LATER, Tricia was alone in her room, sobbing, when a gentle knock sounded on her door. "Go away."

"Tricia, it's me. Halle."

She jumped up and swung the door open, pulling her cousin into the room and slamming the door behind her before *he* showed up.

"Girl, we need to talk."

"About what? I'll figure out a way to tell CJ what happened. He'll believe me."

Halle shook her head. "If he takes a few minutes to listen to Ben and thinks about what jerks Jonathan and Margo can be, he'll come around. Now that I know the truth, I'm not as freaked out as when I had no clue what I'd done wrong."

"You did nothing wrong."

"Right. But I didn't *know* that. Now I do. So, I'm pretty sure things will be fine. Between CJ and me, that is." She cleared her throat.

"But?" Tricia stretched the word into two syllables.

Halle laughed. "But I'm worried about you. And Ben. Ned. Whatever his name is."

"There is no Ben/Ned and me, so you can stop worrying." She emphasized her words with a *harumph*.

"Hand me your bag."

"What?"

Halle nodded toward the boho bag lying on Tricia's bed.

Tricia shrugged, grabbed the bag, and tossed it. "I don't have much cash." She plopped onto the bed where the bag had been.

Halle sat in the desk chair and rummaged through the tote. After a few moments, she pulled out the wadded slip of paper. "You've kept this all these years."

"Yeah. I know. Stupid."

"Do you know why it says 'Arkansas'?"

"Because I had no idea where to go when I packed up and left Mississippi after Ned—*um*, Ben—and I broke up."

"So, you came to my house until you decided. Remember?"

"Yeah. And you had that lame idea to write the names of all the states on slips of paper and draw one out of a hat to choose where I would live. And I had to pinky-swear to move to whichever state was picked, no matter what." She laughed at the memory. "What a dumb plan!"

"I mean, it's worked out well, right?"

Tricia nodded. "Yeah, but I could have wound up in North Dakota and frozen to death!" A touch of horror filled her voice.

Halle shook her head, grinning. "Nope. There was no chance you'd have wound up in North Dakota."

Tricia gazed at her cousin. "There was a *one in fifty* chance ... right?"

"I'm afraid not."

"*Huh?*"

"Nope. Because *all* the slips had Arkansas written on them."

"What?" She paused a moment, noting the cat-ate-the-canary grin forming on Halle's lips. "You wrote Arkansas? On all of them?"

"Yep." She giggled.

"Cheater."

"Wanna know why?"

"Because you missed your favorite cousin after I left for college."

"True. I did. But when you high-tailed it away from Oxford, I got a call. From Ned."

Tricia felt her face scrunch. "And? He didn't ask you out, did he?"

"Oh, mercy, no! Like you said, we'd never officially met. Anyway, he got my number from CJ and told me he'd figured you were heading this way. He had a plan to get you back."

"Get me back?"

"He was distraught. He really loved you. And since he's never sought a serious relationship after y'all broke up, he probably still does."

"I doubt it." Tricia wiped an errant tear. "So, the pick-the-state-out-of-the-hat game wasn't your idea?"

Halle shook her head, bobbing her short black curls. "He asked me to convince you to move back home. I mean, I guess we could've thrown darts at a map, but I don't have a huge map, and darts are sharp and pointy. Plus, you might have missed."

"So, *he* had you put Arkansas on all the slips?" Tricia asked.

"It figures. Because he definitely didn't want me to come back to Mississippi."

"He wanted you *here*, Tricia. Because *he* wanted to come here when he graduated. CJ said he had it all planned out. But then Doc Ballard got sick and retired a year early. Before Ned-Ben—I'm never going to get used to that—finished eye doctor school. Doc put a notice about selling the clinic in the optometry school's newsletter or bulletin board or something, and Kent saw it. He graduated a year ahead of Ben, so the timing worked perfectly for Kent."

Tricia's brain muddled as she processed what she'd just heard. "Ben wanted to come here? He never spoke to me about his plans."

Halle sighed. "Did you give him a chance?"

Tricia put her head in her hands.

"When he had me fill out those paper slips, he had hoped to finish optometry school four years after your breakup, then buy Doc's clinic, and *boom!* Show up here and win you back." She let Tricia absorb her words. "My job was to keep you single while he was in grad school. But that was no problem, of course, because you'd sworn off men for good. Easy-peasy for me."

"Because I thought if God had wanted me to get married, He would send me somebody."

Halle moved next to Tricia and put her arms around her. "Maybe He just did."

FIVE

"Come on, man. Think about why you fell for Halle in the first place. What attracted you to her?" Ben's convo with CJ was falling flat.

"What caught my attention? She was a flirt. That's what." CJ took another sip of his frappe, his expression as cold as the icy drink. "Just like she's always been and always will be. No wonder she was with Jonathan."

"She wasn't *with* Jonathan." Ben shook his head. "For five minutes, I want you to use your brain. You're smart. Tricia said Jonathan liked Halle way back when, but she refused to give him the time of day because he was a jerk. Do you remember that?"

CJ stirred his drink, watching the liquid swirl in the cup. After a moment, he glanced up at Ben. "Yeah. I'd forgotten about that. But—"

"But nothing. So, dude has held a grudge against you this entire time. Since high school. Now that you're about to embark on your happily-ever-after, he can't stand it, so he puts in one desperate jab to try and ruin it for you. And you're about to let him."

"But the purse. He had it."

"Yeah, he had it. Because his slimy friend Margo helped him out. From what the girls told me, she'll do anything for a dollar."

"The girls? Wait. I thought you'd just talked to Tricia. You've seen Halle? Is she—" he cut himself off. "Never mind."

"She's devastated. Is that what you want to hear? It's the truth. You humiliated her in front of her closest friends without even asking her what happened. She's going to be your partner in life. Your helpmeet. You've got to learn to work together. Work things out." Ben sucked in a deep breath and let it out slowly.

"So, I'm supposed to take expert love advice from someone whose one and only relationship flopped and who never got up enough guts to try again? What about you and Tricia? Are you going to work things out with her?"

Ben held up his hand. "We're talking about you and Halle—"

"The way I see it, the situations are the same. You want me to give Halle another chance. Don't you think Tricia deserves another chance too?"

Ben put his head in his hands. "I don't know. She was all whiny and strident when she threw that fit and ran away." He focused his gaze on CJ. "She packed up and left college, never thinking about how much her parents had invested, much less not allowing me to explain things. It was pretty immature and selfish."

"Yeah. She was what, nineteen? Twenty? Who's mature at that age?"

Ben sighed. "Probably no one."

"Do you know why you came here? Why you agreed to work Kent's clinic for him?"

"It's a favor. His mother-in-law might not pull through."

"*Um-hmm.* Keep telling yourself that. You're here because of Tricia. And the sooner you admit that, the better off you'll both be."

CJ ignored Ben's attempt to lighten the conversation. "Think back to what attracted you to her in the first place."

"Really? You're using my own line of questioning against me?

And you accuse me of missing my calling. *You* should've been a lawyer." He took another swig of coffee. "Well, what are you thinking? Will you give Halle another chance? Talk to her? And be nice about it?"

"Tell you what. I will if you will."

Ben swallowed quickly to keep from choking. "If I will what?"

"I'll take Halle on a nice date where we can talk things through. But you have to do the same for Tricia."

"Seriously?"

"Yeah. Seriously. You want me to give Halle another chance? Then you've got to give Tricia one. Deal?" He held out his hand, ready to shake.

Ben threw up a quick heaven-help-me prayer and stuck his sweaty hand into CJ's. "Deal."

No. No. No. No. This couldn't be happening. Things were going just fine. Tricia didn't need God to send her a man. She had her house. Her home. And she spent all her spare time directing handyman traffic around the place as soon as she had money for each project. But now, this leak had her bumfuzzled, and her bank account was dwindling.

She refused to ask her dad for money. Then she'd have to hear the whole you-shouldn't-have-dropped-out-of-college spiel. She sucked in a deep breath and dropped her iPad on the desk. She'd watch another half-dozen plumbing tutorials later. For now, she could do something simple.

Tricia fastened the chain to the back of the house's new sign. *Messina.* Italian for "port." True, there was no ocean in Arkansas, but the previous owner had immigrated from Italy and lived by the sea. She'd hired Tricia to help her during her aging years. And when the woman—known as Nonna Amalia to the community— entered a nursing home two years ago, she set up a lease-to-own contract, which included allowing Tricia access to Nonna Amalia's prized recipe collection.

Sign under one arm and stepladder under the other, Tricia grabbed her toolbag and headed to the front of the wraparound porch. Glancing at the space she'd chosen to hang the sign, she pulled a hammer and level from her bag and poked a handful of nails between her teeth.

The sound of tires on gravel caught her attention. A courier van parked, and a harried-looking young man jumped out, holding a large envelope. "Morning, ma'am." He tipped his hat. "Sorry for the late notice, but Mr. Conrad said there was an error on the address his client gave him, so we had to track you down." The man tucked the envelope under his arm, pushed a clipboard toward her, and handed her a pen. "Sign here, please."

She spit the nails into her hand, dropped them into her toolbag, and wiped her hand on her jeans. "*Um*, what exactly am I signing?"

He showed her the envelope. The return label read Conrad, Simpson, and Heath, Attorneys at Law, with a Little Rock address.

"A law firm? What's going on?" A sick feeling crept into Tricia's stomach.

"I'm not privy to that information, ma'am. I'm just the delivery boy." He gave a nervous grin.

She scribbled her name on the indicated line, and he handed her the parcel.

"I'm sorry for your loss, ma'am." And with that, he hurried back to the van and left.

"My loss?" Tricia's thoughts immediately went to her parents. *Please, God, no!* How had Ben handled the news when his parents were killed? An inkling of sympathy hit her in the gut. And guilt. He must still be reeling from the loss, and she hadn't exactly treated him well.

Rushing into her office, she ripped open the envelope. Skimming past the legal mumbo-jumbo, her eyes focused on the sentence "Reading of the last will and testament of Amalia Giordano." *Nonna Amalia was dead?* She sucked in a breath and ran her finger across the page. The will was to be read at three in the afternoon. Today. Had Nonna Amalia willed the property to her? Or would she be homeless by the end of the day? She glimpsed at her FitBit. Ten o'clock. Still time to finish hanging the sign and get ready.

Tricia returned to the porch, stuck the nails in her shirt pocket, moved the stepladder into position, and climbed the four steps. Within a few seconds, she felt the ladder wobble. A creak sounded, followed quickly by the sound of splintering wood. She yowled as one leg of the stepladder crashed through a rotting porch plank.

Flailing her arms, the hammer flung in one direction and the level in the other. She felt her body moving in a downward spiral, almost in slow motion and braced herself for a hard landing. Instead, she hit something soft. Strong, but not the wooden porch deck or stone steps she'd anticipated.

She heard an "*oof*" just before she and the somewhat soft thing thudded to a halt. Time immediately sped up to normal tempo, and she realized the *thing* that had broken her fall was a person. Ben. Ned. Whatever. And she was sprawled out across his chest.

"*Um*, thanks for breaking my fall."

He eased her off him and stood, reaching a hand to help her stand. "I would say anytime, but after ducking the hammer and nearly breaking a rib, I hope this is a one-and-done situation." A smirk crossed his mouth.

She smiled. A second later, she scanned the space in somewhat of a panic.

"What's wrong?"

"The sign. Where did it go? Did it break?"

Ben pointed to the wooden plaque, leaning safely against the side of the house. "That sign?"

Ugh. She'd grabbed the nails, hammer, and level but forgotten the sign.

"I'm guessing you wanted to hang it there?" He pointed to the spot she'd picked out.

"*Um-hmm*." She nodded.

He pulled the ladder from the porch's clutches and scooted it over a bit. "You know, it's okay to ask for help when you need it." He retrieved the hammer and level and reached into her tool bag for two nails. "I'm going up. Hand me the sign, okay?"

Tricia stood guard at the ladder's base, sign in hand, waiting for his signal. Five minutes later, the slab of carved wood hung from its new home beneath the porchlight.

Ben descended the ladder and bent over, running his hand along the broken slats. "Most of these boards look okay, but those two need to be replaced. You got any orange caution cones?"

"I have a wet floor sign," she said sheepishly.

"That'll work for now. Straddle it over the hole. I'll make a lumber yard run and repair that spot before someone gets hurt." He unconsciously rubbed his side while he spoke.

Six

Grateful the porch repairs had gone well, Ben took a quick shower and dressed in business casual attire. As he towel-dried his damp hair, a grumble from his stomach reminded him he'd only drank coffee during his early morning chat with CJ. He checked his room's bedside clock. Just after twelve. Plenty of time to make a quick lunch before his afternoon appointment.

He'd had no idea his family owned land in Arkansas, and the notice he received didn't offer much information—just a time and location for Ben to appear. Within a few hours, his curiosity would be appeased.

Rounding the corner toward the guest kitchen, he paused at the sign on the door. Use at Your Own Risk. A chuckle gurgled in his throat. From what he'd overheard, the issue was a leaky faucet. Or sink. Maybe he could help Tricia with the repairs.

Tricia.

He sighed. Everything he did or said upset her. Was a relationship with her worth pursuing? An ache in his heart nudged him. *Yes.* If only she felt the same way. He shook his head, wiped the stray water droplets trickling from his damp hair, then strode across the room and opened the fridge.

Within a few minutes, he assembled sandwich makings—ham, cheese, bread, a tomato, leaf lettuce, mayo—and set them on the counter. Crime scene tape crisscrossed the sink. Grinning, he pulled open the cabinet doors below. A slow drip fed into a shallow container beneath the garbage disposal. Was that all? Probably needed some PVC cement. He could pick that up while he was out.

After rinsing the tomato, he located a cutting board and a sharp knife. He cut a couple of slices, tossed the stem end and bottom into the garbage disposal, and ziplocked the remainder.

Footsteps sounded in the hallway. Tricia stuck her head through the doorway. "What are you doing?"

"Fixing lunch. Is that included in the room rate?"

"*Um*, yes. Of course." She moved a few feet into the room.

He gave her a quick once-over. "You're dressed up." Did she have a lunch date? *Not your business, pal. Let it go.* But she was gorgeous. Auburn waves pulled back in a messy bun with a few tendrils snaking along her neck. *Stop.*

She shrugged. "I have to run an errand but should be back in time to fix supper. If not, you can order a pizza and charge it to the B&B."

He nodded. "I have to go out too. I'll grab something to fix this drip while I'm gone if that's okay." He turned on the water and flipped the disposal's ON switch. A rumbling noise emitted from beneath the sink. "What is that?" He flung open the cabinet doors.

"No, don't!" Tricia's warning came out in a half scream, half shout.

The rumbling intensified, and before Ben could flip the switch down, the pipe leading to the garbage disposal popped out of place, drenching him with a geyser of water and tomato sludge. He reached to turn off the monster appliance but slipped on the slimy floor and fell on his backside.

She took a step forward and called over the clamor, "Let me—"

"No!" he cut her off, regretting how harsh his voice sounded. Ben grasped the counter and hoisted himself up, then shut off the switch and the faucet. Glancing at the goopy water seeping across the floor, he whooshed out a deep breath.

"So, *that's* the issue with the 'wonky' sink?"

"*Um-hmm.* I'm so sorry." Her voice was barely above a whisper.

He ran his hand through his hair and sighed. "It's okay. Go run your errands. I'll clean this up." His eyes skimmed his soaked clothes, and he made an up-and-down sweeping gesture. "And this too."

"But—"

"It's fine. Really. Go on. He that maketh the mess, cleaneth it up, right?" He managed a laugh.

"Well, if you're sure." Pity filled her eyes.

"I am. Go on. I'll see you this evening." Ben gave a finger wave as she tiptoed toward the hallway.

Well, Lord, if this is what it takes to soften her heart toward me, then so be it. He smiled and trudged toward the closet labeled Cleaning Supplies.

TRICIA FORCED her nerves to calm as she entered the lawyer's waiting area. Glass-doored mahogany bookcases lined the wall. Blue overstuffed wingbacks faced a low table strewn with a few magazines. A coffee service angled across one corner. She regretted declining the receptionist's offer to serve her a cup and seated herself in one of the chairs. She hadn't even processed the fact that Nonna Amalia was gone, which likely meant so was their lease-to-own agreement.

Twenty minutes passed, according to the grandfather clock

opposite the coffee bar. She fidgeted. How long until she learned her fate?

A few minutes later, a squat, balding man entered. "Miss Waters? Leo Conrad." He reached to shake her hand. "I apologize for your wait. I'd hoped the other party would have arrived by now, but there has been an unavoidable delay. Let's go into the conference room, shall we?" He motioned toward a hallway and padded across the plush carpet.

Mr. Conrad held the door open for her. "Are you sure Felicity can't bring you some refreshments? Water? Coffee?"

She shook her head, fearing her stomach would rebel against anything she put in it. They'd barely sat at the large formal table when the door swung open, and in walked a harried-looking Ben.

A gasp escaped from Tricia's lips. Ben appeared as shocked to see her as she was to see him. *What a good actor.* She crossed her arms and forced her focus toward Mr. Conrad.

The attorney cleared his throat. "First, I wish to offer you the firm's sincere condolences for your loss."

"*Um*, excuse me," Ben cut in. "But who died? The notice I received mentioned something about property my mother's family owned."

"Yes. Your mother was mentioned in her great-aunt's will. However, due to her ..." He skimmed the papers in front of him before returning his gaze to Ben. "Again, I'm sorry not only for the loss of your great-great-aunt but for your parents as well, Mr. McIntyre."

Tricia spun her head toward Ben. "You're related to Nonna Amalia?"

"Who?"

Either he should get an agent and go to Hollywood, or he seriously had no clue. "Amalia Giordano. *Messina's* owner."

"Miss Waters, Mr. McIntyre, I believe if you both grant me a few moments, I can clarify the situation." He flipped through the pages, selected one, and set the others aside.

Tricia angled her body so she could read the top line. Last Will and Testament of Amalia Lucia Giordana.

"Mr. McIntyre is the great-grandnephew and only living relative of Ms. Giordana." Mr. Conrad turned toward Tricia. "And you, Ms. Waters, were like a granddaughter to her, caring for her during her latter years until her health declined to the point you were no longer able." He ran a finger down the page. "Ms. Giordana has named you both equal heirs in her estate."

Her mind froze at the words 'equal heirs.' With *Ben?* Was God having a good laugh over this? A thousand thoughts muddled her mind as Mr. Conrad continued in a muffled *wah-wah-wah* voice. Tricia caught a few words, such as limited funds and long-term care facility bills. She jerked her head back toward the head of the table when he said, "Free and clear." *What* was free and clear?

"I'll have my clerk prepare the deed to the property and call you when it's ready. Thank you for coming." Mr. Conrad stood, indicating the meeting was over.

Ben held the door for Tricia as they left the building. "Wow. I didn't see that coming."

"Me neither." She noticed his dark curls glistening in the sunlight. Undoubtedly, he'd had to take another shower after the plumbing fiasco. And she almost felt sorry for him. *Almost.* She stopped walking and faced him. "Now what?"

"Business as usual? I'll be busy at the clinic, and you can do your thing at the Bed and Breakfast."

"You won't interfere?"

"No. You're doing an awesome job. Just let me know if you need anything."

"How long do you plan to stay there?"

"Is it really that horrible with me there?" He laughed.

She sucked in a deep breath and shrugged. "It's just … awkward, okay?"

He nodded. "Fine. As soon as my house deal goes through, I'm out of there."

"You're buying a house?" Her stomach tightened—from excitement or dread?

"Yeah. I have an accepted offer, contingent upon it passing the home inspection." He glanced at his watch. "Actually, the inspector should be done by now. I should know soon."

They continued walking in step to the parking lot. A moment later, his phone buzzed. He swiped to answer and mouthed to Tricia, "It's the real estate agent."

She didn't want to be nosy, but he didn't step away to take the call.

"Seriously?" she heard him say.

A frustrated expression crossed his face, and he sighed. "So, it'll take a lot, then. Right?"

After another exchange, he thanked the caller and punched the END button. Ben turned to Tricia. "It failed inspection. It'll need a new roof, plus the foundation isn't level."

"Wow. That would take a lot of time and money to repair."

"Yeah," he said, running a hand through his now-dry curls. "So—"

"So, I guess you'll be stuck at *Messina* for a while." She paused for a moment. "Oh, and we'll refund your stay since you're half-owner now."

He shook his head. "Keep what I already paid. I'll find another place as soon as I can."

SEVEN

When she returned, a work van with a full wrap advertising Paul's Plumbing was blocking Tricia's normal parking space at the B&B. She pulled her SUV into the guest parking area, tromped across the walkway, and stormed past the reception desk. When she reached the common area kitchen, a heavyset man stood beside Ben, using animated gestures to emphasize his case.

"Yeah, but that'll be like putting lipstick on a pig. These pipes are ancient. This place has to be at least a hundred years old. You'd be better off to replumb the entire house."

Tricia pushed her way between them and spun to face Ben. "Business as usual, *huh?* You won't interfere, *huh?* Yet the moment I stop by the dollar store, you beat me back and call a plumber? You know that's not in the budget!"

"*Woah, whoa, whoa.* Settle down." Ben put his hands on her shoulders. "I called Paul before I left for the meeting. And I'll foot the bill, so no need to worry about your budget."

"I don't need you traipsing back into my life, flaunting your money." She brushed a tear.

Ben stiffened. "Look. My parents were the most generous people I've ever known. And I don't need you—"

"I'm still here," Paul butted in. "And as much as I'd love to listen to your lovers' quarrel, I must remind you that I charge by the hour. So, what's the plan, Doc?"

"You had to tell him you're a doctor? Show off!" She turned toward the door.

Ben grabbed her arm and pulled her toward him, perhaps a bit harder than he intended. The momentum pushed her against his chest. Before she could step away, he bent down and kissed her. Gently at first, then with urgency. He eased his fingers to the nape of her neck, intertwining them in her hair, and deepened the kiss. Without warning, she found herself kissing him back. Her mind screamed to pull away and run, but her traitorous heart won out, and she melted into his embrace.

When the kiss ended, Plumber Paul guffawed loudly. "Well, that's one way to shut her up!"

An expression Tricia couldn't read crossed Ben's face. He angled his head toward the man and said, "Whatever we decide to do about the plumbing issue, we won't be using you. I'll pay for your service today, but we are done here."

Her hands were still pressed against Ben's chest when he pushed away and ran out of the room.

Turning toward the back of the house, he flung open the door leading to the deck. Plopping in a patio chair, he ran his hands through his hair before settling his face in his palms.

Idiot! Why'd you kiss her?

He'd kissed Tricia before. Many times. But this kiss was different. She was different. Yes, she was the same beautiful woman he'd fallen in love with years ago. Vulnerable. That's what he sensed during the kiss. Life had dealt her some blows, and she'd built a tough barrier. But today, during the brief moment when she transformed from being kissed to kissing back, a bit of that wall crumbled. Although the crack in her protective barricade was a tiny one, he'd taken advantage of her hint of openness. In front of that arrogant plumber, no less.

The startled look on her face when he stormed away haunted him. He sat up and palm-slapped himself on the forehead. What to do now? Straggle back to the kitchen, where he'd left her alone to deal with Plumber Paul? Weak. Apologize? Weaker. Words without actions mean nothing. Send flowers? Maybe.

He descended the steps and paced the backyard, nearly stumbling into a building he hadn't noticed. A pool house, perhaps? Although there was no pool and no recessed area in the ground to indicate there'd ever been one. He turned the doorknob, surprised when the door opened.

Light filtering through the front window's caked-on dirt revealed what was once a quaint cottage. At first glance, he didn't notice any major structural issues. No stench of mold. Just dust.

As he was contemplating the building's potential, the door creaked open.

"There you are. I've been looking everywhere. Paul is done."

Ben's brain whiplashed back into reality. "*Um.* Yeah. Sorry. I'll go pay him."

"Thanks."

He placed a hand on her shoulder as she spun toward the exit. "Tricia—"

"Not now, Ben. Ned. Whoever you are." She muttered the last part and tromped across the grass toward the main house.

Tricia retreated to the attic. Perhaps a bit of the peace Halle found in this place could find its way into her heart. She bounded across the room and practically pounced onto the couch. So many emotions swirled together in such a short time. She brushed away a tear.

That kiss. Dreams from the past—and hopes for the future—

filled her mind when Ben pulled her close, and she let him in. Before she could savor the moment, he'd pushed away and stormed off. Had she done something wrong?

She should have kept her shields up. Not let him know how she felt. The growing attraction. No. Not *growing*—revived. All the feels from her college days that she'd buried deep inside rose to the surface, reviving her love for him. What should she do about it? Was pursuing the relationship worth the turmoil? Would he even want to pursue their past? Not from the way he reacted. He obviously regretted kissing her.

A text notification buzzed her phone, interrupting her musings. Dare she look at the screen? Praying it wasn't from Ben, yet hoping it was, she pulled the device from her jeans pocket. Halle.

Girl, where are you? I've got HUGE news!

Glad Halle's situation was improving, Tricia forced a smile. Her fingers hovered over the screen to answer when another text appeared. Ben/Ned.

We need to talk.

Chaos instantly flooded her mind. Ignoring him was the best plan. She'd type a quick response to Halle before deciding what to do about Ned/Ben.

I'm in the attic. Wanna join me?

As soon as she hit send, she realized the messages app was still open to his text. What had she done? A moment later, heavy footsteps on the stairs answered her question. She's just invited Ben to her sanctuary.

EIGHT

Ben took another bite of his loaded potato skin. He pointed to Tricia's plate. "You've barely touched your food. Are you not hungry?"

A sheepish look crossed her face, and she poked a fried pickle in her mouth. Talking around her food, she said, "Sorry. I guess I just got wound up."

He smiled. Asking her to lunch had been a good idea. Just apps at the local diner. Simple. Nothing fancy. He knew he'd still owe her a formal dinner, or CJ would call him out on their bargain. But that could wait. Along with a discussion about the past. The future. And yesterday's kiss. Today, he kept the conversation focused on her vision for the bed and breakfast. Something she was excited about, considering how animated she'd been while sharing her ideas.

"What about the backyard cottage?" He pointed to her notebook of goals. "Any plans for that?"

Tricia shrugged. "At one point, I thought it'd be a comfortable place to live, but every dollar I make is already promised to another project. It'll likely be way down the list."

"Yeah. Simply maintaining the house is a major financial

undertaking. But repairs and improvements can cost a small fortune."

"That's for sure."

He regarded her eyes, noting how golden flecks shimmered within her green irises. "I'm proud of how much you've accomplished."

Her mouth turned up at the corners, and his gaze dropped to her lips. He chastised himself for focusing on them. "Thanks for sharing your plans for the place. I can see you have great vision and passion for *Messina*. Nonna Amalia was smart to put you in charge."

A blush graced her cheeks, converting her confident appearance into one of a shy schoolgirl. The same shy schoolgirl he'd fallen in love at first sight with. "Thanks." Head tilted downward, she batted her eyelashes—not in a flirty, seductive way but in a modest, embarrassed manner.

Ben steepled his fingers in front of him. "I have a proposition."

Tricia's eyes widened, and a deer-in-the-headlights look overtook her expression. "Wh-what?" She fiddled with her napkin.

Placing one of his hands over hers, he smiled. "I want you to be able to do everything you've shared about fixing up the bed and breakfast. From repairing the plumbing problems to picking the perfect paint. All of it."

Her breath whooshed out in a half-laugh. "Right. Any idea how much all that would cost?"

"I have a pretty good idea since you put estimates on most of your list items." He grinned. "What if we split this fifty-fifty?"

She jerked her hands from his. "Ben, I know you've been gone a while, but I didn't win the lottery while you were away." Sipping her iced tea, she peered at him over the top of the glass.

He nodded. "I don't want you to take this wrong because you've already accused me of flaunting money, but I could be your financial partner, and you could oversee the planning and coordinating the work. I can set up an account, and—"

She held up a hand. "Ben, stop."

"Please. I want to help. I want you to be happy." The last part wasn't in the speech he'd so carefully planned. But it was true. He did want her to be happy.

Her face softened, and she let out a long sigh. "So, I get to be happy. What do you get? What's in it for you? What percentage of the profits will you receive?"

The question took him aback. He gathered his thoughts before responding. "None."

"You can't be serious."

He shook his head. "I imagine your margins are already thin, and you must keep some retained earnings for your personal income. I'll have a salary from the clinic—whether I work there temporarily or wind up buying that business."

"So, you *are* serious?" Shock filled her face. "You're offering to foot the bill and asking for none of the revenue? Surely you want *something*."

He wished she could trust him. Let him take care of her the way he truly wanted. But her self-sufficient stubborn streak would never allow that. He sucked in a breath and held it for a few seconds before blowing it out. "Does it sound too hokey to say it would make me happy simply to help you to be happy?" She didn't answer, but she didn't follow her typical course of action and run away, either. He took a chance and extended his hand toward her. "Partners?"

~

WHAT HAD SHE DONE?

Although Tricia didn't feel like she'd sold her soul to the devil, the newly minted partnership with her ex-fiance felt ... *awkward*. That was the word. She cast a side glance at Ben as she accepted the bank signature card. The teller waited less-than-patiently while Tricia's pen hovered over the document. After another moment's hesitation, she scribbled her name on the line beside Benedict McIntyre's.

He'd insisted no contract was necessary since they were equal owners of the property. And she'd used the argument to convince herself that, if nothing else, his monetary contributions were an investment in his property. *Their* property. *Ugh*.

Ben's one request in granting her the ample capital improvements allowance was that she include renovating the separate cottage where he intended to live. She cringed a little at the thought because Tricia had had her eye on the small house as a possible home for herself one day. However, budget constraints due to maintenance of the main house never left any money to start that project. A small sigh escaped her lips.

"You okay?"

She gave a slight nod. "Yes. Still processing. I appreciate your generosity. I-I—"

He placed a finger to her lips. "It's fine. Really. I'm going back to the clinic now. I imagine you have some projects to coordinate." He gave a quick wink and clicked his truck's key fob.

Thirty minutes later, Tricia spilled the day's details to Halle over banana splits. "There's got to be a catch," she said, twirling her spoon in the whipped cream.

"Why? It makes sense to invest in the place by sprucing it up. That way, if y'all ever decide to sell—"

"You think he's planning to sell *Messina?*" She almost choked on a chunk of pineapple.

Halle pointed her long sundae spoon toward Tricia. "Stop. I said, 'If *y'all* decide,' as in *both* of you. You're joint owners. He can't just up and sell the place without your knowledge or consent." She shook her head. "I bet your guardian angel is exhausted at the end of the day."

"What?"

"You worry too much, Tricia. The old people call it

'borrowing trouble.' The Bible says, 'Do not worry about tomorrow.' You need to learn to trust."

Trust. There was that word again. Tricia blew her breath out so hard her bangs flopped, prompting a giggle from her cousin. "So, tell me about you and CJ. Things going better?"

Halle's face lit up. "First of all, yes." She held her left hand toward Tricia, the sparkling diamond back on her ring finger as it should be. "But don't think I didn't see what you did there. Changing the subject."

Tricia suppressed a chuckle. "Busted!" She dipped another spoonful of ice cream. "I'm just glad you two worked it out."

"*Ben* worked it out. CJ is so stubborn, but Ben found a way to convince CJ to give me another chance."

"Even though you did nothing wrong." Tricia stabbed the maraschino cherry, topping the middle mound of frozen scrumptiousness.

"Yeah. Whatever. It's still my word against the world's, but who cares? As long as we're back together again—that's all that matters." Halle wiped a drip off her chin. "And guess what!"

"What?"

"He's taking me on a fancy date tomorrow night."

"Where to?"

She shrugged and giggled, her face brightening even more than before. "I have no idea, but he said it would be special and to dress up." She held her ring at eye level, smiling. "I can't believe the wedding is just a few weeks away."

"Yeah. It'll be here before we know it."

And so would the end of Ben's commitment to Kent. Did she want him to live here permanently? Now that his house deal had fallen through, was half-ownership in *Messina* enticing enough for him to stay?

She knew she certainly wasn't.

NINE

Tricia sat at her desk the next morning, determined to make a thorough list of all the repairs and projects needed to spruce up *Messina*. The Debbie Downer part of her niggled, asking countless questions. "Why'd he give you the money?" "What does he really want?" "Are you sure you can trust him?"

There was that trust word again.

Her phone buzzed, nudging her thoughts back to reality. She read the text.

> Wanna celebrate?

Ned. Ben. Whoever. She'd never get used to his name change. Not that she likely needed to. She figured he'd be gone after the wedding—less than four weeks.

What did he want to celebrate? Their newly minted business partnership? CJ and Halle's reconciliation? Ben's imminent departure? Something else?

Her fingers hesitated. Before she could change her mind, she punched in a response.

> What's the occasion?

> The restoration of Messina to her glory
> days.

Yes. That was worthy of celebrating. She could get on board with that.

> Awesome. And thanks again for making
> that possible.

> She deserves it. YOU deserve it.

Why'd he use all caps? Before she could push that thought aside, he sent another text.

> I'll pick you up at 6:30. Dress up. ;)

A winky face? Ben didn't strike her as the winky-face type. And he'd pick her up? Not hard, since they lived under the same roof. His last text was more light-hearted than she'd expected from him. Maybe she didn't know him as well as she thought.

BEN PATTED the small square lump in his suit jacket pocket. *Patience. It may be too soon.* He'd promised himself to see how the evening went before attempting to pick up where they'd left off. But things had gone well. Plans for the house. His hopes of relocating here if Kent was game. And that kiss. He'd mentally relived it dozens of times, hoping to repeat that special moment more than just mentally.

He knocked on Tricia's door, and when she opened it, he sucked in a deep breath. "You look gorgeous."

"Thanks." She subconsciously brushed her hands down the swirly green skirt, and a skeptical look crossed her face. "So, what's this really about? Is there something you're not telling me?"

"Nope. No more secrets. I promise." Except the box in his pocket.

As they walked past the front desk, he gave a slight wave toward Lauren, who peeked up from a novel she was reading. She hollered, "Y'all have fun."

Keeping his hand at the small of Tricia's back, he guided her to the passenger side of his truck and opened the door. He paused for a second before placing a soft kiss on her cheek. "Thanks for coming tonight."

A shy smile crossed her lips. Lips he must stop thinking about in order to concentrate on driving. Small talk. That would distract him. But what could he say to this woman he hoped to spend the rest of his life with?

She must have sensed his nervousness, for she said, "I'm working on a projects list for *Messina*."

The house. Safe topic. "Okay. What's up first?"

Tricia prattled on about her plans—from repairs to decorating to landscaping. Her voice burst with enthusiasm.

"Sounds like you've put a lot of thought into this."

She nodded. "Two years' worth." She turned toward him. "The only thing stopping me from proceeding was the lack of budget. I don't think you know what a blessing your gift will be. To me. To this community." She reached past the console and placed her hand on top of his. "I can't thank you enough."

He savored the soft warmth of her touch. "Just hearing happiness in your voice is all the thanks I need." Ben rubbed his thumb in gentle circles along the palm of her hand.

TRICIA HADN'T THOUGHT it possible for a restaurant to be fancier than the one where CJ and Halle's engagement party was held, but Ben's choice for their celebration dinner was all that and more. A slight gasp escaped her lips as they stepped into the lavish atmosphere. "Wow."

Ben winked. "Like I said, *Messina* is worth celebrating." Then, his expression grew serious. "And so are you." He reached for her hands and kissed the back of each, his gaze never wavering from hers.

That ooey-gooey feeling traveled from her gut to all her extremities, and she was grateful when Ben extended his elbow. She gladly looped her hand through it, needing every ounce of his strength to steady her wobbly legs. Her mind made a feeble attempt to recap the warnings, but she ignored it. Ben had been nothing but kind and generous since his unannounced return to Arkansas. And she had no doubt those actions would continue. She had no worries.

He placed his hand on hers as they followed the *maître d'* to their table. They continued light conversation about the house, the clinic, and the upcoming trip to the Mississippi Gulf Coast for CJ and Halle's wedding.

From the exquisite presentation of their salads to the melt-in-the-mouth deliciousness of the filet mignon, Tricia couldn't remember ever having a date so pleasant. Wait. Was this a date? They were simply celebrating the launch of *Messina's* return to her former beauty. Right?

When their server set the ramekins of *crème brûlée* in front of them and poured the most aromatic coffee Tricia had ever smelled into their cups, she dreaded the end of the magical night. Would he kiss her again? A tingle crept up her arms at the thought, creating visible goosebumps.

"Cold?"

She shook her head slightly. "No. Just taking it all in. The food. The setting." She paused and dared to meet his eyes. "The company."

His lips parted to speak when a guffaw behind him broke the spell. "Don't you look lovely, Miss Waters?" CJ bowed and kissed the back of her hand. The sensation of his lips wiped away all the tingly feels created only moments ago by Ben's touch.

"Thank you."

Before she could speak to Halle, CJ bent toward Ben's ear and said loud enough for the diners two tables away to hear, "Good to see you're holding up your end of our bargain." He slapped Ben's shoulder and escorted Halle toward the exit.

"What bargain?" Tricia trembled as she searched Ben's face for a reasonable explanation. His pause was too long. "What bargain?" she repeated.

Ben cleared his throat before responding. "When I met with CJ about giving Halle another chance, he challenged me to give our relationship," he pointed his finger back and forth between them, "another chance." Another pause. "We've been getting along well lately, and I decided to ask you out."

"So, this, whatever it is," she mimicked the back-and-forth finger-pointing, "is part of some sort of deal you made with CJ? What *exactly* was the bargain?" Her voice pitched upward.

"Listen, Tricia—"

"Don't you 'listen Tricia' me. I thought we'd agreed no more secrets. I asked you a question. Answer it." A woman at the table nearest theirs cocked her head toward them, then gave her date a questioning expression.

"Fine. The deal was that CJ refused to listen to reason. He believed Halle had cheated on him, and he was done with her. He even said, 'She is dead to me.' And he wasn't kidding." He pinched the bridge of his nose and refocused his gaze on Tricia. "No amount of reasoning was working. Then, he turned things back on me and said I hadn't given you another chance, so why should he give Halle one."

If he expected Tricia to insert a comment, she didn't. Couldn't. Was this glorious date simply a plan concocted to reunite CJ and Halle? Was everything they'd experienced together recently all part of some scheme? Did he even care?

"What happened between Halle and CJ is different. She was set up. And you—"

"What about me?" Her voice rose from whisper and screech.

"You wouldn't give me a chance. Back in college. You know

there are always two sides to every story—in that case, what you thought you saw and what really happened—but you didn't trust me enough to listen to mine."

"And I should trust you now? After you use me as a bargaining chip? Why did you even ask me to come here with you?" She stood and moved away from the table, hot tears streaking down her cheeks.

Ben stood to block her path. "Oh, no, you don't." He put his hands on her shoulders and pushed her back into her chair. "You've run off without hearing me out too many times. I don't care whether or not you choose to trust me, but you're going to listen to me this time." He removed his hands and ran one of them through his hair before he returned to his seat. "The girl from college—the one you saw me hugging—her name is Lorraine. Her brother had just died. He was a friend of mine. Remember? The one who had cancer? She'd come to tell me he'd passed."

Tricia had never been at a loss for words, but the only one she could find at the moment was "*Oh.*"

"So, not only was I devastated by the loss of my friend, but my fiancée, my soulmate, the love of my life, abandoned me. But that may have been for the best because it toughened me to withstand trials without help from anyone. It taught me to lean on God rather than other humans. And that's the only thing that got me through the loss of my parents."

He paused to catch his breath. "Did I use you as a bargaining chip to save Halle's engagement? Sure. But I didn't do it for that reason alone. I thought about CJ's words. About the fact that I was encouraging him to do the same thing I'd refused to do. For years. I knew where you were. I could have reached out to you. I could have begged you to kiss and make up. But I was too stubborn. Too prideful. Too self-sufficient to need another person to have and to hold.

"When Kent called, I thought long and hard before I agreed to man the clinic, and then I only committed for a few weeks.

But I did so in hopes of reconnecting with you. To see how you were. To determine if there was any hope of reconciling."

He blew out a breath. "I didn't intend for tonight to fulfill some 'bargain' with CJ." He used air quotes as he spoke. "I wanted to spend time together because I loved how our relationship has rekindled recently. And I've realized that I still love you. Always have.

"Why did I even ask you here tonight?" He reached into his pocket, pulled out a black velvet box, and tossed it onto the table. "Because I had planned to propose."

With that, Ben pushed away from the table, grabbed the ring box, stuffed it back into his pocket, and stormed out of the restaurant, leaving Tricia with her thoughts.

And the check.

TEN

Over three weeks had passed since what Tricia had dubbed "The Big Brouhaha." She'd barely seen Ben. Lauren had rescued Tricia after he'd left her at the restaurant, bringing along a large sum of petty cash to cover the meal's cost. When they returned to the bed and breakfast, she discovered he'd moved out of his room, hauling his meager belongings into the yet-to-be-repaired cottage.

He'd thrown himself into work at the clinic and, she noticed from the receipts he'd left with Lauren, improving his new "home." In a futile attempt to take her mind off him, Tricia had marched down her projects list with gusto, coordinating contractor schedules and material deliveries like an expert circus juggler.

Two days before she was to leave for Halle's wedding, Lauren asked, "You ready to go?"

Tricia shrugged. "Yeah. I guess." After a minute, she added, "I need to pick up my bridesmaid gown from the alteration place. And I should probably get my tires rotated. That would make my dad proud." She tried to force a smile.

"I'm about to grab lunch. Want me to follow you in the beast so you can drop your SUV off at the tire shop and pick up your dress?"

"Can two people *and* a dress bag fit in that thing?" Tricia had only ridden in Lauren's Mini Cooper once, and that was enough to spark a near-claustrophobic fit.

"The Beast is a lot roomier than you give it credit." Lauren laughed and grabbed her keys. "C'mon. Let's go while it's quiet here."

When they returned to *Messina* an hour later, Lauren swerved to miss the pothole in the driveway. The milkshake Tricia had held between her knees sloshed all over her.

"Sorry. I always forget about the monster hole. I hope that's on your to-do list."

Tricia half-laughed, wriggling to prevent the milky mess from sliding onto the Beast's seat. "It will be now."

Lauren jerked the car into Park and jumped out. "Let me help you." She ran to the other side and took what was left of Tricia's milkshake, allowing her to maneuver out of the minuscule vehicle. "Go clean yourself up. I'll grab a rag and take care of the car."

"Thanks! I think I need a shower."

TWO DAYS until time to leave. Then, the day after arriving in Mississippi, Ben would walk down the aisle with Tricia on his arm. Only they'd be headed in the wrong direction—away from the altar. *And* they'd be at someone else's wedding. Not theirs. Because he'd blown any chance he'd ever have with Tricia.

He shook off his memory of the night he'd abandoned her. Did he regret what he'd said? No. He'd needed to tell her. But the way he did it. In a public place. And walking out—no, running away—the same thing he'd been frustrated with her about. He pounded the steering wheel of his truck, mumbling a bunch of would've, could've, should've thoughts.

His phone buzzed—a thumbs-up from Kent, who had begged Ben to stay here a few more months. Kent's mother-in-law's condition had worsened, and his wife was leery of leaving. Ben had reluctantly responded to Kent's earlier text and agreed to stay as long as necessary. He blew out a breath, pulled his truck into the service department lot, and headed for the counter. Maybe he could find another place to live.

"Hey. What's up, Doc?" The attendant, one of Ben's recent patients, laughed.

The poor attempt at humor forced a chuckle out of Ben. "I'm going out of town and need to get the oil changed. Fluids checked. All the things to make sure she's ready to roll."

"Sure thing. But we're backed up at the moment. Can you leave it until tomorrow morning? We'll have her ready for you before noon."

Ben checked his watch. He'd hoped to wait and drive back to the cottage, but walking would probably do him good. "Sure. Thanks."

He signed the estimate agreement and handed the man his keys. Good thing he'd finished at the clinic and had changed into jeans and tennis shoes.

Thirty minutes later, he was back in his tiny house, pulling a water bottle from the fridge, when his phone rang.

"Hello, this is Ben."

"Dr. McIntyre?" Panic filled the man's voice. "It's Red. I was grinding something after I'd welded it, and I think I got some metal shavings in my eye. Rhonda called the clinic, but there was no answer. Is there any way you could see me today?"

Ben's thoughts swarmed. The clinic was on the opposite edge of town. A much longer walk than he'd just finished. He hadn't seen Tricia's SUV in her normal parking spot. Not that he'd relish asking her for a ride. CJ was busy doing honey-do things before he and Halle headed to the Gulf. Perhaps Lauren ...

"Sure, Red. Can you give me thirty minutes?"

He whispered a quick prayer for transportation and headed

to the main house. After explaining his predicament to Lauren, she said, "Here, take the Beast," and tossed him her keys.

"The what?"

"My Mini Cooper." She laughed. "I think you'll fit."

He waved his thanks and folded his six-foot-two-inch frame into the driver's seat, whispering another "Thank You" for the answered prayer.

TRICIA DUG THROUGH HER TOTE, searching for the ringing phone. She grabbed it just as it stopped ringing. Missed call from Halle. Before she could click to return the call, it rang again. "Hello?"

"Are you home?" Halle sounded out of breath.

"Yeah. Just going through my list of must-dos before I leave."

"Margo had a wreck."

"What? Is she okay?" Not Tricia's favorite person, but she didn't wish her any harm.

"Yeah. She's fine. But ... Tricia, Ben was in the vehicle she hit."

"Wow. Then Margo's lucky because his truck is huge."

There was a pause before Halle answered. "Tricia, he wasn't in his truck. He'd borrowed Lauren's rig."

Tricia took a moment as reality hit. "The Beast? It's so tiny. Is he—?"

"He's at the hospital. They may transport him to Little Rock."

She couldn't breathe. Halle's words jumbled in her ear as she grabbed her keys and rushed out the door.

"Wait! I'm coming to get you. Be there in five."

"I'll be at the hospital in five."

"Tricia, wait. Seriously. I'm sure you're upset. You shouldn't be driving—"

"Hanging up now. Love you, Hal."

As soon as she ended the call, she realized her car was in the tire shop. *Ugh!* She punched to call Halle back.

She heard her cousin laughing as the call connected. "You just remembered you're on foot, right?"

"*Um*, yeah."

"Well, I'm turning onto your road right now. Be right there."

A few minutes later, Halle pulled into a spot as close as possible to the hospital entrance. The glowing Emergency sign blurred through Tricia's tears as she rushed toward the automatic doors.

A white-haired woman wearing a pink vest smiled when they approached the counter. "May I help you?"

"I'm here to see Ned—Ben—*um*, Benedict McIntyre."

Molly, according to her nametag, spoke gently, "Are you immediate family?"

"No, ma'am. I'm—" What was she to Ben? The word *nothing* hovered on her lips as she remembered him leaving the restaurant. "I'm—" She couldn't get any words to form.

"She's his fiancée," Halle's voice came from behind her. Then she muttered, barely audibly, "Or she was." She attempted to cover the last bit with a cough.

Molly raised an eyebrow. "I see." She tossed a skeptical scowl back and forth between them. "Have a seat, you two. I'll have to check with the nurse."

"But I *am* a nurse." Halle flashed her APN credentials at the gatekeeper.

She grasped the badge and peered over her glasses. "That's nice, dear. But you don't work at this hospital." Molly pointed toward the row of beige plastic chairs. "Have a seat. I'll be right back."

The automatic doors opened behind them, and a young woman flew toward them.

Halle turned around. "Margo?"

The girl flung herself into Halle's arms. "I'm so sorry. I've ruined everything."

"Are you okay?"

Margo nodded and took a moment to catch her breath. "I wasn't hurt. What about the other guy? The witness called an ambulance."

"We're waiting to find out now."

"I-I have to tell you about ... about Jonathan—what he did. What *I* did."

Halle put her hand on Margo's arm. "Everything is okay now between CJ and me. We're getting married this weekend."

Margo was either too focused on her own thoughts or didn't hear Halle because she plowed through her next series of words as if her very life depended upon her uttering them. "It was supposed to be a prank. Jonathan said it was an old inside joke between him and CJ, and that it was all in fun. So, I played along. Took your purse. I didn't take anything out of it, of course. But I got it and gave it to Jonathan." She sucked in a deep breath. "I just told CJ that nothing happened between you and Jonathan. That you were never with him. I'm so sorry." Tears streamed down her face.

"Everything is fine. Seriously. Ben talked to CJ. All is well." Halle pulled Margo in for a long hug. When she stepped back, she turned toward Tricia. "Margo, have you met my cousin, Tricia?"

"You've been crying," Margo observed. "Oh, we're at the hospital. You must be waiting on someone. Have you heard bad news? I'm so sorry."

If the girl apologized one more time ... Tricia forced a smile. "We're waiting to hear about my—" She stopped, again unsure how to label her nonexistent relationship with Ben.

Before Margo could respond, Molly entered the room and moved toward them. "All the nurses are busy back there. I didn't interrupt. I'm afraid you'll need to wait a while."

Tricia wrapped her arms around her waist and nodded, silently praying as she shuffled toward an empty chair. She barely noticed when Margo left.

Halle plopped down beside her. She peered past Molly, retrieved her phone from her pocket, and typed in a text. A moment later, her phone buzzed. "We're in!" She looped her arm through Tricia's and pulled her toward the door separating the waiting room from the treatment area. The door swung open, and a young doctor wearing scrubs greeted them.

"Thanks, Jared." She turned toward Tricia. "Tricia, this is Doctor Jared Hughes. I worked with him during our ER rotations. Jared, this is my cousin, Tricia Waters."

"Tricia? Pleased to meet you." He shook her hand and turned toward Halle. "Is this the one here to see Dr. McIntyre?" The doctor nodded toward her.

"Yeah. Can she go back?"

"Yes, of course, but I must warn you—he's unconscious." He punched in a code and motioned for them to follow.

As she hurried past the desk, Tricia noticed Molly returning to her station, wearing a huffy expression. She offered an apologetic smile and followed Halle and Jared toward an area partitioned off with a curtain.

Tears welled in Tricia's eyes at the sight of Ben. A large bump had formed on his forehead, and bruising shone beneath his left eye.

"His vitals are stable." Halle pointed toward the monitor. "If you'll be a while, I may step out. Gotta finish packing."

"I'm not leaving."

"I didn't think you would." Halle planted a quick kiss on Tricia's cheek. "We'll be praying hard," she called over her shoulder as she ducked past the curtain.

Tricia nodded. *Hard.* The word spoke to her. Ben had called her out about running when things got hard. She stared at him now. Pale. The sound of his shallow breaths mingling with the beeps.

"We'll need to run some tests."

She jumped at Dr. Jared's voice, forgetting he was still there. "Checking to see if he sustained a *coup-contrecoup* injury."

"A what?"

"It's a type of traumatic brain injury. I want to do a brain scan."

Traumatic Brain Injury? Talk about hard ... A ball of fear welled up in her gut, threatening to grow. She fought back with a prayer. Faith, not fear, she reminded herself. For better or worse. In sickness and in health. Not that she'd ever hear those words directed at her, but if she could show Ben she wasn't running anymore. Prove to him she could weather the storms. Maybe he'd be willing to give her another chance. The look on his face when he stormed out of the restaurant appeared in her thoughts.

"Stop," she said, not realizing she'd spoken out loud.

Ben stirred. "Hey," he choked out the word.

"Hey, yourself." She searched for any other obvious injuries. "You decided to wake up?" She swiped away a tear with the back of her hand.

"Yeah. How long was I out?" The blood pressure cuff whirred as it filled with air. He grimaced as it tightened against his bicep. After a short time, the air whooshed out, and the reading flashed on the screen.

She shrugged. "At least a few hours." After a moment's pause, she added, "I was pretty scared."

He reached for her hand. "I'm okay. The other person? The one who hit me?

"She's fine."

His lips moved in a silent prayer, then he met her gaze. "Sorry about your dress."

"My dress?" Tricia suddenly remembered leaving her gown in Lauren's car.

"Yeah. I think it's messed up. Lots of glass."

"Oh. Don't worry about it." She scooted a chair beside him and took his hand. "You trying to get out of escorting me at the wedding?" Tricia tried to smile through the threatening tears.

Ben reached up and wiped one off her cheek. "I wouldn't miss it." He pulled her hand to his lips. "I-I'm sorry about—"

"*Shh*. It's okay."

"But—"

She pressed two fingers to his lips. "Rest now. Heal up. We can talk about it later."

He leaned back into his pillow, and within a few minutes, she could hear the even sound of his breathing. Tricia whispered a prayer of thanksgiving.

"A what?" Tricia listened carefully as the tire technician repeated his explanation. "Okay. Thanks." She punched the END icon and whooshed out a long breath.

"What's up?" Lauren peeked up from her work.

"Well, considering your Beast is totaled, my worries aren't that important in the grand scheme of things." She paused to sip her coffee. "But my car won't be ready for the trip tomorrow. Something about wheel bearings. And I was supposed to drive Ben."

"Is he coming home today?"

Tricia checked the time on her phone. "I'm supposed to pick him up in thirty minutes." Without a vehicle.

The desk phone rang, and Tricia jumped, startled at the noise.

"Good morning. Thank you for calling *Messina*. How may I help you?"

Tricia took another sip of coffee, amazed at how cheerful Lauren sounded this early.

"Yes, but he's not available at the moment. May I take a

message?" Lauren waited for the caller to respond. "Oh, I see. So, it's ready now?" Another pause. "Perfect. *Um*, sir, is there any way someone could deliver it?" Lauren winked at Tricia. "Fifteen minutes? Perfect. And yes, that's the correct address. Thanks so much."

"What's happening in fifteen minutes?"

"Your chariot will arrive."

"My what?" Tricia hadn't consumed enough coffee yet this morning to play mind games.

"A guy from the mechanic shop is going to drop off Ben's truck."

∼

"YOU SURE YOU'RE ready to travel? I mean, we don't have to leave until tomorrow." Tricia gave Ben a sideways glance.

"I want you to have time to find a dress since I ruined yours."

She gave him a half-hearted punch in the arm. "You did not *ruin* my dress. I'm just grateful you weren't hurt any worse. When I saw the car—"

"You weren't supposed to see it. But I'm fine. Really." He lightly placed his finger on his forehead lump. "Doc says I'm lucky. I should be fine within a few days. But thanks for driving."

"Like I had a choice! I just hope you're better soon so I don't have to drive this gargantuan truck back home."

"We'll see." He was so grateful to hear the laughter in her voice. "Besides, leaving today instead of tomorrow gives me a chance to reveal my surprise."

She checked the mirror before changing to the passing lane. "I thought we agreed no more secrets."

"I guess surprises could fall into the 'secrets' category. But when I said, 'no more secrets,' I meant the kind that could later cause misunderstandings or ... worse. Does that make sense?" He shuddered at the memory of her storming away after she'd seen him hug Lorraine.

"*Um-hmm.*" She eased the pickup back into the right lane. "So, what's the big surprise?" Her mouth formed a grin.

"You'll find out soon enough." Ben leaned his seat back and settled against the headrest. "Looks like you've got this under control. I'm going to get a bit of shut-eye."

"Sweet dreams." She kissed the end of her index finger and touched it to his lips.

He sighed as he sank deeper into the seat. *God is good.*

A couple of hours later, Tricia pulled Ben's truck into the parking area of the beach resort. "Wake up, sleepy head. We're here."

Ben stretched and yawned. "*Ow!*"

"You okay?" She placed her hand on his.

"Yeah. Just sore. And stiff from too much truck time."

She hopped down and hurried to the passenger side to help him out.

As he slid onto the pavement, he put his arms around her waist and pulled her close. Her heart sputtered at the anticipation of the coming kiss. It did not disappoint.

When he finally pulled away, he winked with his good eye. "And now, let's see about the surprise I promised."

"It can't be better than that kiss." She felt a blush rising on her cheeks.

"There's more where that came from." Ben winked and took her hand.

As they approached the resort office, he pointed toward the adjoining restaurant. "Do you mind getting us a table while I take care of the check-in stuff?" He leaned in for another quick kiss.

She took in the ocean view through the floor-to-ceiling windows that spanned the room's length. He joined her a few minutes later, his grin rivaling the size of the gulf as he sat. A moment later, he smiled. "And now, it's time for your surprise." He pushed himself up slowly, focused on something over her shoulder.

Tricia turned to follow his gaze and squealed. "Mom! Dad! You're back from your trip? And you're here?" She rushed to embrace her parents, then spun back toward Ben.

"You knew?"

He shrugged and joined the group hug. "Guilty."

"It's so good to see you again, Ned. Er—Ben." Her father patted him on the shoulder. "It'll take a bit to get used to that."

"Tell me about it." Tricia laughed out loud.

When they'd returned to their table, Tricia's mom patted her hand and gave Ben a look Tricia couldn't decipher. "We decided we couldn't miss Halle's wedding, sweetheart."

"Okay. But that doesn't explain why Ben knew."

"I—*um*—oh, look. Our server's here."

"You may be saved by the server now, but you owe me some answers, mister." She giggled.

When they'd placed their orders, Ben winked at Tricia's mom. "Ready?"

Mrs. Waters nodded. "More than ready. Go ahead, dear." Her dad took his wife's hand, both of them beaming.

Ben rose from his chair and grimaced as he maneuvered to one knee beside Tricia. He reached into his pocket, and she gasped. It was happening. He was going to propose. *That's* why he'd contacted her parents.

He opened the box and held the gleaming diamond ring out to her. Taking her left hand, he gently placed it on her ring finger. "Tricia Waters, I would be so pleased if you would do me the honor of becoming my wife. Will you marry me?"

A tear escaped from her eye, and Ben gently brushed it aside. "Yes. Oh, yes." She leaned down, cupped his face in her hands, and moved her lips against his. "I love you Ned-Ben." She giggled.

"And I love you too."

Her dad lifted his water glass. "Cheers!" He helped Ben to his feet and gave his daughter a tight hug. "It's so good to see you happy."

And he was right. She was happy. And it was good.

TWELVE

An early text from Ben woke Tricia up on the morning of the wedding. She subconsciously twirled the newly nested ring on her left hand before clicking the message app.

Good morning, my darling. I'm afraid I
won't make breakfast with you, but I
heard Halle and the girls are meeting at 10
in the event bungalow for a girls' brunch.
See you at sunset. All my love.

Wait, what? Engaged less than twenty-four hours, and he was skipping their first breakfast together as a couple? Well, technically not their *first* since they'd been engaged before and had often met for breakfast. But that seemed like a lifetime ago.

Okay. No to breakfast. Probably because of the girls' gig. But lunch? What about lunch? Of course, she still had to make a quick dress-shopping trip, but now that they were back together, Tricia wasn't sure she could wait until the sunset beach wedding to see him. To touch his face. To kiss him.

Trust. God placed the word on her heart again, reminding her to trust Ben—and Him. Maybe the groomsmen had lunch plans.

She sucked in a cleansing breath, held it, then released it slowly before responding.

> It'll be a long day without spending time with you, but I'm sure the girls will make it fun. Praying you're feeling well.

> Actually, I've never felt better.

He followed the text with a kissing Memoji. She smiled. Whenever her life with him as her husband began, it would be a good one.

Tricia stepped into the event bungalow at 9:56, her heart full from the events of the past few days. But today was Halle's happily ever after, and she'd do her best to ensure her cousin's day was perfect.

She was immediately surrounded by a group of giggling young women, with Claire leading the pack. "Lemme see it!"

Examining the exquisite ring, Claire squealed. "I can't believe you're engaged to that hot eye doctor."

Talk about good news traveling fast …

"Have you set a date yet?" another bridesmaid asked.

A wave of claustrophobia washed over Tricia, and she stepped backward from the huddle. "Well, *uh*, we just—"

"Yes. The date has been set," Halle interrupted.

What? Wasn't date-setting on the bride's to-do list?

Halle swung her arm around Tricia's shoulders. "She's getting married today. We're having a double wedding."

"Tricia? Come on, honey. Wake up." Tricia's mother patted a damp cloth on her forehead.

Halle and Claire eased her into a sitting position. Tricia heard muffled voices in the background. She thought she heard one of the girls say, "Wow. That was so cool! I'd never seen anyone faint before."

Had she fainted? She vaguely recalled a strange dream where Halle said she was getting married today. Was it a dream? Dizziness threatened.

"Oh, no, you don't," Halle scolded. "You're not fainting on me twice in one day. Let's get you to a chair." A joint effort from the bridesmaids helped Tricia into one of the cloth-draped chairs prepared for the reception.

Her mother appeared with a water bottle, and a moment later, Ben was at Tricia's side. One of the girls must have sent for him.

He knelt beside her and gently placed his hands on her shoulders. "Hey, there." He tipped her chin up to meet his gaze. "What's this I hear about you fainting? You okay, babe?"

"I-I'm not sure what happened." She touched a balled fist to her eye.

Ben gently pulled her hand away. "Remember what happened the last time you rubbed your eye too hard? Let's not reenact that scene, okay."

She nodded feebly. "Halle said we're getting married today."

He held her hands in his. "I'd like to. That is, if you're okay with it."

Confusion swarmed her thoughts. "But—don't we need a license or something? We just got engaged." Again.

Ben reached inside his jacket pocket and pulled out a brochure-sized folder. He opened it, revealing a marriage license. The one from six years ago. "It's still valid."

"Really? It's not expired or anything?"

He shook his head. "In Mississippi, marriage licenses don't expire. We can get married today, if you want."

Tricia took a moment to process his words as the faint fog lifted from her brain. She could be married. Today. To Ben. She lifted her face to meet his eyes. "But what about Halle and CJ?"

Halle scooted a chair next to Tricia. "It was my idea. It's a practical thing, really. This way, we'd never forget each other's anniversaries. What do you say?"

She leaned against Ben's shoulder and lightly touched his bruised cheek. The happily ever after she'd always wanted, but she'd nearly thrown away. Now, through God's grace and Ben's patience, the opportunity had been restored. With Halle's question still waiting, unanswered, Tricia knew there was only one response.

"What will I wear?"

Halle turned to Tricia's mother. "Aunt Catherine?"

Tricia's mom hurried to a nearby table and returned with a slightly tattered dress bag. Although faded, the Ed's Bridal Emporium logo was stamped in the right-hand corner. Her wedding gown—the one she'd selected six years ago.

THE SETTING SUN glistened off the gulf's gentle waves. Ben stood tall next to CJ in what likely appeared to be a grinning competition. Ben decided he had the edge on his best friend and now best man.

With Halle on his right arm and Tricia on his left, Tricia's father walked slowly across the sand toward the waiting grooms. Each step they took brought Tricia nearer to him, to their future together, to their happily ever after.

Mr. Waters and Halle blurred into the background as Ben focused on the vision of loveliness approaching him. Her silken waves framed her face as gently as the dress—the bridal gown her mother had stored all these years and had cleaned and pressed just days ago at Ben's request—fit her soft curves. *Tricia.* His bride. His love. His wife.

As the minister closed his Bible and finished with the words recited throughout the ages, "I now pronounce each of you man and wife. You may kiss your brides." Ben pulled back Tricia's veil and cupped her face in his hands, placing a tender kiss on her lips. He held her against his chest for a moment, feeling her heart beating in rhythm with his.

"I love you, Mrs. McIntyre," he whispered against her mouth.

"And I love you, too, Ben. Ned. Whatever."

About the Author

Linda Fulkerson began her writing career as a copyeditor and typesetter at a small-town weekly newspaper. She has since been published in several magazines and newspapers, including a two-year stint as a sports writer, and is the author of two novels and several non-fiction books. In 2020, she purchased Mantle Rock Publishing's backlist and founded Scrivenings Press LLC.

She and her husband, Don, live on a ten-acre plot in central Arkansas. They have four adult children and eight grandchildren. Linda enjoys photography, RV travel, and spoiling her two dachshunds.

Sharktooth Island

A collection of Romantic Suspense novellas

Includes "A Passage of Chance," a novella by Linda Fulkerson, and three more stories set on Sharktooth Island, a fabled island that no one dares to tame.

Get your copy here:

https://scrivenings.link/sharktoothisland

Candy Cane Wishes and Saltwater Dreams

A collection of Christmas beach romances

by five multi-published authors.

Includes "A Pennie for Your Thoughts," a novella by Linda Fulkerson, and four more Christmas beach romances.

Get your copy here:

https://scrivenings.link/candycanewishes

parents is less than ideal. How can Ivy ever find love when every man she meets puts career over family?

***Sweet Delivery* (by Heather Greer)**—After winning Cake That, Will Forrester thinks his Pastry Perfect Baking Dreams have come true. The sweetness fades when a chain bakery moves to town, and Will must adjust his plans to keep his customers. Hiring Erica Gerard is one of those changes. As they work together, Erica challenges Will and offers new ideas to improve the bakery. Soon, Erica and Will start bringing out the best in each other. But Erica harbors a secret, and if it's discovered, Will might never be the same.

***The Mermaids, the Ex, and USSS* (by Rachel Herod)**—Braig Sanborn is the most loyal employee the United States Shipping Service has ever seen, which is why he agreed to transfer across the country with only a few weeks' notice. Bailey Bivens is so busy planning a friend's wedding, she didn't expect to fall for the carrier who delivers packages to her house. When they both find themselves in too deep, will they agree the relationship was doomed from the start?

Get your copy here:

https://scrivenings.link/lovedelivered

～

Love in Any Season

A novella collection

Spring Has Sprung—by Regina Rudd Merrick

Laurel Pascal, Assistant City Manager of Spring, Kentucky, is tasked with organizing the town's beloved Daffodil Festival, and she's not happy. An allergy sufferer all her life, she dreads the season from the first Daffodil bloom in the yard to the last coat of pollen on her car. Newcomer Dr. Owen Roswell volunteers to help, and soon finds that not only does Laurel need his expertise as an allergist, but help in appreciating the season she's obligated to celebrate.

What does he want more—for Laurel to fall in love with his favorite season? Or him?

The Missing Piece—by Amy R. Anguish

Beth Norton and Tommy England grew up together with best-friend moms who had a love of quilting and a business celebrating the craft. When high school ended, though, so did Beth and Tommy's friendship.

When Tommy moves back after seven years and his mother's death, he can't understand why Beth is so angry with him. Helping Beth and her mother stabilize the finances of the business, they're forced to work together. As Tommy sorts through his mother's things, he finds an unfinished quilt, and it turns into a joint project.

With each stitch taken, they work toward more than just a completed blanket.

A Sweet Dream Come True—by Sarah Anne Crouch

Isaac Campbell is living his dream of running an ice cream shop but fears he won't last past the first difficult year. Mel Wilson is a busy single mother who longs to be a chocolatier but is too afraid to turn her dreams into reality.

When Mel and Isaac meet at Bestwood, Tennessee's fall festival, it seems like divine providence. But once Mel agrees to help Isaac bring in customers by selling her chocolates at his shop, she realizes how challenging running a business can be.

Can Mel and Isaac trust in God's provision and make a leap of faith? Will their partnership end in disaster, or will it be a sweet dream come true?

Sugar and Spice—by Heather Greer

Emeline Becker, owner of Sugar and Spice Bakery, loves New Kuchenbrünn, except for the gingerbread. As the only bakery, she supplies the annual Gingerbread Festival with the one treat she can't stand. It's gingerbread everywhere.

Things get worse when Ryker Lehmann is hired as the festival photographer. He was her secret teen crush, her sister's boyfriend, and witness to her worst humiliation. Plus, he broke her sister's heart and bruised hers when he left town after graduation. Now, he's back in town, determined to fix their friendship before the festival ends.

With gingerbread and Ryker together, can Emmie make it through the festival with her mind and heart intact?

Get your copy here:

https://scrivenings.link/loveinanyseason

Candy Cane Wishes and Saltwater Dreams

A collection of Christmas beach romances

***Mistletoe Make-believe* by Amy Anguish**—Charlie Hill's family thinks his daughter Hailey needs a mom—to the point they won't get off his back until he finds her one. Desperate to be free from their nagging, he asks a stranger to pretend she's his girlfriend during the holidays. When romance author Samantha Arwine takes a working vacation to St. Simon's Island over Christmas, she never dreamed she'd be involved in a real-life romance. Are the sparks between her and Charlie real? Or is her imagination over-acting ... again?

***A Hatteras Surprise* by Hope Toler Dougherty**—Ginny Stowe spent years tending a childhood hurt that dictated her college study and work. Can time with an island visitor with ties to her past heal lingering wounds and lead her toward a happy Christmas ... and more? Ben Daniels intends to hire a new branch manager for a Hatteras Island bank, then hurry back to his promotion and Christmas in Charlotte. Spending time with a beautiful local, however, might force him to adjust his sails.

***A Pennie for Your Thoughts* by Linda Fulkerson**—When the Lakeshore Homeowner's Association threatens to condemn the cabin Pennie Vaughn inherited from her foster mother, her only hope of funding the needed repairs lies in winning a travel blog contest. Trouble

is, Pennie never goes anywhere. Should she use the all-expenses paid
Hawaiian vacation offered to her by her ex-fiancé? The trip that would
have been their honeymoon?

Mr. Sandman **by Regina Rudd Merrick**—Events manager Taylor
Fordham's happily-ever-after was snatched from her, and she's saying no
to romance and Christmas. When she meets two new friends—the cute
new chef at Pilot Oaks and a contributor on a sci-fi fan fiction website
who enjoys debate—her resolve begins to waver. Just when she thinks
she can loosen her grip on thoughts of love, a crisis pulls her back.
There's no way she's going to risk her heart again.

Coastal Christmas **by Shannon Taylor Vannatter**—Lark
Pendleton is banking on a high-society wedding to make her
grandparent's inn at Surfside Beach, Texas the venue to attract buyers.
Tasked with sprucing up the inn, she hires Jace Wilder, whose heart she
once broke. When the bride and groom turn out to be Lark's high
school nemesis and ex-boyfriend, she and Jace embark on a pretend
romance to save the wedding. But when real feelings emerge, can they
overcome past hurts?